THE DARK VALE

By

Andy O'Halloran.

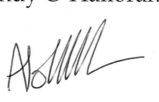

For you Dad,

I miss you.

Rest in peace.

PROLOGUE.

ENGLAND 1596.

The little girl closed the door quietly behind her, trying not to let the latch click too loudly.

'Where are they? Where's he hidden them?' she whispered to herself, as she leaned against the wall of the upstairs passageway.

Her father had left early that morning to collect rents from his tenants in Worcester. As soon as he was gone she began her search, upstairs. She was quite sure that he wouldn't have hidden her presents down stairs.

The door latch of the next room silently fell into place.

'Well, they're not in the guest room.' she said, pausing a moment to listen for any sign that she had disturbed the house keeper. Not that she should worry; Mistress Barker was as deaf as a post. She smiled to herself as she remembered her father's quip about the old woman.

She lifted her skirts and padded across the cold oak floor stopping at her father's room. Carefully she lifted the latch and pushed the door open, just enough for her to quickly step inside.

1.

Whilst she stood looking around the room she could feel a prickle of excitement on the back of her neck. She wasn't usually allowed in here. Her father's room looked dark and cold, as the curtains had only been opened wide enough to allow a thin sliver of daylight to cut through the gloom. Normally she didn't like the dark, but on this occasion she was determined to find the hidden presents. She had never managed to find them before, father was just too clever.

She quickly ran across the room and pulled open the heavy curtains.

'That's better!'

When she glanced around the room, she was surprised to see that it was quite Spartan in its furnishings. Apart from a modestly sized four poster bed, with a crimson, velveteen canopy, the only other items in the room were an oak desk with a high backed chair and a large linen chest.

Her small feet made gentle slapping sounds on the bare floor as she hurried over to the linen chest at the end of the bed. On the top was a bowl of old lavender flowers, which had long ago lost their scent. She lifted it off and placed it carefully on the bed. Slowly, she opened the chest. Her delicate features twisted into an uncomfortable grimace, just in case squeaking

2.

hinges announced her curiosity to the household. The room stayed silent as the lid flopped back against the bed and she breathed a sigh of relief. Eagerly she looked inside and was disappointed to see that there was just a pile of neatly folded sheets and nothing else.

Once she had closed the chest and replaced the bowl, she turned towards the desk. On the top sat her father's bible, a huge leather bound tome, that was always locked from prying eyes by a large brass clasp. She had always liked the intricate swirls of the strange pattern on the cover. She remembered that he had once shown her where the day of her birth had been recorded. He had sadly refused to show her the entry for her mother's death. She still didn't understand why.

Shortly after, she left the room, closing the door behind her. She stood by the wall and glanced down the passageway. There were only two doors left. The door to her room and the door that led up into the attic.

'Mmm, I've looked in my room,' she said to herself, 'but I'm sure father wouldn't hide them in there anyway.'

Before creeping down passage she stopped and listened again for a few moments. The house remained quiet.

Reluctantly, she started walking towards the attic door. She had never been allowed up into the attic before. 'There's nothing up there for a little girl,' he would say to her.

She reached the door and stopped, knowing full well it was locked. When she looked up she saw that the key was still where it had always been, hanging from a nail, high up on the door frame. Whilst she had been growing up in the house, the key had always been out of reach, but soon she would be seven years old and she had grown taller.

Standing on the tips of her toes she stretched her arm up and tried to grab it. She grinned broadly as her fingers brushed the tip, spinning it around on the nail. She tried again, with a little jump. This time the key spun around several times before circling off the end of the nail and clattering loudly to the floor.

She immediately froze, waiting for a shout of alarm or the sound of heavy foot steps on the stairs. Her heart pounded in her narrow chest, clammy hands trembling at her sides. She stood motionless for what seemed like hours.

She waited for a few more moments, just to make sure, before bending down and picking up the key. Without looking behind her, she pushed it into the lock and turned.

It turned easily enough, with only a dull click as reward. Then she hesitated, before turning the handle and pushing the door open, the enormity of the situation was finally dawning on her. She had never been into this part of the house before, it had always been forbidden.

She stood silently, at the bottom of the short flight of stairs, looking up into the gloom. The actual task of finding her hidden birthday presents had long been forgotten. This was her chance to dispel the ghosts of her childhood curiosity, mere fascination had given way to cold dread. Slowly she started to climb the stairs, being careful not to put all her weight on any steps that might creak.

When she reached the top, the stairs opened out into a dark, cavernous attic room. It was dimly lit by a small dirty window, high in the wall at one end, which allowed in a few thin rays of light. She wrinkled her nose at the damp, musty smell.

At first glance the room looked empty. All she could see through the darkness were bare floor boards. Then she saw something at the far end of the room, in one of the corners.

She started to walk, cautiously, across the room. Tiny dust motes floated aimlessly around her, as she momentarily broke the pale beam of light. When she neared the far corner of the room, she could see that the mysterious shape was a large casket.

When she finally reached the casket she stopped and knelt down. Gently, she ran her hand over the smooth polished surface of the lid. Her small fingers traced around her father's gold inlaid initials that had been beautifully carved into the wood.

She started opening the lid and was relieved to find that it wasn't locked. Opening it as far as it would go and being careful not to let it fall back against the wall, she peered inside.

'Oh bother! It's empty,' she mumbled, frustration washing over her.

Feeling dejected, she reached over to close the lid. Suddenly something caught her eye and she stopped.

At the bottom of the casket she could just see a small pile of folded cloth. She reached in and touched the cloth. It felt smooth and light in her fingers, like nothing she had ever felt before. When she lifted it out and held it up she saw that it was a robe. She stared spellbound as the black material glistened in the dull light.

As she was about to put the robe back into the casket, she noticed something else at the bottom.

She leaned in closer to see what it was and gasped. Lying in the bottom of the casket was a large knife.

Fear gave way to curiosity and she reached in. Her fingers closed around the handle and it felt cold. Slowly, she lifted it out. It was heavier than she expected. She could see that the blade was razor sharp by the way light glinted off the edge. Then she noticed something else, the strange symbols that were etched along the length of the blade. She recognised one of them in particular.

'That's the same as the shape on father's bible,' she said quietly.

Suddenly there was a noise behind her and she stopped. Icy beads of sweat rolled down her back. She could feel the silence thumping in her ears as she listened. Then she jumped as she heard a cold familiar voice behind her.

'Put the knife back inside the casket and close the lid.'

Tears of fright appeared at the corners of her eyes. Her hands began to shake uncontrollably.

She placed the knife back inside the casket and closed the lid. Then she stood up and slowly turned round to face the direction of the voice.

'You know it is forbidden to be here, do you not?'

'I'm sorry father.' Her answer was no more than a whisper as she started to cry.

CHAPTER 1.

ENGLAND 1610.

The dull quiet of the dawn was interrupted when Jasper hawked and spat on the ground. As he stumbled along the track he pulled a sour expression and then wiped his mouth on the sleeve of his coat.

'I gotta stop drinking that stuff,' he said, 'I can't feel me mouth and me 'eads ringin.'

'You gob on my foot Jasper Cotter an I'll be ringin' yer 'ead an all,' grunted Dag, the shorter and stockier of the two men. 'You gotta learn to control yourself when you're drinking Simon Hawkins's ale, you bloody idiot!'

The two men had set off for work early that morning, making their way into Cowley Wood, just north of the village of Honeybourne.

They worked for the local Squire, cutting wood, game keeping and any other general labouring tasks he thought they were capable of.

After a few moments of uncomfortable silence, trudging along the deserted path that divided the fields, the taller man spoke.

'What you got yer ass in yer 'ands for, any way?' Jasper asked rubbing his head, whilst looking at his companion.

Dag let the silence linger, content to listen to the sound of their boots scuffing the ground.

'I 'aint', he answered eventually and then looked away, 'I just think that tavern is a right shithole. I don't know why we go in there.'

'Where? The Black Dog?' Jasper said sounding puzzled, his lanky frame almost tripping over as he slipped, stepping in a rut on the muddy track.

'That's where we were last night, wern't it yer daft lump!' Dag replied, becoming irritated. He shifted the weight of the bow saw on his wide shoulders. 'Now drop the questions! It doesn't matter.' He felt embarrassed and quickened his pace, putting some distance between them. But as they started to enter the woods, Jasper caught up with him.

'I know what it is!' he said with a look of realisation on his dirty face, 'Sarah! You were trying to have a crack at her last night, but Daniel got there first!' Jasper saw the look on his friend's face and suddenly realised he had gone too far.

'Bastard blacksmith! I bloody hate him!' Dag seethed, causing the younger man to flinch. 'Anyway, I said bloody drop it. We got work to do and these fucking trees don't cut 'em selves down'. He stormed ahead again causing Jasper

10.

to hurry to keep up.

They followed the winding track deep into the wood until they got to a clearing. Once they had stopped Dag slipped the huge bow saw off his shoulder and leaned it against a stacked pile of sawn tree trunks, the evidence of the previous day's labour. He pushed his hands into the small of his back, to try and ease the nagging pain that he seemed to get more often than he used to.

Jasper sat down on a tree stump and breathed out loudly, cradling his head in his hands. Dag looked at him and shook his head and smiled, his mood lightening a little. He had known the younger man since they were children, both of them growing up in the village. Together they had been the cause of all manner of mischief, sharing a camaraderie that was known and admired amongst the other children. In a word they were inseparable, which is how Jasper had found work. The Squire had been reluctant to take the younger man on at first. But Dag, who was regarded as the sensible one of the pair, felt quite protective towards Jasper and managed to persuade him otherwise.

'How's yer 'ead?' he said calmly, looking up and surveying the tree line. 'Any better?' There was no answer. 'I said how's....' He glanced down and saw that Jasper's face was frozen in a

11.

mask of utter terror. 'What is it?...eh what yer seen?' He looked up sharply and followed Jasper's gaze.

The colour instantly drained from his face. He felt unable to move or speak and the only sound he could hear, over the cawing of the crows, was Jasper being violently sick on the ground behind him.

CHAPTER 2.

Months later, on a cold October night, a dull moon appeared over a quiet, sleeping village. Ghostly clouds drifted aimlessly across the endless sky. Pale moonlight gently tainted the squat chimneys and roof tops of Honeybourne.

A man appeared in the lane that led out of the village, hurrying as if being chased, his clerical robes billowing out behind him. Once he had got to the church he ducked through the gates and entered the grounds, his quick footsteps echoing off the walls of the Church.

The verger followed the path to the safety of the vicarage, which nestled amongst the trees that surrounded the graveyard. He nervously glanced behind him whilst he walked, in an attempt to spot any hidden pursuers.

Eventually and with visible relief, he reached the front door of the vicarage. He turned to look a final time, staring into the shadows for any sign of pursuit. Once he was satisfied he entered, closing the door silently behind him.

A dark figure watched, hidden among the shadows of the gravestones. As soon as the frightened verger had disappeared inside, the figure turned and crept out of the graveyard, disappearing into the night.

The verger locked the door, then turned and leaned against the oak panelled wall of the entrance hall.

'Justin, is that you?' a voice called.

He hurried down the passage to the room at the end of the hall and without waiting pushed the door open. He relaxed slightly when he recognised the familiar odour of burning candles and felt the warmth from the roaring fire that welcomed him.

Seated behind a huge polished desk in the centre of the room, was the thin willowy figure of the Minister of St Georges, the Reverend William Farrow.

William had only recently turned fifty; many of the villagers in the parish would swear he looked more like a very old seventy. His diminutive frame and waspish features easily misled them. But one look into his intelligent, passionate eyes and any doubts that he was just an old country vicar were quickly dispelled. After twenty five years as a minister, his enthusiasm and kind heart had made him a popular local figure.

'I'm glad to see you returned safely, Justin,' the Minister said smiling his usual warm smile.

'William, you were right. They were visiting, in Evesham.'

The Minister's smile disappeared.

'And you delivered the message?' he asked.

'Yes!' Justin replied solemnly.

'Then it is out of our hands.' The old man sighed looking at the verger.

Some distance away from the vicarage, deep in the woods, a small, bound, figure was being held captive at the edge of a brightly lit clearing. Without any warning the cloth sack that covered her head was removed. She gasped the moment her terrified gaze fell on the horrific scene to her front.

Gathered together, illuminated by torches positioned around the edge of the clearing, was a large circle of people. Some of them, she saw, were partially dressed, most were entirely naked. All of them wore hideous, bestial expressions on their sweating faces, as they danced.

The cacophony of noise scared her more than the sights around her. Intermittent screams, low harmonious chanting and moaning sounds of pleasure came from the grotesque revellers.

She tried to cover her ears, but couldn't move, the strong grip of the brutish man holding her arms tightened, causing her more pain.

When she was eventually forced into the clearing she noticed that in the centre of the circle, there was a goat tied to a post by a length of rope. The animal's glazed eyes seemed to stare ahead in a trance, its body standing motionless as if unconcerned at what was going on around. Then one of the revellers walked slowly into the circle.

The naked man stopped by the goat and raised his arms, which caused his ugly, bloated body to quiver. He looked around the gathering and then shouted.

'Let the obscene kiss beckon forth our lord Satan!'

The circle of people, now quiet, watched as the man lowered his arms and knelt down behind the animal. He bent forward and, lifting the tail, kissed the goat on the anus.

After the man had got to his feet, the revellers lined up and one by one did the same.

When each one had completed their foul task they rejoined the circle and continued the low hypnotic chant, whilst gently swaying from side to side to the droning rhythm.

16.

The man walked forward again into the centre of the circle. This time in his hand was a long, black handled knife. He slowly raised his arm and pointed the thin blade in the direction of the girl. He then passed the knife, in a wide sweeping motion, to his other hand and gestured to a tree at the end of the clearing.

'Tie her to the altar!' he shouted.

Whilst the girl was being dragged across the clearing she franticly looked for a means of escape. As if sensing her thoughts the hands holding her squeezed tighter, causing her to cry out in pain.

When she neared the altar tree the girl saw, to her horror, a congealed, reddish brown circle glistening around the base of the tree. A rank, coppery odour hit her nostrils. Suddenly, panic gripped her when she realised what it was.

'The blood alter is cast!' the fat man shouted, 'The dark lord is near.'

She started to struggle again when the filthy gown she was wearing was torn from her, revealing her nakedness. Strong hands held her arms in place, whilst she was tied to the tree, her back towards her captors. Tears rolled down her pale cheeks as she wept at the helplessness of her situation.

'It will soon be over my dear,' a voice hissed

close to her ear.

The chanting grew louder and louder as the congregation reached fever pitch. They were now surrounding the tree, their gruesome faces screaming and baying for blood.

Somewhere amongst the crowd someone had begun frantically beating a drum, which only seemed to incense the crowd further.

'Lord Satan! Receive our offering,' a loud voice bellowed, silencing the crowd instantly.

The girl suddenly screamed as a hand roughly grabbed a handful of her hair and violently yanked her head back. She started to cry as she stared wildly at the stars of the night sky. The next thing she felt, through the sobs, was the cold edge of the knife as it touched the side of her neck.

Without another word the blade quickly sliced across her throat. The last thing she knew, as the warm lifeblood trickled down her front, was the eruption of noise from the foul gathering. Then blackness.

CHAPTER 3

The next morning the minister's skeletal frame was sat hunched over his large desk. The house keeper, Mrs. Simpton, would joke that it was more of a banqueting table than a desk. 'It's too big for you vicar!' she would fuss. Secretly he enjoyed the attention. Lately, though, he had started to feel that recent events were beginning to weigh on him.

He put his quill down and leaned back into his chair, rubbing his tired eyes.

'The bishop will be furious with me for ignoring his advice, you know Justin,' he sighed, his face a mask of worry. He folded his arms and pushed his hands into the folds of his robes, trying to relieve the cold that gnawed at his fingers. He watched fondly as Justin, who sat by the dying embers of last night's fire, was pulling his gown tighter round his narrow shoulders.

'I've asked Mrs. Simpton to revive our poor fire. She'll be along shortly.'

Justin nodded.

'Thank you.' He sat up and blew on his clasped hands. 'Anyway, I think you'll find William, that it wasn't advice, it was an order.' He stretched his legs as the house keeper quietly entered the office and added more fagots of wood to the barely glowing embers in the hearth. Once she seemed happy that the fire had taken hold again she left, bowing slightly as she closed the door.

'It matters little now,' William said. 'As soon as the members of The Order arrive, the Bishop will have no other choice but to relinquish all power to them.'

'You said earlier, William that you would explain to me, just who The Order of St Michael are.' Justin's mood was starting to brighten a little, now the warmth of the fire had brought some life back to his limbs.

'Quite right!' William said, sitting upright. 'It's only fair that you know what you are now involved in.' He exhaled slowly, looking Justin in the eye 'The Order of St Michael is what remains of the old knightly orders. After the fall of Montseguer, the Cathars were all but wiped out. The French King, Philippe, turned on the Templars accusing them of heresy.' The old man leaned a bit closer, 'It was rumoured that he only wanted their gold, but with the backing of His Holiness they were arrested, tried and found guilty. Many members of the order were executed, dying a heretic's death at the stake. This threw the other orders into question. At the end of it all the orders, as they were then known, ceased to exist.

As the years passed, the Church realised that they still had need of men with the unique abilities and strengths of the old orders, so the Pope decreed that from the remnants of the old orders, the chosen few would form The Church of the Order of St Michael.'

Justin looked at William, mouth agape.

'So really, they are warrior monks?'

'Warriors yes, monks no. Not any more. They now act as magistrates and all manner of other clergy,' the Minister said, as his right hand fingered the small crucifix that hung around his thin neck. 'But they have also been called many other things, such as Witch Hunters, Inquisitors, Examiners and Torturers. St Bernard called them Christ's Legal Executioners.' William paused as he stared into the fire. 'Now they live their lives in waiting. Ready for when they are called upon to carry out their true task.'

'Are you sure they are the best people to help us?' Justin asked still looking nervous.

'I do truly believe, in this situation, they are our last hope. The local Constable and the Magistrate are both at a loss at what to do.' William looked down and crossed himself. 'Four bodies found in the last month and the sickening way in which they have been left, I'll confess, it terrifies me!' He looked at Justin 'They are the only ones who can save the people of this parish and the Church.' he sat back looking thoughtful, 'I'm surprised they're here though, but I suppose His Majesty must have approved or he wouldn't have granted them permission to act in England'

'How many will come?' Justin asked trying to sound more confident.

'Only one,' William answered.

'Only one!'

'Oh, he will have a companion, of course,' the older man said. 'Every member of the Brethren travels with a companion, specially chosen by themselves.

Make no mistake Justin; the Brethren are hard, capable men. They can survive in the most severe situations and they are also amongst the most feared combatants in Christendom.

The authority given to them, which was agreed when the King allowed them to enter England, means that they do not have the legal restrictions of a secular court to stop them passing judgement and administering the punishment.' The Minister stood and walked slowly over to the fireplace to warm his hands by the fire. 'I will admit I do find some of the tales of the

Order's actions, in other countries, quite terrifying.'

'Such as?' Justin enquired turning towards the Minister.

'In Germany, just outside the Archbishopric of Treves, the inhabitants of two entire villages were found guilty of practicing witchcraft and burned at the stake!'

William glanced at Justin with a look of grave concern.

'God have mercy!' the verger whispered 'What have we done?'

CHAPTER 4.

A few days later the moon illuminated a cold, dark evening on the way from Evesham to Honeybourne. The muddy road wound its way through the ridges and furrows of well- tended farm land. It was a dangerous route with only a few villages and some dense woodland along the way. Woodland which was often the haunt of some of the Shire's more desperate thieves and rogues. Some of whom now occupied a copse beside the road to Honeybourne.

The cluster of oaks, silver birch and bushes concealed them well, whilst still allowing them to watch out for any unsuspecting travellers on the road. The three hidden figures shivered as they quietly waited.

The Cooper brothers were three prime examples of the human flotsam that roamed the more inhospitable areas of the Shire. Isaiah Cooper, at 29, was the oldest, followed by his two younger brothers, Saul who was 19 and Eli who was 16. All were distinguishable by their thick mass of red hair.

They had not always been so desperate. Ten years ago they had been living a happy family life, in a cottage near Bretforton, with their God fearing mother Wendy Cooper.

Unfortunately one winter she died of the pox, leaving the young grieving Isaiah to fend for the family. After only a brief time in which to mourn he had set about looking for work. For weeks he tried various jobs in local villages and coaching inns. Eventually he found work on a farm that paid well and things started to improve.

But disaster struck again the following summer. One hot day Isaiah got into a fight with another one of the workers, who happened to be the farm bully, and he lost his position.

When he returned home that night he found their cottage in flames. Apparently, during the day Eli and Saul had stolen some scrumpy from the market in Badsey, taken it home and drank the lot. In their drunken state they had started fighting and during the scuffle a lantern was kicked across the floor, setting some of the furniture alight. Consequently the cottage burnt to the ground and stayed that way, none of them had had the money, the skills or the will to rebuild it.

In the weeks that followed they wandered the countryside. Occasionally they stayed with some of their friends' families. But after it was clear that they had outstayed their welcome they would move on. When the cold winter nights started to draw in they found themselves often being turned away by the farms and villages that had once welcomed them. Soon, all they had to look forward to was the occasional uncomfortable night in a barn and a meal of a poorly roasted capon, which they had poached off the squire's land. They decided that they had to find a way out of their predicament and eventually, in their minds, their only other choice was to turn to a life of crime, which they had been doing ever since.

'Issy, there's someone coming!' whispered Saul, a little too loudly for his elder brother's liking.

'Right you pair of daft buggers,' he said quietly, turning to them, 'You both know what to do and remember, I'm doin' the talking.'

He looked back to the road and saw two figures, both on horseback. Thanks to the full moon he could get a good look at them. They were wearing big riding cloaks, with the hoods pulled low over their faces. 'A bit far from home aren't we lads?' he thought to himself.

'Ready you two? Let's go!' he said and ran out from the cover of the trees. His brothers both followed him, leaping over roots and bushes as they ran. When they stopped they took position, one either side of Isaiah, who was now standing in the middle of the road.

26.

'Good evening gentlemen,' Isaiah said in a loud cheerful voice. He raised a large horse pistol from under his cloak, and aimed it at the two approaching riders.

The men slowed their horses to a walk and stopped a few yards away from their 'would be' assailants.

Isaiah couldn't see either of the riders' faces; their hoods were drawn too low over their heads. He thought it made them look a bit like travelling monks. The heavy riding cloaks, they were wrapped in, entirely covered their clothing as well. He noticed, now that he was closer to his quarry, that their horses were not the usual half starved, swaybacked nags that he'd seen most other travellers riding on. These were strong, well fed mounts. Huge warhorses that looked strong enough to carry an armoured warrior full pelt across a battlefield and smash an enemy line.

'Some fine animals you have their gentlemen. I'm going to have to ask you to hand them over.'

Saul and Eli looked at each other and smirked.

'Think of it as an act of charity. You'll be helping the poor.'

One of the riders urged his horse forward a few steps. Moonlight glistened off the flanks of the beast as it moved. He stopped and his hood shifted slightly when he cocked his head to one side, as if he was trying to prompt some form of recollection.

'That's close enough, matey. I don't want to have to shoot you out of the saddle of that expensive horse now, do I?'

'You won't shoot!' said a deep humourless voice.

The rider's response had taken him by surprise.

'Say again, friend,' he answered after a few moments, with a note of caution.

'You heard what I said, Isaiah Cooper!' the man answered, his grim voice resonated across the road. 'You won't shoot.'

Eli and Saul nervously glanced at each other, their smiles disappeared.

Isaiah slowly lowered the heavy pistol. 'Do I know you, friend?'

'No, but I know you Isaiah Cooper. I assume your accomplices are your brothers, Eli and Saul,' the man replied sternly. 'I also assume your mother has no knowledge of what you are doing?'

'She's dead,' Isaiah answered warily, 'Gone eight or nine summers ago.'

'I'm sorry, Isaiah. She was a good woman,' the man said respectfully. He tied the reins he still held to the pommel of his saddle and sat upright, pulling back his hood.

The rider revealed a shaven head, with a neatly trimmed black beard and moustache. He also had a single, piercing blue eye that stared back at them, boring into their very souls. The other was covered with a black leather eye patch. At the sight of the rider's frightening visage the three brothers each took an involuntary pace backwards. Fear suddenly gripped all them.

The hulking figure of the other rider then raised his arms and removed his hood. All three of the Cooper brothers gasped, Eli actually fell backwards in surprise, landing on his backside.

The man's face that glared down at them was more frightening than the first. His fierce eyes stared at them with utter contempt. His harsh features were framed by a wild shock of dark hair and long thick beard. As they looked at his brutal face they also noticed a long livid scar, running down the right side of his face, from his forehead to just under the right cheek, raising the corner of his mouth into an almost bestial snarl.

The one eyed man introduced himself, 'I am Master Thomas Wayland and my large friend here is Mr. Samuel Bolton.' The harsh tone of his voice softened slightly, 'And you, Isaiah, and your brothers, now have a problem!'

'A problem?' Isaiah replied raising the weapon again, a note of defiance in his voice as he tried to regain some composure. Deep down he was starting to get worried. The sight of the pistol was not having the same effect on these two as it usually did on other folk, even though he knew it wasn't loaded.

'That's right Mr. Cooper. You and your… fearsome band here,' Thomas said, ignoring the presence of the heavy pistol aimed at him, 'have attempted to commit an offence against servants of the Church on His Majesty King James's highway. Your lives are now forfeit!'

'What do you mean, forfeit?' Isaiah stuttered.

'I mean, Mr. Cooper that you now, all have to be brought to justice and punished.'

'The nearest courthouse is Evesham, an' that's miles away.' Eli cried out shaking his head. 'And I aint dangling from no gallows on Merstow Green.'

'Hold your tongue boy!' Samuel snapped, his forceful tone instantly plunging Eli in to silence.

'Thank you, Mr. Bolton,' Thomas said turning his head slightly to his brutish companion, giving him a brief nod. He looked back to the terrified trio, 'Unfortunately for you gentlemen, the authority that I have allows me to carry out my blessed duty with the full jurisdiction of the court.'

'Might I ask how you and Mr. Bolton serve the Lord, sir?' Isaiah asked hesitantly, hoping his guess was wrong.

'Of course! My companion and I serve the Lord as members of The Blessed Order of St Michael. By your blank expressions I see you are none the wiser. Would it be clearer if I said that in Europe we were referred to as the inquisition?'

'Mercy!' Isaiah whispered falling to his knees, dropping the firearm. Saul and Eli both copied their older brother crossing themselves.

Thomas looked at the tree line and slowly walked his mount over to one of the larger oaks, with branches that stretched out over the track. He looked up, reverently at the ancient boughs,

'Isaiah! Do you or either of your brothers know how many people I have hanged from this great tree, whilst serving the lord?'

'No master.' Isaiah quietly replied, wishing he was anywhere else but there.

Saul risked a sideways glance at Eli and saw tears rolling down his brother's cheeks. He turned back to where Master Wayland sat on his huge horse. He glanced at the thick branch and realised he couldn't stop his hands from trembling, as he imagined the noose tightening around his neck.

'None!' Thomas shouted, causing the three kneeling figures to flinch. He turned and fixed them with a serious stare 'But that can change right now...unless,' he paused again, enjoying the drama of the moment, 'you all agree to serve penance to the Lord, under my instruction.'

All three of the brothers instantly stammered their relieved agreement.

'Thank you master. Our lives are yours.' Isaiah spluttered.

'Your lives belong to God, Isaiah, as does mine,' Thomas said crossing himself. He walked his horse back over to the road and stopped along side Samuel. 'Do you know the Black Dog?'

'The tavern in Honeybourne? Yes master.' Isaiah answered.

'Be there tomorrow night. Do not be late!'

Without waiting for an answer Thomas and Samuel dug their heels in to the flanks of the horses and galloped away.

The three brothers, still kneeling in the middle of the track, watched them ride off.

'Master! You said you hadn't hanged anybody from that tree?' Samuel asked the other man, as they rode away, 'But I clearly saw rope marks on the bough!'

'Ah, yes.' Thomas answered with a laugh, 'I thought it prudent not to mention that I have actually sent a soul for judgement from that very branch.'

'Who was it?' the big man shouted out, trying to make himself heard above the sound of thundering hooves.

'Their father.' came the answer.

CHAPTER 5.

The next evening Reverend Farrow knelt in prayer at the altar of St Georges. The small medieval church had served the parish for over two hundred years. The part timbered, part stone construction stood on the south side of the village. It had survived the Reformation virtually unscathed and up until recent years had continued to be the place of worship for the community.

Over the years though, William had become worried about the size of the congregation. The number of worshipers had started to reveal more and more empty places amongst the pews. During Holy Communion on Sundays he could, more often than not, reckon the number of parishioners on the fingers of one hand. A far cry from Easter and Christmas, years ago, when he remembered there was standing room only.

He then thought about the bodies of the poor children that had been found, each of them mutilated beyond recognition. The mood of the parish was now one of fear and mistrust. It saddened him to realise that with every death, the spirit of the community was dying a little as well and he felt powerless to stop it.

His clasped hands trembled as a draught ran

across his hunched shoulders causing him to shiver. He looked up at the altar and noticed the flames of the candles briefly dance, as if brushed by an unseen hand. The tragic face of Christ looked down on him sadly unable to provide the answers.

'William!' A deep hollow voice sounded behind him, jolting him out of his thoughts.

He spun round, managing to still keep hold of the altar bar to steady himself. He gasped in surprise at the sight of the two frightening figures that were standing behind him.

'William it's me, Thomas!' A heavily set man in black robes stepped forward and removed the hood that hid his face.

William stared in bewilderment at the single blue eye that regarded him and then at the black leather eye patch. Then recognition suddenly dawned across his face.

'God have mercy...Thomas, it's you!' The old vicar got to his feet and slowly walked towards him, holding his hands out in greeting.

'Hello old friend, it's been a long time.' Thomas smiled as he returned his old friend's grip, his harsh features instantly softening.

'Thomas, I thought you were dead!' The minister stared in disbelief 'With my own eyes ...you were dead!'

Thomas shrugged.

'The brothers at the almonry are skilled physicians and I suspect the Lord still had need of me in this life.' He turned and beckoned forward the enormous form of another cloaked figure. The other man took a step forward and removed his hood. 'Don't be alarmed William. This fierce looking gentleman is my companion, Samuel Bolton, and as far as I can remember he has never smiled.'

Samuel slowly bowed his head.

'Good evening sir,' he offered in greeting, 'Please forgive my master's dry wit.'

Thomas grinned. 'We received your message whilst we were at All Saints, William. Now tell me, what troubles this place?' he asked the old man.

'You and your companion must come over to the vicarage. I will explain there.' The Minister gestured to the Church's east door. 'Please follow me.'

Once inside the vicarage they relaxed in the warmth of the Minister's office whilst William explained the disturbing events that had recently beset his parish.

As he spoke he saw that both men wore breastplates that were slightly dented and battered in places. Their green tunics and black breeches were worn and travel stained. Finally, his eyes settled on the long basket hilted broadswords that hung from their wide leather belts. In all, he thought, they looked more like two warriors that had just marched from some ancient battle field, rather than men of god on a mission for the church.

Samuel listened as he stood by the window and looked out at the ranks upon ranks of ancient, worn gravestones that rose from the shadows of the church yard.

Thomas sat by the fire looking thoughtful.

'Where did you say the remains were found?'

William winced at the term Thomas used for the bodies. 'Cowley Wood. It's about a mile north of Honeybourne.'

'And they were all found in the same manner?' Samuel enquired gravely, as if already anticipating the answer.

'I fear so, but the Constable would have to give you the exact details. He lives in the village.' William paused and looked anxiously at his old friend. 'These are good people Thomas....'

'I understand your concern William but good people should not stray from the path of God.' Thomas answered sternly. 'Good people do not kidnap and mutilate innocents! No… with God's

Grace we will bring these disturbing events to a close.'

William's hand unconsciously moved to take hold of the small gold crucifix that hung round his neck. He closed his eyes and said a silent prayer for his unfortunate parishioners.

The Verger had been cowering silently in the corner of the office throughout the whole relaying of events. As soon as they had arrived he had felt paralysed with fear at the sight of the two nightmarish visitors. Finally he managed to find the courage to speak.

'M...Master Wayland w...would you and your companion be staying here with u...us while you are in the area?'

'A kind offer indeed. No we would save you the distress Mr. Mathews,' Thomas replied, smiling at the Verger, 'We need to be in the village, I think.' He turned to his companion, 'Samuel.'

'Yes master?'

'Find the tavern and secure us some rooms, if you would.'

The large man nodded and left the room. Thomas turned back to the two clergymen.

'And so it begins, gentlemen.'

CHAPTER 6.

The Black Dog Tavern was one of the largest and busiest buildings in Honeybourne. It started off, back in the medieval age, as a small cottage on the end of a row. The village then was no more than a nameless hamlet in the middle of nowhere. As the years went by more people settled, a church was built, then more homes and the hamlet then became a village. The small cottage that had served ale for all that time had then become too small.

After a time a man arrived and bought all the cottages in the row. Soon after he turned all the cottages into one large tavern. From then on the Black Dog became the second most important building, after the church. It was soon renowned for its entertaining and sometimes rowdy evenings in the taproom and tonight was no exception.

'A word of advice lads….Don't ever venture into Cowley Wood after dark!' Toby Watts, the local gossipmonger, paused for effect whilst taking a long drink of his ale. He looked at the faces of the little band of patrons that had gathered at his usual corner booth.

The men glanced at each other, none of them daring to ask why. Then a quiet voice broke the silence that had fallen over the table.

'Why not T…Toby?' stuttered Guy, the hunchbacked simpleton who worked at the tanner's yard.

Toby smiled 'Cos it's so bloody dark you'll trip over and break your bloody neck!' the gathering erupted into loud hysterics spraying each other with ale.

The landlord's daughter, Sarah Hawkins, weaved her ample frame between the tables carrying trays loaded with mugs of ale and rough cider, that she held high in the air. But because of her size this usually resulted in her knocking over chairs and barging innocent drinkers out of the way, an occurrence that most of the locals were used to.

'You clumsy, fat sow!' shouted Duncan Fellows, the burly tanner. He quickly jumped up, revealing his ale soaked lap. The regulars rewarded him with loud a raucous cheer.

The portly landlord leaned across the bar.

'Sit yer backside down Duncan. I'm coming over to refill yer pot now,' he shouted.

Simon Hawkins had been running the Black Dog for the last twenty years. He had already had a successful pub in the city of Worcester, but after a bout of the pox that had swept through the city, wiping out a quarter of the inhabitants, including his wife and two sons, he decided to start afresh somewhere else.

He left Worcester with Sarah, who was only six at the time, and moved to the countryside. Whilst staying with his sister in Evesham he heard tell of a tavern being up for sale in one of the villages. Now a score of years later he and Sarah were proprietors of the village tavern.

'That Duncan has had a skinful tonight already,' Sarah moaned as she reappeared back at the bar.

'…And as long as he holds his temper, I want him to come back again tomorrow night!' Simon said, his back to his daughter, as he filled a stone jug with ale. He turned and saw Sarah's worried face. 'What's wrong dear? What's the matter?

Normally her father's worrying nature would annoy her, but tonight she was grateful of for his concern, 'Lately, Dad, people have been acting strange. I don't know what it is. But I'll not lie to you… it bothers me.'

'You know people, my love.' Simon answered, giving his usual neutral answer.

'I used to,' she said picking up another mug, before slumping back against one of the large barrels that were stacked behind the bar. 'It's not like it used to be. People seem…Oh I don't know.' She looked back at her father, but he was glancing around the busy taproom with his usual worried expression on his face. 'It doesn't matter.' She said quietly.

'What was that dear?' he asked quickly, still watching what was going on in the room.

She picked up a tray of drinks and held it out to him, 'You'd better take that over to Duncan's table before he gobs off again.'

'Oh yes! Thank you my love,' he replied absentmindedly, snatching the tray from her.

As he hurried from behind the bar the front door opened and three travel stained, rough looking characters entered the room, their faces hidden under the wide brims of their hats. They pushed through the crowd and sat down at one of the empty booths in the corner, nearest the door.

Sarah started to weave her way through the crowd, towards their table. When she got closer she saw the unkempt, red hair hanging down their backs.

'Oh not tonight, please!' she muttered, 'Evenin' lads, what can I get you?' she asked, cheerfully as she could, when she reached the table.

'Three ales please Sarah!' Isaiah mumbled keeping his head low.

Something's wrong, she thought. The Cooper brothers were definitely not acting themselves tonight. Usually they were the loudest and the most boisterous drinkers in the pub.

'Alright, but no trouble tonight Isaiah. Please?' Sarah asked in a soft voice. She had always had a soft spot for Isaiah. She loved his wild red hair and his loud jovial manner, and she also remembered how he had never made fun of her about her size. Tonight, though he seemed different, subdued for some reason. She looked at each one of the brothers in turn, 'A quiet night tonight from all of you...Please, eh lads?'

'There'll be no trouble started by us tonight Sarah. Anyhow we're waiting for someone.' Isaiah glanced around the crowded taproom with a barely concealed look of concern.

'What do they look like? Perhaps they've been in already?' she asked helpfully.

'No. You'd know if they'd been here,' Isaiah answered with a humourless chuckle.

'The Cooper brothers...You mean the Highwaymen?' the landlord spluttered as he started to shake. 'Why are they here? They're from the other side of Bretforton!'

'Isaiah said they were waiting for someone.' Sarah said trying to reassure her frantic father, 'Anyway, they've never been caught!'

'Only because there's none round here brave

enough to arrest 'em.' Simon said, his voice rising to a squeal. He looked over at their table, before leaning in close to her, 'They said they don't want any trouble?' he asked.

'That's right! They said they were waiting for someone,' she replied, 'and something else. They looked…scared.'

The landlord looked down and started shaking his head.

'I'll tell you what, I just don't know any more.'

Just then, without warning, the front door swung open and an immense black clad figure stepped in to the room. He turned slightly, reached a long arm out and slowly closed the door behind him.

The noise of the taproom died down to a dull murmur. All eyes were now on the newcomer as he turned to face the room. His hood shifted slightly, as looked to see in which direction the bar was, before carefully winding his way through the crowded tables. Half way across the packed room a leg shot out in front of him, barring his way.

'Good evenin' master and what brings you to our humble watering hole?' asked the slurring, husky voice of Duncan, the tanner.

'Let me pass,' Samuel answered menacingly.

'What's that bloody idiot, Duncan, doing?' Eli

whispered to his brothers.' He's going to get a right slap in a bit.'

'Yeh, I know.' a smiling Saul whispered back.

Duncan looked up at Samuel and smirked.

'You know my friend, you're a long way from the sanctuary of the...'

Suddenly a huge hand shot out from the gigantic man's sleeve, grasping the tanner around the throat. Duncan's hands started to frantically claw at the heavily muscled arm, as he choked. He then felt himself being lifted off his stool and into the air. All eyes stared, dumbfounded, at the sight of one of the village's largest men being lifted into the air as if he were a small child. The giant hooded figure leaned closer to him.

'It is you who needs sanctuary...My friend!' Samuel hissed.

'Samuel!' A loud voice called from the Taverns open doorway. 'We are all God's creatures!'

All eyes turned to the figure in the door way, with disbelief etched on their faces.

The next sound was the still twitching body of the choking tanner, hitting the floor after the monstrous hand had released its grasp.

Samuel glanced down.

'For some master, creatures is an apt term.'

A few from the crowd crept forward to help

Duncan, as he fought for breath.

Thomas closed the door and walked across the room, 'Come Samuel we need our rest.'

Together they weaved their way through the still dazed patrons, stopping at the bar.

'Is the landlord here?' Thomas asked loudly.

A chubby hand that was slowly raised into the air caught Thomas's attention. He glanced down at the plump figure, at the end of the bar,

'Ah! Master landlord, I am Master Thomas Wayland. You have already met my less tolerant companion, Mr. Samuel Bolton. Both of us are merely humble servants of the Lord and members of the Blessed Order of St Michael.'

Several people in the crowd gasped.

'Witch Hunters!' someone said under their breath, but still loud enough to catch Thomas's ear. He spun around, his hand moving quickly to the hilt of his sword. The sudden movement caused several people to stumble backwards in surprise. He grinned at their reaction.

'We have been called many things during our service to the lord. But when all is said and done, we are naught but humble servants of God'

Then a soft voice broke the tension.

'Please masters can I help you?' Sarah said as she stepped forward. 'I am Sarah Hawkins, my father is the landlord.'

Thomas smiled kindly.

'Thank you dear lady. We would like rooms and some food and water if possible.'

Sarah bowed her head and showed them to a table by the wall. As Thomas was about to sit down he noticed Isaiah and his brothers at the table in the corner. After a short while Sarah came back with some bread, cheese and cold ham and placed them, with a stone jug of water and some cups, on the table in front of them.

Thomas looked up at Sarah.

'Dear lady, if I'm not mistaken, I saw Mr. Cooper and his two younger brothers by the door. Could you ask them to join us?'

She curtsied and made her way over to the Cooper's corner table.

'Isaiah, Master Wayland wants talk to you three,' She noticed how all three blanched as they looked at one another. She leant closer to their table, 'How in heaven did you meet them?' she asked.

Isaiah looked up at her and shrugged, 'We tried to rob them on the Badsey road. We didn't know who they were, Sarah. That's the God's honest!'

She stared at them in shock.

'You bloody idiots! They could have hanged

47.

you all, there and then you know.'

'Yes, we know.' Saul answered.

Sarah shook her head slowly in disbelief.

'Well he wants you three, over there, now!' she said and then stormed off.

'She's definitely got a thing for you, Issy,' Eli said chuckling.

'Come on, or the only humping me and her will ever do, is when she helps to carry my box.'

The atmosphere in the taproom struggled to return to normal. People quietly wandered back to their tables and more ale was ordered.

The Coopers stood up and reluctantly walked over to Thomas's table.

'Good evening' masters,' Isaiah said trying to sound confident.

'The three of you will be back here at dawn,' Thomas said not looking up from his food.

'Right you are, sir. 'Isaiah answered. After a few moments of being ignored the brothers looked at each other and turned to walk away.

'And gentlemen…'

The brothers stopped.

'Do not be late!'

The Coopers left the tavern. Thomas and Samuel finished their simple meal, in silence. When they were ready Sarah showed them to their rooms, at the back of the building. Once she had let them in, she bid them good night and left.

Thomas looked at Samuel and nodded.

'Well…tonight should set tongues wagging.'

CHAPTER 7.

Dawn broke with a heavy mist hanging lazily over the sleeping village. The intermittent caw of the ravens that were in the trees, echoed across the wet roof tops.

Suddenly the calm of the dawn shattered as the frantic, misshapen form of Guy, the tanner's apprentice, ran into the main street, heading towards the tavern.

When he reached the tavern he began frantically hammering on the front door.

'Simon! Sarah!' he shouted, 'Hurry up, open the door.'

One of the upstairs windows opened and Simon poked his head out.

'Guy? You noisy bastard. What do you want? It's too early, bugger off!'

'It's Master Roberts. He sent me to fetch the two church gentlemen that arrived last night.'

'Tell the Constable that they've already gone out,' Simon replied sleepily, with a frown. 'They went to find the pillory. Why does he want them anyway?'

'They've found another body in Cowley Wood,' Guy shouted over his shoulder as he started to run off in the direction of the pillory.

'Who is it?' Simon called after the boy.

'They don't know,' he shouted back, almost slipping in the mud. 'There's no head!'

Simon watched guy disappear around the corner. He looked around the quiet street then ducked back inside, closing the window after him. Somewhere in the village a dog started barking.

Thomas looked at the pillory; its pathetic wooden frame was clearly in a state of disrepair. The contraption hadn't been used for years.

'Mr. Cooper, do you know if there is a joiner in the village?'

'Yes there is, Master,' Isaiah replied, 'His name's Abel Winter. He's got a workshop next to the village hall.' He felt rough this morning. Last night's ale had turned his stomach sour and being woken early had done nothing to help his delicate condition either.

Eli and Saul were sitting quietly on the wet grass of the village green; both of them were also feeling the effects of the previous nights drinking. In their state neither of them cared that the morning dew was soaking through their breeches.

'This morning Eli, I want you to go to Master Winter's workshop and tell him that I require this wooden structure repaired. Today!'

'I can't see Able Winter doing this today, Master Wayland.' Eli called over.

Thomas slowly walked over to Eli, who now wished he had kept his mouth shut. He stopped in front of him and smiled.

'Give Master Winter my complements and tell him that if the village pillory is not repaired today, I will find another carpenter to do the job!' He paused. The coopers looked at one another. All had puzzled expressions on their faces. 'You may also tell him that he… will pay this other man to make the repairs and once complete, Master Winter himself will be the first soul to be confined to the device.'

Eli nodded.

'Yes Master.'

Desperate footsteps sounded in the street behind them and they all turned.

'What's that halfwit want at this time of the morning?' Saul muttered under his breath.

'He's probably got lost on his way home again!' Eli chuckled.

'Silence!' Thomas snapped. He held his hands up as Guy reached him, 'Stop boy, stop…Calm yourself!'

'Master Wayland, sir, Mr. Roberts has sent me. He begs your assistance,'

'Who is Mr. Roberts? And what does he want,

boy?'

'He's the constable sir. There's been another child's body found in Cowley Wood.'

Thomas immediately looked at the other men.

'Mr. Bolton and Isaiah will come with me; Saul and Eli stay in the village and carry out your tasks.' They then set off through the village, following Guy's stumbling form.

After a mile or so Isaiah found that he was struggling to keep up with the powerful strides of the two men. He noticed that both of them were carrying sturdy looking quarterstaffs. 'They don't need them for leaning on!' he thought to himself wryly. After a few more miles, the seemingly vast expanse of Cowley wood came into view.

Once they were in the wood, Isaiah noticed that he couldn't hear any sounds, no birdsong, no breeze, nothing. There was only the damp odour of wet earth and rotting leaves. In places daylight was barely able to shine through the thick, canopy of the trees.

They trudged quietly along a muddy track, that wound its way through the trees. After a while, up ahead, they could see some figures standing at the edge of a brightly lit clearing

Thomas noticed that the three men standing inside the tree line had their backs to the scene.

He pushed his way through the group and stopped at the edge of the trees. At once, he was gripped by the gruesome sight in front of him.

'Samuel,' he said in a level tone, lifting the staff on to his shoulder. Slowly he started to walk around the edge of the clearing, his eyes vigilantly scanning the area around the grisly scene in the glade.

Samuel turned around and looked at the group of men.

'Stay here; do not enter the clearing!' he growled. He then set off in the opposite direction, with his quarterstaff resting on his shoulder, also keeping to the edge of the site.

Isaiah carefully walked forward to see what Thomas and Samuel were doing. He watched them as they skirted around the outside of the clearing, hardly making a sound. He noticed the way that they stepped through the damp undergrowth, carefully trying not to disturb anything on the ground.

'You keep strange company, Cooper!' Martin Richards, the local Constable, said moving closer.

Isaiah could smell the stink of body odour and stale ale on the man's clothes.

'It's not by choice Mr. Richards, I can tell you. Anyhow, the way I see it, no one else is trying to do anything?' He glanced slyly at the Constable, out of the corner of his eye. 'I mean, how many kids have been cut up so far? Has anyone been caught yet?'

Richards bristled at the insult.

'These two are just a pair of mad men. They'll try and destroy this community, you mark my words.'

'Seems to me that it takes a mad man to catch a mad man.' Cooper grinned. The constable stormed off, back to where the other group of men stood.

Thomas stopped. Behind him he could just hear Samuel moving. He waited a moment until the big man stopped beside him.

Samuel saw that Thomas was looking straight ahead and took the chance to scan the area immediately around him. He could see that all around the clearing there were scorched patches of earth. There were also odd articles of clothing scattered about, a stocking here, a shirt there, a few hats.

He also saw that animal bones littered the ground. When he looked closely at some of them he saw what he thought were bite marks in the bone. It looked as if a live animal had been torn apart and eaten. A goat he thought, noticing hoof marks in the soil. Then he followed Thomas's gaze. What he saw at the end of the clearing overshadowed everything else.

'The altar tree?' Samuel asked quietly, stepping closer. Thomas nodded, his gaze still locked on the spectacle to their front.

Tied around the tree in a macabre embrace was the headless, naked body of a small child. The open neck wound glistened in the morning light, flies buzzing around the exposed tissue and bone. Some of them settled where the head should have been.

'Baphomet.' he whispered.

'How can you be sure?' Samuel asked, unable to take his eyes off the mutilated body.

Thomas raised the butt of his staff and pointed to the dark ring that encircled the base of the tree.

'The blood shrine, the embrace and the missing head.' He turned to face the centre of the clearing, 'The goat was tethered in the centre and then eaten, alive, at the end of the ritual. The coven all remained sky clad through out.' Thomas straightened and looked back at the body. 'We must find this, Baphomet,' he paused, 'It will be difficult I'll wager. He has the coven to hide him and we have no idea who they are.'

CHAPTER 8.

'Master Wayland, may I ask you a question?' Isaiah caught up with Thomas whilst they walked back to the village. Samuel followed a distance behind, his cowl pulled down over his head.

Thomas blinked out of his deep thoughts.

'Of course Mr. Cooper, please ask,' he said continuing his steady pace along the track.

'Back in the wood, you said that we're going to try and find the demon?' Isaiah inquired, unable to hide the nervous edge to his voice.

'No Mr. Cooper. I said we "will" find the demon, because find him we will.'

'What! Are we going into hell itself to drag him out?' Cooper started to panic, not reassured by Thomas's air of indifference, 'Pardon me Master, but how can be you be so certain?'

Thomas laughed, showing his white teeth through his thick, black beard. 'Isaiah let me explain; Baphomet is not a demon as such, he is just a man who has adopted the name and characteristics of his patron demonic entity.'

'Which still makes him a monster,' Samuel added.

'Quite so!' Thomas replied.

After a while they entered the village, along a

road that threaded between two derelict looking barns. Both constructions were no more than skeletal oak frames, squatting over stacked bales of straw. As soon as they walked out into the main street Thomas held up his hand, signalling them all to stop. The village seemed deserted apart from a dirty mongrel puppy sniffing amongst some rotting piles of straw, hungrily looking for scraps of food. Cooper was about to open his mouth, to ask what was happening but stopped when Thomas spoke.

'Isaiah are you armed?

Cooper looked stunned, 'Err…no Master!' He felt a light jab at his stomach, when he looked down he saw Thomas's hand holding a stout, heavy looking cudgel.

'Take this, and don't lose it.' Thomas turned away and hefted his heavy quarterstaff staff out in front of him, taking up a guard position. 'Samuel?' he uttered in a low voice.

'Four in front, two behind, Master,' replied the big man's thick, gravelly voice.

Isaiah turned and saw that Samuel was facing back the way they had came, with his staff also held out menacingly.

Suddenly Thomas pushed him back against the wall of the nearest building and told him to keep out of their way. It stung his pride a little when he realised that he was a more of a hindrance than a help, to the two dangerous looking men. He gripped the handle of the club anyway and gave it a few practice swings, it felt a bit heavy but it would have to do.

He saw a movement out of the corner of his eye. Four figures, their faces covered with scarves, ran out from the building in front them. When they stopped, they spread out across the street and blocked their way forward. Two more, again their features hidden, appeared behind them from the back of the other barn. Isaiah noticed that they were all armed with sturdy looking clubs.

'Good morning gentlemen! How can we be of assistance?' Thomas cheerfully cried out in greeting.

'You're not wanted round here!' an angry voice called out in reply from the group of four. The same man pointed at Samuel, with an out stretched club, 'And that big bastard is owed a beating.'

'Can I assume then, that you good people have not come to talk?' Thomas asked. When no answer came he smiled and turned to Isaiah. 'Mr. Cooper when the fun begins, would you please fetch a cart and some twine. I would guess that Master Winter would be able to help.'

Without waiting for a response he looked back to Samuel. 'Don't kill any of them, Samuel. We'll need to question them after.'

The big man nodded in reply, then he moved the staff to his left hand and knelt on one knee. He closed his eyes, bowed his head and crossed himself. Isaiah looked in disbelief at the two men. Both were kneeling in silent prayer, almost treating the threat from their advancing attackers with contempt.

Samuel suddenly jumped to his feet, 'Come on then!' he bellowed.

The attackers looked at one another and then charged. Their shouts of defiance echoing off the walls of the narrow street. The first man to reach Samuel swung his club and missed, as the big man ducked under the blow. Before he was able to swing again he doubled over with a grunt, pole axed on the end of Samuel's out stretched staff. Then, in one fluid movement the large man stood to his full height and swung the weapon around his head, knocking the next attacker into one of his accomplices. Both men landed with a sickening thud. He then calmly walked forward and thumped each one of them unconscious, with a sharp blow from the butt his staff. He looked round for the last attacker, but the man had already fled.

Cooper turned away from Samuel's one sided exchange, whilst he searched for his last opponent. He saw that Thomas had already rendered unconscious one attacker and was hammering the other into submission, with a short succession of quick blows that reduced his nose to a bloody mess across his face.

Isaiah was stunned at their brutal efficiency. He then remembered he had to look for a cart. Whilst he ran he stumbled on the cobbles, still shocked at what had happened, he'd never witnessed anything like that in his life.

After a short while and a quick argument with Able Winter's red faced wife, he returned to the street pulling a heavy barrow. The five assailants had already been tied up and were sitting back against a wall, their bruised faces uncovered. One of the faces was familiar. It was Duncan Fellows, whose severely broken nose was causing him to wince with pain.

'What're you playing at Fellows you bloody idiot?' Isaiah asked smirking. The tanner looked away.

'Mr. Fellows is going to help us by answering some questions,' said Thomas wandering over. Samuel had started loading the barrow with the trussed up attackers, lifting them as if they were weightless. 'I think we will do our interrogations in the village hall,' he said.

Isaiah shivered involuntarily at what he thought was to come.

CHAPTER 9.

There was a light tap on the door of the private chambers.

'Your Grace! Your Grace!'

'Enter,' came a weak reply from inside.

The Curate, Owen Naish, hurriedly opened the door and entered the plush chambers of the Bishop of Worcester, Henry Phillpots.

'Your Grace, I have just got back from Evesham.'

The gangly, sycophantic curate, although irritatingly efficient, grated on Henry's nerves. Even down to the way his oversized Adam's apple bobbed when he spoke.

'What is it, Owen? Did you speak to the Canon?' The Bishop, his head still held in his hands, was not in the mood for one of the Curate's unctuous retellings of some menial task.

'Yes, Your Grace. The Canon sends his blessings and the two visiting gentlemen have left the Almonry.'

'And gone where?' the old man demanded, looking up.

Owen avoided the Bishop's steely gaze. Tales had often been told that the old Bishop could see straight into a man's soul stripping him of any deception.

'The Canon told me that they went on to Honeybourne, at the request of their minister.'

Henry lowered his gaze and crossed himself.

'William, no!' he whispered to himself. When he opened his eyes he looked up. 'What were the names of the visiting gentlemen?'

'If I remember correctly, I'm sure the Canon said they were a Master Thomas Wayland and, his apprentice, Mr. Samuel Bolton.' Owen looked pleased with himself at his feat of memory. His smile disappeared though, when he realised the bishop still remained silent, staring right through him.

'Man of sorrows,' Henry said eventually. He stood up from his large desk, pushed the chair back and walked slowly over to the window.

Owen looked at the slight form of the Bishop as he looked out across the grounds of the cathedral. His faded purple robes seemed to hang limply off his emaciated frame.

'Sorry your grace? Did you say… Man of Sorrows?'

'It's what they called Master Wayland in Germany,' Henry answered, his back to the Curate. 'The Bishop of Treves asked The Order of St Michael to send some of its brethren to him, to help with the questioning and prosecution of some of the locals that were suspected of witchcraft.' The Bishop turned, a grave look on his face, 'When all was done, two entire villages were eventually burned at the stake. Every man, woman and child…Master Wayland was the man that the Order sent.' Henry turned back to the window. 'It is said that he stood and wept as he watched them burn.'

Owen stared in disbelief, struggling to accept what he had just been told. 'Lord have mercy!' he said softly.

CHAPTER 10.

Duncan blinked as consciousness returned, the pain of his injuries hitting him as his body came back to life. After a while the dull ache in his head started to subside. He then became aware of the intense burning around his ankles and wrists, as his bindings cut in to the skin. Doing his best to ignore the pain, he opened his eyes. At first all he could see was that he was lying on the floor of a dark room. About an arms distance away he could see, what looked like, a body, lying on the dusty floor next to him with its legs trussed up behind. He stopped moving for a moment and listened, he was sure he could hear someone else breathing somewhere in the room. He tried to look around and see where it was coming from.

'Who's that?' he whispered. There was no reply. 'Oi…Who's that?' he said, this time slightly louder and a little desperately, wincing as he pulled against his bonds.

'Duncan? Is that you?' a voice whispered slowly. 'Where are we?'

'Who's that? Duncan answered, straining his ears, trying to locate the direction of the voice.

'It's me Toby…Where are we?' Watts replied, sounding relieved and scared at the same time.

The Tanner lay still listening for other sounds.

'Quiet!' He hissed, 'There might be someone listening.' He tried to look around the rest of the room, to see if he could spot any other signs of movement. Pain suddenly lanced through his shoulders when he twisted his neck trying to try and get into a more comfortable position. 'I think we're in the village hall,' he said quietly, spotting something, 'I can see two of the lads here by me. They 'aint come round yet.'

'There's someone by me but I can't see who it is.' Toby offered, sounding anxious 'D'you think those two bastards are in here as well?'

'No, I don't think so. I've had a look round and I can't see anyone else.' Duncan replied, the pain in his head was starting to ease a bit more. 'What happened back there? I thought we had 'em!' When he closed his eyes he could still remember the speed and the ferocity of the two men. They had overwhelmed his little band of ambushers as easily as if they were just children.

Toby breathed out silently.

'I've never seen anything like it. They were all over us like a dose of the pox.'

'I know, I'm hurting all over,' Duncan said closing his eyes, as he tried to block out the pain in his wrists.

A low moan suddenly came from the shape

next to him.

'Ow! My head!'

Duncan listened.

'Abel! You alright!'

'No I'm bloody not!' Abel fidgeted trying to ease the pain digging into his wrists.

'You won't get out of them,' Toby called. 'They've tied us too tight.'

'Shut up! And you Fellows, you bastard! You said we could have 'em.' Abel could feel his anger rising.

'Don't you start on me, Winter! It was the gaffer who said we had to do it.' the Tanner explained.

Toby started to think about what was going to happen if they got away.

'He's going to kill us for messing this up.' he said. 'Still, as long as we don't tell those two bastard's about him, it might not be too bad.'

'We've just got to keep our traps shut,' Duncan added feeling a bit more confident, 'They'll have to let us go sometime.'

'You are going nowhere gentlemen!' a voice boomed out of the darkness, causing the captives to cry out in alarm. 'Until you have told us everything we need to know!'

'God in heaven! They've been here all along,' the startled Tanner squealed.

A loud, almost inhuman, voice filled the room.

'I will punish the next one of you that takes the Lord's name in vain.'

Duncan recognized the voice instantly and he started to shake with fear.

Suddenly a bright ray of light pierced the darkness. Pain exploded in the captives eyes, causing them to all yell out. Thomas had pulled a board away from the window, lighting up the room sufficiently to see five pathetic shapes curled up on the floor of the village hall. He smiled as saw that all five men were averting their eyes from the bright sunlight.

'Gentlemen, as you can hear, Mr. Bolton is not in the mood to tolerate any uncooperative attitudes.' Thomas's voice was heavy with regret, and just a hint of sarcasm. He paused for a moment, letting the words hang in the air, 'I'm not sure how long I will be able to placate my brutal companion. My influence will only reach so far.'

'Master, please! We can not tell you anything,' Toby pleaded.

'He's right Master. Our boss will kill us if we name him. We'll not tell you.' Duncan said, trying to sound reasonable, hoping to appeal to Thomas's better nature.

'Mr. Bolton?' Thomas gave the captives an

unsettling smile. 'Since you have been my apprentice, and even before that, assuming that crude tales of my deeds have been mentioned by others in The Order, have I ever unsuccessfully examined a prisoner, failing to gain full information?'

'No Master, you have not!'

'Master Wayland. Have mercy, please! We can't tell you,' the tanner spluttered. 'He'll kill us all.'

'Only our Lord God can show mercy, Mr. Fellows. I can not!' Thomas turned and walked to the end of the room, where a rope had been thrown over one of the rafters in the roof. A loop had been tied at one of the ends, whilst the other end was curled on the floor. Next to the coils of rope was a pile of large stones in a rope net. 'Strappado, I think Mr. Bolton. Bring the first one please.'

The enormous black shape came out of the shadows and walked over to where Toby lay. Two powerful hands seized his wriggling body and lifted him effortlessly off the floor. Samuel then turned and carried him over to where the rope dangled from the rafters. The young man yelped in surprise, as he was dropped to the floor. He froze in wide eyed terror as he watched Samuel pull a large knife from his sleeve.

70.

He started to struggle, but stopped when he felt the cord that tied his feet to his wrists being cut. He let out a sigh of relief, when he saw the wicked looking knife being returned to the big man's voluminous sleeve.

Then he felt his arms being raised up behind him and the other end of the rope looped round his wrists. All of a sudden his arms were pulled up into the air behind him, forcing his head forward and lifting him to his feet. Toby screamed as an unimaginable pain that exploded in his shoulders.

'Toby!' Duncan shouted in despair. 'Master, please! We can't tell you.' He started to panic as he listened to his friend's screams echo off the walls of the room.

'This can end now, gentlemen,' Thomas said. 'You must give me your master's name. It's the only way.' He squatted down next to Duncan. The tanner turned away, trying to hide the tears in his eyes. 'Duncan, you can save your friend.' He said softly.

'Toby!' Duncan cried, closing his eyes as the feeling of helplessness gripped him.

Thomas stood up and turned back to the half conscious form of Toby, who whimpered quietly. He nodded to Samuel. Watts screamed as he was violently lifted into the air again, his arms almost being yanked from their sockets.

'Squire Danvers!' the tanner yelled, tears running down his cheeks, 'It's Squire Danvers. He's our master. He wanted you two beaten and sent out of the shire,'

'Thank you, Duncan,' Thomas said adjusting his eye patch. He calmly turned back to Samuel,' Lower Mr. Watts, please Samuel, and release the other captives. We have to pay our respects to Squire Danvers.'

At the same time, eight miles away Brother Godfrey sat in the gatehouse of Evesham's almonry, dozing. Suddenly a loud hammering on the main door startled him, almost causing him to fall off his stool.

The old man struggled as he got to his feet.

'That better be the devil himself beating these doors down, for he'll need the whole host of hell to protect him from me, when I get my hands on him.'

The old man's hunched frame tottered over to the Almonry's big wooden gates and opened the shutter of the small postern door. He looked out to see who had woken him from his revere.

'Who is it? What do you want?' he snapped. When he peered out, his view of the street was blocked by the sweating flanks of a huge horse.

An enormous voice bellowed from the horse's rider.

'Old man! Before you wrench these gates open, come out into the street and show me the error of my ways. Would you bless me with some information? I need to find the whereabouts of some visiting gentlemen?' Loud hysterical laughter echoed outside the gates.

'Why do you want to know? And I asked you, who you were?' Godfrey replied in a clipped tone.

'It's no business of yours, old man, but because I'm in a good mood,' the voice chuckled, 'I will tell you. We are seeking two armed men who wear black cloaks. Both large fierce looking fellows, although one is a head taller.'

'The older one has only one eye?' Godfrey asked, 'Yes they were here but I advise you stay well clear of them, St Michael is the patron of their Order; if you know what that means? They are not to be trifled with.' He craned his neck to try and see who the rider was.

'Old man, your concern for my safety warms my heart!' Loud laughter broke out again, but this time from more than one voice, 'We'll take our chances all the same. Now, in which direction did they leave? If that is not too big a secret!'

'They do not need my help to protect them,' The old man chuckled mockingly, 'they are more than able to do that themselves…They went to Honeybourne, and may God have mercy on your souls.'

'He does old man, every day!' the voice laughed back, before being drowned out by the deafening thunder of hooves that quickly disappeared off into the distance.

CHAPTER 11.

That evening in The Black Dog the mood in the hazy taproom was subdued. The few people who were present sat quietly hunched over their drinks, keeping their conversation low. Thick, harsh wood smoke hung in the air causing unsuspecting drinkers to explode into coughing fits as they first entered. The villagers, who drank regularly in the pub, would laugh about the first conversation people had when they walked in, "When's the landlord going to get round to clearing that bloody birds nest that's blocking the chimney?"

Saul was sat with his two brothers in their usual corner booth. He glanced around at the tavern's other two occupants, Jasper and Dag. Before he turned back he thought how sad the two woodsmen had looked lately, not their usual madcap selves. It was a shame, he thought to himself, he and his brothers had had some good, rowdy nights drinking with those two in the past. But that seemed so long ago. He took another swig of his ale, wincing at the bitter taste.

'Did you hear him scream,' Eli said sounding uneasy. 'What were they doing to them in the village hall, Issy?' He shook his head and stared at his older brother.

'What ever was done to them, they had it coming.' Isaiah answered quietly, glancing at Eli. 'Boys I saw what happened when Duncan and his lot tried to beat up Master Wayland and Mr. Bolton, and believe me lads, what ever is going on around here, we're on the right side.'

'Where are they now?' Saul asked watching the door.

Isaiah placed his mug back down on the table and wiped his mouth with his sleeve.

'I think Master Wayland said they had been invited to see the Magistrate.'

'I thought they were off to see the Squire, to sort him out?' Saul smiled.

'Oh don't worry they'll see that bastard alright! Mr. Bolton said that anticipation would keep the Squire at bay for now.' Isaiah winked at his smirking brothers.

Three miles away two shadows stood in the trees, watching the gates of Bretforton Manor.

'Sir Nicholas Dickinson… I wondered when we would be meeting him.' Thomas said softly.

They saw that the manor's large wrought iron gates were set into a formidable looking stone wall. Both men had also noticed that the area running along the wall had not been cleared, even when a number of the larger trees had grown over the top of the wall.

Samuel saw that in a few places tree roots had even buckled the brick work.

'It seems Sir Nicholas was not able find professional guards.' He said, 'The ground has not been prepared for defense.'

'Not necessarily my friend. The condition of the grounds could have been left for a reason, namely…'

'To appear inept.'

'Exactly! Come, let us meet our host.'

When they approached the gates a uniformed figure stepped out from behind the wall. They saw that the guard, wearing a highly polished morion helmet, was armed with a heavy sword. He wore a multi- coloured, pleated tunic and breeches with black leather boots, typical of the professional Swiss mercenaries they had seen many times before.

'This is a private estate!' snapped the guard, in a Germanic accent. 'State your name and your business.'

'Of course!' boomed Thomas smiling broadly, causing the guard to blink in surprise. 'I am Master Thomas Wayland and this is my companion, Mr. Samuel Bolton. We've been invited here tonight by Sir Nicholas.'

'Wait here.' the guard ordered before disappearing back behind the wall.

'Cheerful fellow,' Thomas muttered, he was rewarded with a grunt of agreement from Samuel.

After a short wait the guard reappeared and opened the gates. He stood to one side to allow them both to enter the grounds. Once they were inside, the gates slammed behind them, the loud clang echoing across the courtyard as they were locked. The stern faced guard instructed them to follow before leading them along a cobbled pathway.

Thomas and Samuel noticed the neatly cut lawns and trimmed box hedges of the grounds whilst they followed their escort. They both desperately tried to look into the furthest shadows of the gardens, without looking concerned. The only sound they could hear was the guard's heavy boots echoing off the cobbles. As they walked up to the Manor house Thomas was sure he could see dark figures watching them.

After a few minutes they could see the silhouette of the building, distinguished against the night sky. Bright lights shone through large leaded windows, the mullioned glass throwing bizarre shapes across the lawn. Both men could see that the black and white frontage created a magnificent façade, typical of the grand country retreat of the local gentry.

Finally, they arrived at an impressive oak door. Before the guard could knock, the door was opened and they were shown into a wide hallway. The dull white washed walls reflected the candlelight poorly, giving the hall a hollow, cavernous appearance.

'Good evening gentlemen,' said a pinched, rising voice behind them. The two men turned to see a gaunt, smartly dressed figure addressing them from the end of the hall.

'I am Cawthorne, Sir Nicholas's aide.'

The man's cold smile was framed by a neatly trimmed beard and moustache.

'Master Wayland, Mr. Bolton, would you please follow me.'

As the aide turned Thomas glanced at Samuel and raised his eyebrows in mock surprise. His companion, already on his guard, betrayed no emotion. They followed the slim, dark figure silently along the blank passageway until they reached a pair of polished walnut panel doors.

'Wait here please gentlemen.' the aide disappeared into the room.

Thomas glanced up and then down the passage. At one end he noticed that a door was ajar, shadows under the door showed that there were figures standing on the other side. He quickly glanced at Samuel, who nodded back. Suddenly the double doors were swung wide open to reveal the smiling face of Cawthorne.

'This way gentlemen please!' he said stepping to one side, motioning for them to enter.

Thomas and Samuel walked into a very impressive, oak paneled room. A fire blazed away in a wide stone fireplace, allowing bright flames to cast a warm glow across the hearth rug. Ornate candles positioned around the walls in fashionable brass candelabras added to the room's lavish feel.

'Gentlemen may I introduce Sir Nicholas Dickenson.'

A tall, grotesquely fat figure stood up from behind a large table with his arms spread wide in greeting.

'Master Wayland and Mr. Bolton, may I say that it is a pleasure, nay an honour to finally meet you both!' the magistrate effused. The large man wore a billowing, crimson robe and a high ruff in the seemingly crass mockery of a clergyman.

On the table in front of him was a vast array of

food. Pies of all sizes, plates of roasted capon smothered in gravy, sweet meats, loaves of bread and baskets of fruit. In the centre of the table dominating all the dishes was a large ham of bacon. He gestured to two chairs that were positioned near the table, 'I hope you both will sit and dine with me? Cawthorne fetch our guests some wine.'

'Sir Nicholas, you are too kind but we've already eaten,' Thomas interrupted, 'I'm also afraid that the rules of our order permit us to drink water only.' Thomas noticed that the man was sweating and red faced, he also seemed a little nervous.

'Oh well, I hope you gentlemen won't think me rude if I finish my humble meal, while we talk.' Sir Nicholas sat down and carried on eating a large plate of bread and cold meat.

During his meal he described to them the surrounding areas and how all the food on his table was grown and sold locally. He talked about his lands and how, in his own opinion, he was a fair employer and that he got on well with his tenants. Meat juice dribbled down his fleshy chin as he spoke.

All the while Cawthorne silently stood a few paces behind his master's chair. His eyes blankly staring across the room avoiding the gaze of the two men.

Thomas eventually found the opportune moment to interrupt.

'Sir Nicholas please forgive me, but did you invite us here for a specific reason?'

'I did indeed Master Wayland, I did indeed.' He smiled at them as he wiped his chubby hands on a towel. He appeared to be more at ease now that he had finished his enormous meal. 'I am aware of the circumstances which have brought you and your companion here.' He paused to allow Cawthorne to refill his wine glass. 'I would like to offer you my assistance with your investigation into these… unfortunate matters.'

Thomas looked at the man for a few moments before realizing that he was serious.

'Thank you sir, but I regret we must decline your kind offer…' He stopped when an idea came to him. 'Unless Sir Nicholas, if I may be so bold, I could ask you to provide us with some information?' He watched the smile on the magistrate's face change to a frown.

'Anything I can do to help, Master Wayland. I am at your service.'

'Thank you, sir. Firstly, are you aware that you have a 'witch problem'?' Thomas didn't take his eyes off the bloated figure across the table.

'Any information would be invaluable.'

'A 'witch problem' you say!' The magistrate looked thoughtful. 'You don't mean the old crone who lives Fladbury way, do you? Cawthorne, what's her name? The old woman who lives in the woods?' The fat man strained his neck as he turned around to look at his aide.

'I believe her name is Charlotte, sir,' the man replied. 'The villagers refer to her as 'Old Lottie'. I believe she sells medicines and cures, sir'

Thomas smiled 'I fear the problem is worse than the local medicine woman, Sir Nicholas.' He gave Sir Nicholas one of his intense stares. 'You say sir, that you are aware of recent events?'

The fat man nodded.

'Well we believe that the murders could be the work of a coven of witches.'

'Are you sure man?' the magistrate asked as he sat bolt upright, 'I mean, I confess that I have not personally seen the bodies but surely it is just the act of some wandering lunatic?'

'I'm quite sure sir. Mr. Bolton and I have seen the site of the last murder and we are convinced it was the site of a witches' sabbat.' Thomas noted the shocked expression on the fat man's face. 'The unfortunate girl was sacrificed in some form of satanic ritual.'

Sir Nicholas drained his wine and held the empty glass up towards Cawthorne again, who stepped forward and silently refilled it.

'Do you have any knowledge as to who the members of this coven are? No, this is a quiet country area, Master Wayland. These people are farmers and woodcutters, not murderers.' The magistrate shook his head in exaggerated disbelief.

Thomas and Samuel stood up slowly; both of them looking at their host. After a moments pause Thomas smiled, coldly.

'That may be so, sir. But someone is murdering local children and what we saw leads us to believe it was the work of witches. We will find them and when we do by the grace of God, they will all hang.'

It was only a brief twitch, but Samuel was sure he had witnessed the magistrate stifle a grin. Cawthorne then walked forward to stand next to his employer.

Sir Nicholas pushed his chair back and stood up.

'Must you leave so soon gentlemen?'

'I'm afraid so Sir Nicholas, we must depart. But you have been a most gracious host and we look forward to the next time we meet.' Thomas bowed his head. 'Your servant, sir.'

'Master Wayland, Mr. Bolton, it has been my pleasure. Cawthorne show our guests out, if you would.'

The aide silently led the two men from the room. Sir Nicholas sat down as the door closed behind them. He took his wine glass and raised it up.

'Till next time.'

CHAPTER 12.

The next morning was cold and damp. During the night a heavy downpour had turned the muddy roads into a quagmire.

Across the town the slow tolling of the bell of St. Lawrence's reverberated through the murky streets and alleyways.

'I hate Evesham; it's a right shit pit.' Saul said as he shivered in his sodden cloak. He was stood next to Eli who was equally as cold and wet. Together they were standing in a doorway trying to shelter themselves from the elements, whilst they waited for the Red Horse pub to open. Bulstrode, the town draper, had turfed them out of his shop several times, clearly not believing Eli's tale that they were traveling haberdashers, seeking a new line in broadcloth.

They looked out across the market square whilst they waited. All around them there were traders setting out their stalls. Some of them constructed flimsy canopies for their wares, in a vain attempt at protection from the weather.

Above the other sounds they could hear the intermittent, staccato ring of the smiths hammer, from the town forge. At the far end of the square they could see the grey walls of Evesham's gaol.

'We haven't been here for a while. Do you

think they will have forgotten us?'

'It was last summer, if I remember rightly,' Saul replied, pulling his hat lower. He recalled the horse doctor they had robbed the previous year. 'The sheriff didn't catch sight of our fizogs then, so I think we got away with it.'

'What's that mean?' Eli asked with a forced, puzzled look on his face.

'It means face, you twerp! It's welsh.'

'When did you learn to speak welsh then?' Eli asked grinning. Saul ignored the question, refusing to rise to the bait. Eli chuckled in triumph, but his smile quickly disappeared as he caught sight of the men who were constructing the scaffold. 'Have you ever thought about what it's like to be hanged?'

'No! Any way they've gotta catch us first.' Saul answered with a curt tone, before looking at his brother, 'Bloody hell you're of a good mind this morning.'

'I reckon if Sammy had had his way he would have had us strung up, by now.'

'If Mr. Bolton hears you call himself Sammy, he will.' He turned back to the scaffold. The men had finished the construction and were testing their handiwork. One of them was swinging from a rope that they had tied to the crossbeam. 'I need some ale.' he said gloomily.

Back in Honeybourne Isaiah was at the back door of the Black Dog, leaning against the door frame. The rain had stopped a few hours ago and the mud on the roads now looked deep enough to get stuck in.

He knocked on the door again and listened for any sounds of activity from within. After a while he gave up and started to walk away. Just as he turned the door suddenly swung open to reveal a very scared looking Sarah. Straight away he noticed that she must have got dressed in a hurry, because her bodice wasn't fully buttoned up.

She caught him looking down her front, so she hastily started to fasten the buttons.

'It's a might early Isaiah.' Her voice trembled slightly as she spoke.

'I know, but I need to speak to you.'

She looked at him for a while, shaking her head, 'Come in.' she said finally.

'With a sight like that to greet a man I'll be here this hour every morning,' he said following her through the door.

'You'll get a night pot emptied over you next time,' she replied walking through the narrow passageway and into the taproom. 'What do you want this early anyway?'

He sat down at the table by the bar and briskly

rubbed his hands together. Sarah frowned. She was not in the mood for pleasantries.

'Firstly a mug of your best and then I need to ask you a few things.'

His mischievous smile instantly stopped her next sharp comment. She shook her head again and wandered off in the direction of the bar.

When she returned her mood had lightened a little. She banged two mugs down on the table and sat down opposite him.

'What do you want to know?' she asked warily.

Isaiah regarded her silently. After a few moments she raised an eyebrow, still waiting for an answer.

'Where do I find Old Lottie? He asked eventually, picking up his mug and taking a big swig. He tried to make the question sound innocent. He remembered Thomas telling him to be cautious during his inquires.

'How did you hear about her?' Sarah replied looking at him suspiciously.

'Oh just someone mentioned the other night that she makes remedies and cures.'

Sarah grinned at him.

'Ave you caught something you shouldn't 'ave?'

'No it's not for me. It's...Er...Eli he's got a

condition, shall we say.' He fought the urge to laugh out loud at how red his brother would have gone, if he had been there, 'He doesn't like talking about it. He's a bit embarrassed, see.'

Sarah looked around the room before turning back to him. She lowered her voice.

'I know why you want her, Isaiah Cooper!' She glared at him intently. 'And believe me when I say this to you. You don't want to find her.'

He drained the last of his ale and placed the empty mug back on the table.

'And why don't I want to find her?'

She placed her hands on the table and leaned closer.

'Because it'll cost you your life!'

'I wonder how many's dangling today.'

Saul was in a better mood now that they were both sat in the warmth of the Red Horse. Outside, the market square was bustling with activity.

'Altogether there's four,' the land lord said as he placed two pots of cider down on the bar in front them. 'The worst one though is a bastard called Allslopp.'

Eli looked at the dour looking man.

'Why what's he done?'

'Sodomy. The bastard kidnapped some young lad from the poor house and rogered him to death.' The man shook his head in disbelief. 'That poor child.'

Saul turned around after the landlord had walked away, 'That's more like... Murder, isn't it?'

'Well, he'll be in hell tonight. Whether it was sodomy or murder,' Eli said looking out of the window at the scaffold in the square. 'Those damn bells are getting right on my nerves.'

'Don't fret, it's almost time.' Saul stood up straight and dropped some coins next to his empty mug. 'Come on lets get back to the square.'

Eli drank up and they walked out of the pub to see that crowds had started to gather near the gates of the gaol. The townsfolk in the market square were reveling in the occasion. Proud fathers waited with smiling sons on their shoulders, mothers huddled together with their daughters, all enjoying the cheerful mood of the day.

The spectators that were gathered in the square were eager to get the best view. Even the buildings that overlooked the square had eager faces leaning out of every window. The towns

shopkeepers had always seized the opportunity
to make a bit of extra coin, renting out their
upstairs windows for the day.

Saul and Eli pushed their way through to the
back of the crowd. Eventually they managed to
find a space in a doorway that gave them a good
view. Both of them were a head taller than most
which meant that they were pleased with their
position.

When the gates of the gaol started to open a
loud cheer went up. Two lines of armed guards
filed out, each of them holding halberds out in
front of them, and started to push the
congregation back. Once a route had been
cleared from the gates of the gaol to the scaffold,
the procession came into view.

The crowd erupted into loud applause and
shouts of approval when the tall, well dressed
figure of Sir Richard Walsh, the High Sheriff of
Worcestershire, stepped into the daylight.

Behind him followed the rotund and red faced
Sir Nicholas Dickinson. His long dark robes of
office and large powdered wig, immediately
sending most of the crowd into fits of hysterical
laughter.

The guard captain saluted smartly when Sir
Richard walked over to him.

'Well done captain!' he boomed to the soldier,

'Your men are looking sharp today and a well cleared route sir, I do declare.' He walked a few paces away from the soldier and paused. He eyed the crowd and then the route to the scaffold. 'You may bring them out Captain.' he said in a stern voice.

'Yes Sir. Thank you Sir.' The captain turned to the gates. 'Bring out the condemned!' he ordered in a loud, clear voice.

The condemned were led out of the gates and into the light, their arms pinioned behind their backs. The wretched figures shuffled along with their heads bowed low as boos and cries of hate echoing from the crowd. The three men and one woman were escorted by armed guards who flanked them as they made their way to the scaffold.

Saul joined in with the shouts of abuse that was being hurled at the prisoners. The man at the back of the line was getting most of the attention. He pointed to him and nudged Eli.

'That bastard must be Allslopp.'

'He even looks like a beast. I hope it hurts him.' Eli shifted to get a better view when the procession stopped. Suddenly his eyes locked on to another face in the crowd. 'Hey look,' he said pointing across the square.

'What? Who is it?' Saul tried to spot who Eli

was pointing to. Then he saw, 'Oh bollocks! When did he get here?'

'What do you mean 'it'll cost me my life'?' Isaiah repeated staring at her. She wouldn't meet his gaze. 'Sarah, tell me!' He reached out and grabbed her arm, stopping her as she started to stand up.

She winced as his grip tightened.

'Ow! You're hurting me!'

'Not yet I'm not,' he hissed. He heard a noise and quickly released his grip.

Simon appeared from a room out the back.

'You alright there, my love?' He looked a bit worried when he saw Isaiah's angry face.

'We're fine thank you, Dad.' she said regaining some of her composure, 'You can go back into the parlor now, we'll be alright.' Simon quickly disappeared and she turned to Isaiah. 'You must find some other way to get help for Eli,' she said rubbing her arm. 'I'm sorry.'

'Just tell me where I can find her,' he asked trying to sound calmer, annoyed that his quick temper had flared up. 'Sarah, please?'

Even though she was scared of the Coopers, she had always liked Isaiah. Sometimes in her dreams, he would appear at her window and ask for her hand in marriage, but that was just sheer fantasy. She closed her eyes as tears rolled down her cheeks.

'Lottie lives in Poden,' she whispered.

Isaiah reached forward and held her hand.

'Thank you, love.' He lifted her chin and smiled at her. 'Now, where is it?'

'It was just north of the Littletons.'

He looked puzzled.

'What do you mean 'was'?

'The whole area there was wiped out by the pestilence years ago.' She looked down at her mug. 'The only person left there now, is Lottie.'

'No. That's not Mr. Bolton; he's got no beard for a start.' Saul said glancing at his brother. 'Why would he shave it off? And anyway, why would he be here?'

Eli craned his neck as he looked over the heads of the crowd. 'He's gone.' He said leaning back against the shop door. 'No. I don't know who that was? But it wasn't Samuel.'

'Never mind. We'll ask him later,' Saul said nudging him. 'Come on they're getting on the stage.'

The brothers pushed their way through the mass of people, who were also trying to get a better view. Eventually they got into a position they were happy with, both of them having a quick look around to make sure they had a few escape routes, just in case they were recognized. When they turned back to the stage the noise of the crowd had started to build again.

Waiting on the stage was the executioner, his cleanly shaved a clear sign of his profession. In his gloved hands he held several coiled lengths of rope, each one with a noose tied at one end, ready for the prisoners. The man's stern face betrayed no emotion at all as he watched the condemned step up onto the scaffold. The crowd's cheer grew louder, all eager to witness the final demise of the guilty four.

Once all the prisoners were on the stage, the sheriff's men started to shove them into position. They were all quickly pushed in to a line, under the sturdy crossbeam and in front of a long bench.

The executioner then faced the first prisoner, who was the only woman on the scaffold. He looped one of the nooses over her head. She trembled visibly. Seeing this the crowd's jeers and shouts of abuse flared again.

'What's she done then?' Saul asked out loud.

The old woman in front turned around and grinned at him.

'She stole one of Squire Danvers's pheasants,' she answered and quickly turned back, eager not to miss any of the action.

On the scaffold the last prisoner in the line had just had a noose looped over his head. The executioner took a step back, turned to the officials and nodded.

With exaggerated, official pomp Sir Richard stepped up on to the stage and raised a hand for silence. After a short while the noise of the crowd started to die down. He paused for a moment before he spoke.

'People of Evesham. It is my solemn duty as High Sheriff of this shire to carry out the sentence of this court.' He looked over the heads of the townsfolk and suppressed a smile at the sight of all the enthusiastic faces staring up at him. Without taking his eyes off the crowd, he raised the scroll he was holding.

After a nod from Sir Richard the executioner helped the prisoners, one at a time, to stand on the bench. His assistant, who had climbed up a ladder, was leaning against the scaffold, ready to check that each rope was tied securely around the crossbeam. Once he was satisfied that his assistant had properly tied the knots, he stepped away from the bench. He walked back along the line and stopped in front of the woman. He then pulled one of the white linen bags over her head. Now all eyes looked at the tall figure of the High Sheriff.

From the scroll he held out, Sir Richard read the woman's name and the crime with which she had been found guilty. He did the same for the second and third, each time a white bag was placed over the condemned's head. The crowd shouted and hissed when each name was read out. Before he was about to read out the last name he paused a few moments, to let the atmosphere build.

'Simon Allslopp. You have been found guilty of…' he stopped. Slowly he looked up and crossed himself, '…the sodomy and murder of a child.'

As he said the last words the crowd went berserk. The curses and threats that they screamed at the scaffold were deafening. The armed guards that surrounded the scaffold pushed the spectators back as they surged forward, in an attempt to reach the stage.

Sir Richard waited for the last white bag to be pulled over Allslop's head. He then turned to face the condemned and the noise of the crowd faded to a dull murmur. The tolling of the church bell suddenly stopped.

'May God have mercy on your souls.' He

nodded and the executioner quickly kicked the bench away.

The crowd erupted into loud cheers and shouts of applause as the four prisoners swung from the gallows. Their legs kicked and their bodies jerked as the life was slowly choked from them.

'Saul?' Eli said sounding anxious.

'What?'

'Is that what it's going to be like for us?'

CHAPTER 13.

Isaiah trudged wearily through the village as the last of the daylight was disappearing. He was following the muddy road that led back to the vicarage when a horse suddenly appeared from behind one of the cottages. The startled beast's thundering hooves kicked mud and earth in all directions, knocking him off his feet.

For a few moments he lay dazed in the road, before angrily jumping to his feet.

'Damn and blast your eyes man. Will you watch where you're going,' he shouted, brushing the mud off his clothes, but when he looked up at the rider his next words instantly caught in his throat.

In the saddle sat a stunningly beautiful young woman, wrapped in a heavy green riding cloak. By the cut of the bright emerald cloth and the soft ermine collar he could tell she had means. He quickly gathered his wits and snatched off his hat, bowing low.

'My deepest apologies Miss, please forgive my outburst.'

She looked down at him and smiled.

'I'm sorry sir. I fear the beast is testing me.' The magnificent bay gelding was still skittish as she patted its broad neck. 'I've named him Lancelot.

Do you think it suits him?'

'A noble name indeed Miss,' He replied, captivated by her innocent face and impish charm. 'Certainly worthy of a fine animal such as this.'

'Thank you, good Sir.' she answered, pleased with the compliment. Now the horse was becoming calmer the girl sat up straighter in the saddle. 'I don't believe we've met before sir.'

'I'm afraid not Miss, for I would never have forgotten such a moment.' the girl blushed as he replied. 'My name is Daniel Archer.' He had learnt a long time ago never to give his real name. 'Would you honour me with your name my lady, so I may forever live a happy man.'

She giggled clearly enjoying the attention.

'I will reward your kind words Sir. My name is Mary Danvers.'

'Bugger it', he thought to himself, 'She's the squire's daughter'. His heart sank as he felt the hopelessness of the situation wash over him. He knew the class divide alone made it impossible for him to get to know her any better, never mind the jealous father. He paused longer than he intended to.

'Is there anything the matter Mr. Archer?' she asked. His blank look was making her feel uncomfortable.

'Miss Danvers please, I beg you to forgive my rudeness. It has just occurred to me that I'm late for an appointment.' He again took off his hat and bowed, his eyes never leaving hers.

'Till we meet again, Sir.' she inclined her head, blushing deeper this time.

'Your servant, Miss.'

She turned her horse slowly and walked away into the dusk. When she took the chance to look around one final time, the street was deserted.

Two dark figures stood in the shadows of the wool merchant's yard, which looked out over Merstow Green, Evesham's other execution site.

The last body from the afternoon's public display now hung in an iron cage from the town gibbet. The abandoned body of Simon Allslopp swung in the cold night air as an example of what happens to those who chose to engage in sodomy and murder. The other three bodies had been secretly reclaimed by their families after the crowds had dispersed.

'There's nobody coming, I tell you.' Eli whispered in his brother's ear.

'Master Wayland said that someone would turn up after dark.' Saul replied watching the cage swing on the gibbet. 'All we've got to do is wait for 'em, watch 'em and follow 'em. Now shut your noise.'

As they watched, clouds drifted across the night sky, uncovering the moon. The green was instantly bathed in a bright translucent light. The tension between them had evaporated when Saul nudged his brother's elbow. Eli looked at him and saw that he was pointing in the direction of the bushes, on the other side of the Green. When he looked over he saw that a fox had emerged from its dark, leafy hiding place. Its ears were pricked up, listening for any signs of danger. After a brief moment it broke from the cover of the bushes and trotted over to the gibbet. It stopped next to the post and gazed up at the silent corpse.

Suddenly a sound broke the silence, startling the fox from its trance. The animal quickly spun around and sprinted off across the open ground, disappearing into the darkness. Without warning a figure walked from the shadow of one of the buildings on the other side of the green and strode over to the gibbet.

'What's this one doing then?' Eli whispered

'There's another one over there, look.' Saul said, quietly. He pointed to a spot on the other side of the green as another dark figure stepped into the moonlight.

The two brothers watched the second figure

walk over to his companion. The first figure reached up and took hold of the cage with both hands. His companion produced a long bladed knife from under his cloak. He then climbed up the ladder that was leaning against the post and reached into the cage.

Saul felt a slight tap on his arm.

'I know,' he whispered. He couldn't believe his eyes. The figure standing on the ladder had pulled the corpse's hand out of the cage and had started sawing at the wrist with the knife.

In no time at all, the knife had easily worked through the dead man's wrist. The figure that stood on the ladder triumphantly held his gruesome trophy in the air, before tossing it down to his companion. He then reached into the cage and started working on the corpse's other wrist.

Once he had completed the grizzly task, he climbed down the ladder and gave the other hand to his accomplice.

'What are they doing now?' Eli whispered as he watched the figures huddle together around the gibbet post.

'Quiet!' Saul answered.

After a while the two shapes turned and walked back across the green, disappearing into the shadows. Saul grabbed his brother by the arm.

'Go, get the horses and meet me on the other side.' he said quickly. Eli turned and sprinted back into the yard.

Saul waited until he was sure the two figures had gone before running out of the yard and over to the gibbet. When he reached the post he stopped and looked up at the corpse. He saw that the mutilated arms were now hanging out through the bars of the cage, with his sawn wrists exposed to the moonlight. It made it look as if the dead man was just casually watching the world go by. He shuddered involuntarily as he looked at the exposed sinew, but just then he noticed something else. A strange symbol had been carved into the gibbets post. When he looked closer he saw that it was an inverted pentangle. He was not entirely sure what it meant but he knew Master Wayland would want to know.

A noise startled him and he looked round to see Eli leading his horse out of the shadows. He ran over to his brother, who had already mounted up.

'Did you see where they went?' he said climbing in to the saddle.

'They've both gone west and they're mounted as well.'

105.

'Come on then, we don't want to loose sight of the mad bastards'

As soon as the brothers had galloped away two more mounted figures appeared, from the shadows of one of the other cottages overlooking the green.

The features of the two dark riders were hidden under the wide brims of their hats, as they watched Saul and Eli disappear in to the night. Then with out pausing they dug their spurs in and followed after them.

CHAPTER 14.

When his eyes snapped open he recoiled at the sight in front of him. Dancing flames and thick smoke spread as far as the eye could see. A sea of tall stakes covered the field, like a gigantic bed of nails.

As the screams of the tormented assaulted his ears, he fought back the urge to retch at the sweet smell of burning flesh that polluted the air.

'May God have mercy on their souls.' he whispered.

He could feel the intense heat of the fires on his face and the acrid, poisonous fumes burning his lungs. Tortured faces cried out to him, pleading, begging for him to end to their agony. When he could eventually bear no more he turned away, tears rolling down his face.

'God forgive me…God forgive me…God for…'

'Thomas? Thomas…Are you alright?'

He opened his eyes and saw that the fire was still roaring away in the hearth. He glanced round to see that Samuel was still sat at the table, sharpening his knife and the minister was sat up at his desk, looking back at him with a worried expression on his face. Thomas smiled weakly at the old man.

'I'm quite alright William. Thank you.'

The minister nodded in response, although not wholly convinced.

'I was just saying that I think one of the Cooper brothers have returned.'

Thomas stood up and stretched the tension from his back, before walking over to the table. There was a quiet knock at the door.

'Come in Mr. Mathews. I keep telling you, there's no need to knock.' William said, smiling at the embarrassed verger, who had entered the office and was now holding the door open for Isaiah.

Thomas smiled in greeting.

'Good evening Mr. Cooper. I trust you were successful in your task?' He sat down and waved Isaiah to join them.

Isaiah walked over and sat down at the large table. He was still impressed at the welcoming feel he experienced whenever he was in the minister's office.

'Yes Master, I've discovered where the old woman lives.' he answered looking from Thomas to Samuel. The two men still made him feel nervous.

'Well? Enlighten us Mr. Cooper.' Thomas said sensing that Isaiah was reluctant to speak.

'Speak boy!' Samuel snapped, causing Isaiah to flinch.

'Thank you Mr. Bolton.' Thomas said after a few moments, 'Would you care to enlighten us, Isaiah?'

Cooper avoided the large man's gaze.

'She lives in Poden.' He answered.

William slowly sat back in his chair. 'Are you sure Isaiah?'

'I'm sure sir,' he replied, 'Sarah at the Black Dog told me and by the look on her face she wasn't lying.'

The minister ruefully shook his head.

'It seems our mission has become more perilous, gentlemen.'

'What concerns you William?' Thomas looked at his old friend. 'How far away is Poden?'

'It's not too far, but the trouble lies not in where it is, but what has happened there?' He stood up and walked over to the table. 'The village of Poden used to be only a few miles away from here. I say 'used to be' for a reason.' The old minister glanced at the men in the room with a grave expression on his lined face. 'Years ago, the entire population was wiped out by the pestilence. The place has been deserted ever since.' He sat down and rubbed his eyes, 'Years later, rumours of a woman living in the dead village, began to spread. I have heard that some of the older folk have sought her out, to trade with her for her cures.'

'Sarah says the place is cursed,' Isaiah added, remembering the fear in the girl's face as she had told him, 'She said the witch who lives there can raise the dead.'

'Be careful boy. What you speak is blasphemy,' Samuel growled, plunging the room into silence. 'If God has left that place, it is no concern of ours.'

Suddenly, there was a loud hammering on the front door, interrupting the somber mood in the room.

Isaiah frowned, 'That can only be Saul. The idiot couldn't be quiet if his life depended on it.'

'The way events are unfolding, our lives 'might' depend on it.' William said, he looked at the verger. 'Mr. Mathews would be so kind?'

Justin nodded and disappeared from the room.

Moments later Saul entered looking cold and disheveled. Thomas motioned for him to sit in one of the chairs by the fire. Justin poured him a mug of wine. He immediately launched into the retelling of the day's events at the hanging, what they had witnessed happen to the corpse that hung from gibbet that evening, and how they had followed the two figures through the night.

He finished by explaining that Eli was still watching the strangers from a hiding place in the woods. Isaiah suddenly stood up.

'You left him there?' he shouted, 'Is he armed?'

Saul cowered in his chair, startled by his brother's out burst.

'He's got his knife and I gave him the pistol as well.'

'You stupid bastard! That bloody pistol doesn't work, it never has and the last time he tried to use his blade he cut himself.' Isaiah was getting louder. 'Why do you think you went together?' He strode over and gripped Saul by the collar and lifted him off the chair, raising his hand to strike.

'No!' Samuel's harsh voice stopped Isaiah before he landed the blow. The room went silent, the tension in the air, palpable.

Thomas broke the silence.

'Thank you Samuel. Mr. Cooper calm yourself, your brothers have shown remarkable ingenuity. You should be proud of them.' He stood up from the table and slowly walked over the hearth, stopping to stare into the fire. 'So they took both hands,' he said eventually with out turning around, 'That does not bode well.'

Isaiah pushed his brother back into his chair and sat back at the table, his face like thunder.

'Please explain Thomas.' William asked looking confused. 'What is the significance of the dead man's hands?'

'Witches believe that the hand of a dead man is one of the most potent aids to magic, commonly known as the "hand of glory".' Thomas turned to face the gathering, '…And after tonight's events, they have two.'

'We shall have to move quickly, Master.' Samuel said, returning his knife to the sheath hidden in his sleeve.

'Quite right Samuel. We move at dawn.' He turned to Saul, 'Can you find your brothers hiding place again?'

'I think so Master.' Saul said, forcing a smile. 'There was something else, Master.'

'Go on.'

'In the crowd, at the hanging, me an Eli could have sworn we saw Mr. Bolton. Only he didn't have no beard.' He looked at Samuel to see if the he would be amused and was instantly given a black look.

'Are you sure?' Thomas asked warily.

Saul nodded, 'Yes Master he looked straight at us.'

'Stop this!' Samuel boomed, slamming his large hand down on the table, 'You saw nothing boy!' he snapped as he stood up, knocking his chair to the floor. He then turned in silence and strode from the room.

CHAPTER 15.

Early the next morning Thomas pulled on the reins, slowing his horse to a walk. After a few paces he stopped on the brow of the hill and wearily surveyed the view to his front.

As he looked he was pleased to see that, at the bottom of the slope, the early morning mist still hung lazily in the air. 'Good,' he thought 'cover if we need it'. He gazed down, to where he thought the village was and noticed dark shapes starting to become visible in the grey haze. He silently agreed that Poden really did look like a village of the dead.

'Useless, bastard nag!' Isaiah spat as he eventually emerged from the trees. He was still annoyed with himself that he had lost sight of Thomas on their journey. When he looked up to see where they were and noticed that his companion had stopped on the crest of the hill. He righted himself in the saddle before trotting over to join him.

'Glad you could make it Mr. Cooper.' Thomas said without turning, 'You will tell me if I'm leaving you behind, won't you?'

'Of course Master, but the reason I think my horse was slow, was because he had a stone stuck in his hoof.' He patted his mount's neck, hoping the embarrassment in his voice wasn't showing. 'No matter though, I think he's dislodged it now.'

'Indeed.' Thomas smiled. 'Now, what do you see Isaiah?'

The younger man urged his horse forward so he could get a better view. At the bottom of the hill he could see that the mist was beginning to clear. Some roof tops, nestling amongst the trees, were starting to become visible. When he looked closer he could see that there was a thin plume of smoke spiraling into the air from the chimney of one of the buildings further back in the trees.

'A deserted village, overgrown and hidden by trees.' he answered, 'But by the looks of the smoke, someone is there.'

'Good!' Thomas answered sounding pleased, 'And now, I think we should go and find out who this supposed 'witch' is?'

They kicked their spurs back and galloped off, down the hill, towards the village.

'It's just up ahead.' Saul whispered, pointing through the trees. He and Samuel had been creeping through Cowley wood since dawn and he could sense the large man's irritation growing with every step. They had lost their way several

114.

times already.

Samuel then spotted something ahead, a shape, barely visible, but hidden beneath a bush and beyond that he could just see a small cottage.

'Hold on, this is it.' Saul whispered. He pointed to the shape up ahead, 'And there's Eli.'

'Well spotted,' the big man replied, his voice heavy with sarcasm. 'We'll wait over there,' he muttered looking to the right.

They both crouched down and worked their way round to the right of the cottage.
After a while, they found a place that gave them a good view, but still far enough back to keep them hidden. There they crawled forward into the undergrowth, keeping their heads low, until they were happy with their position and there they waited.

Whilst Samuel watched the cottage he noticed that there was a dim light shining through one of the windows. He scanned the rest of the area around the building but nothing else caught his eye.

He looked over to where the other Cooper brother was and nodded to himself, impressed at how still he was laying. Perhaps these boys were not completely useless, he thought, suddenly realising that he was actually starting to like them. He glanced at Saul, who was lying next to him, even he was keeping still. Alright, he had got them lost a few times on the way, but Master Wayland was not the best person for giving or following directions either. A sudden jab in his ribs snapped him out of his thoughts.

'Mr. Bolton. I think there's something wrong.'

When they eventually reached the bottom of the hill both men found that the mist was so thick, that they actually had to calm their nervous horses down before they could coax them into the gloom.

As they entered the ghostly village Isaiah glanced around warily at the derelict buildings. Some of the cottages were little more than sheds, most of them didn't even have roofs. A lot of the thatch that hadn't rotted away was hidden under a thick, covering of damp moss.

The harsh squawking of the watching ravens dogged their every move, as they walked their mounts through the deserted streets, which were little more than muddy tracks.

Thomas sniffed the air and then nodded ahead.

'That's where the smoke's coming from.'

Isaiah looked up and saw a sight that seemed

completely out of place in this abandoned ruin of a village, a beautiful, well kept cottage.

In the garden around the outside, flowers grew in lovingly tended boarders, that framed a neatly cut lawn. The rendered, white washed walls of the cottage were spotlessly clean and even the thatched roof looked newly repaired.

Both men stared in bewilderment at the unusual sight that confronted of them.

'Come on,' Thomas said after a few moments. 'Let us see what welcome awaits us.'

They tethered their horses to the very neat looking picket fence that bordered the garden. Then, cautiously, they made their way towards the small gate.

Thomas pushed it open, stopping to expect a cry of alarm or a shout of warning. But no sound came, so warily they both walked through, Isaiah closed it behind him. They moved guardedly along the path towards the front door. As Thomas glanced around the tidy garden, he noticed all kinds of herbs and plants. Most of them he knew but a few odd looking ones seemed out of place.

'A garden that any apothecary would be proud to have', he muttered to himself.

When they neared the cottage he saw that the

front door was open. Silently he chided himself for not noticing it earlier. Behind he could hear a quiet metallic rasp as Isaiah slowly drew his sword.

'Wait' he said holding out his hand.

Suddenly both men stopped when a voice called out from the cottage.

'I thought you were dead?'

'What do mean, you think something's wrong.' Samuel replied sharply.

Saul looked over to where his brother lay.

'It's Eli, he hasn't moved yet.'

'He's probably asleep.' Samuel answered, watching the shape in the bush. 'He's been their all night, should you care to remember.'

'But we'd know if he was kippin' cos he snores,' Saul replied turning to Samuel, 'Anyway he only kips sitting up, from when he did his back in, falling of a horse we nicked once.'

Samuel looked back to the cottage, shaking his head. They had been there for a few hours now and he was starting to feel a bit suspicious. They had not seen or heard any movement since they had arrived.

'Wait here boy,' he said after a pause.

'Why? Where are you going?'

'I'm going to have a look through the window. I want to see if there is anyone actually in there?' He replied before crawling backwards out of their hiding place.

Once he was out of the bush he stopped and listened for a few moments. When he was happy no one had been alerted he started to make his way through the trees and around the side of the cottage, running in a low crouch with his head down. He eventually worked his way through the under growth, stopping at the corner of the building, a good blind spot.

Saul watched quietly as Samuel crawled slowly out of the bushes and up to the cottage. He was very impressed at the way the big man had managed to keep himself hidden, whilst moving with out a sound.

Samuel stopped again and waited with his back to the wall, listening for any sounds of movement from inside. After a short while he was satisfied that if anyone was in the building they had either not spotted him, or they were asleep. 'Only one way to find out,' he thought.

He carefully turned and looked up to see exactly where the window was. Slowly he got to his knees and raised his head to peer through the corner of the grubby window pane. He could remember Thomas once telling him "There's no better way to get spotted by the enemy than by making sudden movements."

Straight away he saw that the inside of the room was deserted. The bed, that was under his window, had been slept in, but was now empty. There wasn't much in the way of furniture, just the bed and a table, next to a chair on the other side of the room. Cautiously he stood up to get a better look; it was then that he noticed there was something on the floor by the door. 'What's that?' he wondered.

Saul watched Samuel stand up and look through the cottage window. 'By the looks of it there's no one in.' he thought to himself and then crawled out of the bush. As he stood up he saw that Samuel was now at the front door, pushing it open.

With a gentle push the door creaked open and Samuel cautiously peered in.

'God in heaven!' he said, instantly recoiling in revulsion at the sight on the floor in front of him.

Thomas heard the voice and turned to Isaiah, who was already nervously raising his sword.

He looked back to the building and waited for any sign of movement.

'Come in Thomas, you are welcome here.' the voice said with a quiet chuckle. 'You too Isaiah are also welcome. Please come in.'

'Who's in there?' Isaiah shouted suddenly, earning him a reproachful glance from Thomas. But no one answered.

The two men gave each other a brief nod, before cautiously walking through the door of the cottage.

Once inside, they were momentarily blinded by the sudden disappearance of daylight. After a short while though, their eyes started to become accustomed to the dark and they began to see the bizarre interior of the cottage.

All around them it seemed that every available inch of ceiling space had been taken over by plants and herbs, hanging in various sized bundles. A huge, oak dresser dominated one side of the kitchen, with glass and stone jars, of differing colours and shapes crowding every shelf. A wide inglenook fireplace sat at the other end, the embers of the fire still glowing in the grate.

'You know, you haven't changed a bit Master Wayland, champion of the warrior saint.' said a rough, mocking female voice.

'You may sheath your sword Mr. Cooper, I don't bite you know, although I think some would have you believe otherwise.'

Thomas looked in the direction of the voice. Through the darkness he could just see the outline of a shape stood in the shadows, at the back of the kitchen.

'Madam, can I ask you to step into the light, it makes me nervous when I'm unable to see to whom I am talking.'

'Perhaps it is you who should step into the light, Thomas of Treves.' the woman chuckled.

Thomas felt his anger surge to the surface.

'That name means nothing here, woman!' he snapped.

'Not here perhaps, but to the ghosts of Treves may be, 'man of sorrows'.'

Isaiah was completely confused at what was being said. He had no idea what the strange woman was talking about and now he realised that what was making him nervous, was just a mad old woman. He felt a bit foolish.

'Who are you old woman? Speak up now because Master Wayland and I haven't got all day.'

'Be calm highwayman. Your companion will reveal all.' she replied, not at all intimidated by his abrupt tone.

He looked at Thomas, who was staring mutely at the silhouette of the woman.

'Master? What does she mean?'

Thomas's expression softened slightly. 'It seems that the lady has some knowledge of my exploits in the Germanic states.' As he spoke the shape shuffled into the light.

The woman was wrapped in a thick woollen shawl, which covered her completely, and reached to the floor. Beneath the folds they could just see her heavily lined face. By her looks she had once been attractive and when she smiled, to their surprise, she revealed a set of even white teeth.

'I not only know of what has happened in Europe, I also have knowledge of present happenings closer to home, which is the real reason you are here, I think.' Her piercing blue eyes confidently returned Thomas's stare.

Isaiah blinked in puzzlement. He was still unsure at what was going on.

'Who are you old woman?' he blurted out.

Thomas smiled back at her, recognition now dawning on his face.

'She is an old friend, Isaiah,' he replied warmly. 'Hello Charlotte. The years have been kind to you.'

'You never could lie Thomas Wayland.' she said shuffling around the table. When she stopped in front of him, she gazed into his eyes. 'You though, look as if you carry the sins of man on your shoulders.'

'I am fine, thank you,' he answered wearily, removing his hat. 'We have come Charlotte, to ask if you have any knowledge of a coven in Honeybourne?'

Charlotte moved to the table.

'Sit down by the fire, both of you. I will fetch some cider and bread, then we will talk.'

The two men wandered over to the huge fireplace and sat down on the stools that were scattered around the hearth.

As they sat and waited Isaiah noticed animal sculls had been placed all around the hearth, fox, weasel, rat and all other manner of creatures were stacked neatly, their hollow, bestial faces mocking them.

Isaiah jumped when he felt a jab in his side. As he turned Thomas nodded at the ledge above the fire. Staring down at them was a human skull, which had strange symbols carved into the bone.

Charlotte banged a platter of bread and cheese on a small table to their side and handed them each a mug of cider.

'I take it, that you being here means that you're having trouble with Baphomet?' She said sitting down on one of the stools. She then took a long drink from a stone mug, most of the pale liquid dribbled down her chin.

'Do you know who he is?' Isaiah asked, looking from the grinning skull back to the old woman.

'Of course I know who he is and I would wager that you and Thomas have already met him.'

Samuel spun around in the doorway, when he heard Saul walk out of the bushes.

'Wait there boy!' He shouted. When he saw the hurt look on the younger man's face, he instantly regretted his harsh tone. 'Wait there a moment.' he repeated, this time in a calmer tone.

'I was just going to fetch Eli, that's all,' he called back and went to walk off, but he stopped as soon he saw the Samuel close the door and walk towards him, with what looked like a pained expression on his face. As the big man got nearer he did something Saul had never seen him do before, he smiled. Even though it seemed rather strained and uncomfortable, it was still a smile.

'Come, we have to get back to the vicarage. There are no witches here.' He tried to sound casual, but by the look on the young man's face he had failed.

After a few moments Saul nodded.

'Alright, but what about Eli?' he asked, beginning to sound concerned. 'We can't leave him here.' He stepped away from Samuel and shouted over to his brother's hiding place. 'Oi! Come on you lazy bastard, we're off.'

'Leave him Saul, we have to be going.' Samuel reached out to grab Cooper's arm. 'Eli will be along later.'

Saul pulled his arm away quickly and stepped back out of reach.

'What do you mean leave him? Why can't he come with us now?' He could feel himself becoming agitated. '…And why are you calling me Saul all of a sudden? You've never called me by my proper name before.'

'Leave it, boy!' Samuel growled, knowing that he wasn't handling the situation very well, 'We have to go, now!'

'No! I'm getting Eli first!' Saul shouted and he ran for the bushes, ducking under Samuel's out stretched arm.

Samuel immediately set off after him, but the

younger man was quicker. 'Wait boy!' he called out but Cooper ignored him.

Saul could hear the other man running after him as he sprinted off. When he reached the bushes and saw his brother's shape lying on the ground, beneath the bush.

'Wake up you lazy sod!' He shouted feeling angry and confused at the same time, unable to work out what was going on.

He then reached his leg into the bush and kicked Eli's boot. He instantly jumped back when Eli's boot simply fell away.

'Eli!' he cried out in surprise, before frantically crawling into the bush and reaching out for his brother's cloak.

Samuel caught up as Saul was crawling out of the bush. He watched as the younger man stood up and held out Eli's cloak.

'Where's my brother?' he asked, a look of agonised confusion on his face. Suddenly his eyes widened and he turned to look at the cottage. 'You didn't say what you saw inside the cottage, Mr. Bolton.'

Samuel just stared at him, unable to answer, it was then that Saul slowly took a step backwards. Samuel shook his head.

'Leave it boy! Don't go in there.' He said walking towards Cooper, who was still moving backwards.

Suddenly the younger man turned and ran towards the cottage.

'Stop! Don't go in there,' Samuel shouted after him, knowing what was waiting for the younger man when he reached the front door. His heart sank as he began walking towards the cottage.

Saul reached the front of the building and without pausing, kicked the front door wide open. The old lock immediately splintered and the door crashed back against the inner wall.

When he looked inside he instantly stumbled back with a look of utter horror on his face. In front of him, lying spread eagled on the floor was Eli's naked, mutilated body.

CHAPTER 16.

The stone walls of the chamber made the air feel cold and even the fire, dying in the grate, had failed to penetrate the chill. Behind a heavy oak table, seemingly unaffected by the cold, sat the local Squire, Robert Danvers. The tension in the air was palpable. None of the other men gathered in the room could meet his gaze as he stared at them.

The constable, Martin Richards, who stood next to the Squire's table, had seen his master angry before, but today was different. Today, he thought, the squire wasn't just angry, there was something else there as well... hatred. That was it, it was almost if he hated the two strange church men.

'Well?... Why weren't those two bastards beaten black and blue?' The squire asked menacingly, his deep voice echoing around the damp chamber. He glared at the men standing in front of the table. His face was flushed with anger. 'Well? Fellows… you seem to be in charge of this band of half wits. What have you got to say for yourself?'

Duncan looked up, a hurt expression on his face. 'I…err…I don't know what happened Sir. It was if they were ready for us.'

Danvers stood up suddenly, knocking his chair over.

'Ready for you, eh? They're a couple of fucking travelling vicars, and there were more of you, as well!' He suddenly stopped in mid rant and looked directly at Duncan. 'Don't tell me you lot weren't armed?'

'We were armed Squire. We had clubs, but they had those long quarter staffs, of theirs.' He shook his head slowly, the memory of the fight, still clear in his mind. 'I've never seen anybody fight like that before Sir. They were just too fast.'

The squire was walking slowly from behind the table while Duncan was retelling the events of a few days ago. He stopped in front of the tanner just as he'd finished his tale.

Duncan looked into the squire's broad face.

'Shit, I'm for it now,' he thought. He tensed his stomach and screwed his face up, waiting for the inevitable blow from one of the big man's heavy fists.

The Squire just looked at him for a few moments and then smiled. Duncan relaxed, thinking the danger had passed. Suddenly a blinding pain exploded across his face and he collapsed in a heap against the back wall of the chamber. Blood from his broken nose trickled down his chin.

The Squire bent forward so his face was level with the tanner's.

'Oh dear, was that just too fast for you?' He sneered and then walked back to his chair and sat down. 'Listen you useless bunch of cripples. Tomorrow you will have another chance to get those two bastards, but this time I will be there as well.' He sat back in his chair and glared at the line of men, his anger abating slightly. He always felt better after he had hit somebody. 'Now, Constable Richards, I would be grateful if you could get this band of idiots out of my house.'

The constable smirked as he moved around the table and took hold of Duncan's arm.

'Up you get, you great lump.' he murmured.

One of the other men also helped the tanner to his feet, before they all shuffled out the door.

In the hall outside, they all visibly relaxed. Richards looked at them and grinned.

'Right lads be here tomorrow at dawn. You will still need your cudgels but this time the Squire wants you to bring crossbows.' He looked at the men gravely. 'He wants 'em dead this time.'

None of them answered him, instead they just nodded.

After closing the front door the constable went

to go back into the Squire's office, but stopped when he heard Danvers's rough voice.

'Martin go and get Mary. I want to talk to her.'

'Right oh, Squire,' he replied before turning on his heel and hurrying back down the passage to the kitchen.

Mary had just finished pinching the pastry edge around the top of a large pie, which took up most of the space on the kitchen table. The cook, a big woman with a chubby face and thick forearms, was watching the girl as she finished.

'You've done a wonderful job of that, Miss Mary,' Mrs. Potts said, clapping her hands as the girl stood back and admired her handiwork.

'You know Mrs. Potts, I enjoyed making that. I only hope it tastes as good as it looks,' Mary said sounding satisfied, whilst she brushed the flour from the front of her dress.

Both women turned when the door swung open and Martin Richards strode in to the kitchen, with a worried look on his face.

'There you are, Miss Mary. The Squire is looking for you,' he said. Then his eyes fell on the pie sat on the table and he smiled. 'You've done yourself proud there Miss Mary.'

'And where is my father, constable?' she asked sounding rather aloof. She had never liked the man. He had always seemed lecherous and far too friendly for her liking.

'He's in his study, Miss Mary; I'll take you to him.' He grinned at her manner, fully aware of what she thought of him. She'd hate him even more if she knew what he wanted to do to her he thought, already feeling the familiar tingling in his groin.

'No constable, that won't be necessary,' she answered staring at him. 'I'm quite capable of finding my way in my own house.'

He bowed to her, turned and held open the door.

'It's no trouble Miss, I'm just doing my duty.' His kept his head bowed in mock respect as she stormed past him, with her head held high. When he straightened up he looked at the cook and winked. 'See you later, Bette.'

Robert sat up as his daughter walked into his office. He frowned when he saw the black look on her face.

'What is it Mary? Why the angry look?' He stood up and walked around the table with his large arms held open.

She walked into his embrace and allowed her mood to soften.

'It's that man. He always tries to make me feel inferior, and he watches me.' The last words added almost as an afterthought.

'Which man?' he asked, already having a good idea who she meant.

'That man, Mathews. I really don't know who he thinks he is.'

When he let go of her she sat down on one of the chairs by the table. He smiled warmly when he saw that she still had flour on her face. She grinned playfully at him while he leaned forward and brushed her cheek.

'You look so much like your mother when she was your age,' he said softly.

'What happened to her father?' she asked, but frowned when he stood up and turned away.

'Please Mary, I've told you, she's dead,' he replied after a while, wincing when he saw her reaction to his cold tone. 'Please forgive me,' he said, trying to sound more cheerful. 'Let us not dwell on the past, eh?' She nodded mutely and he walked back to his chair and sat down. He hated lying to her, but she just wasn't ready for the truth yet.

Mary felt concerned as she watched her father sit back behind his desk. Recently she had noticed how he seemed to look more tired than usual.

'Is there something troubling you father?'

The expression on his face changed slightly and his smile disappeared.

'I want to ask you something, my love?'

Mary sat up when she realised that he was being serious.

'What is it?' she asked.

'Well, someone has told me that you were talking to a strange man in the village, the other day.' He tried not to let his disapproval show.

She looked surprised at the question.

'Has someone been spying on me?' she eventually replied, stunned at the fact that someone could be watching her.

He instantly held his large hands up in submission.

'Nobody is spying on you my dear, I'm just concerned for your safety.'

She relaxed slightly after hearing the worry in her father's voice.

'There was a gentleman yes, and he was very polite. He introduced himself as Mr. Daniel Archer.'

Leaning forward, he kissed her on the forehead.

'Thank you for telling me and I'm glad that he treated you like a gentleman should.' He smiled affectionately. 'Would you please send the constable in when you leave, my dear. Thank you.' He smiled as she walked out.

Mary left the room in a lighter mood than

when she came in, but her smile soon disappeared as she passed the grinning Richards, who was loitering outside in the passageway.

Once Mary had gone the constable entered the office and sat down in the chair opposite the Squire. He immediately started to feel the stiffening in his groin, when he realised that the seat was still warm from where she had been sitting.

'Well, who was he?' he asked the Squire, mainly to break the silence, but also to avoid the subject of any complaints made by his daughter.

'I'm positive it was that bastard Cooper.' Danvers said eventually, 'Mary said he called himself Archer.'

Richards picked his nose.

'So what are we going to do?' he asked as he examined what was on the end of his grubby finger.

The Squire watched the other man with disgust. Mary was right he really was a piece of work.

'If it is Cooper, he'll die with that bastard Wayland tomorrow.' He waited until the constable had finished what he was doing. 'You really are a foul creature, aren't you, Richards?'

The constable started to grin as he looked up,

thinking the Squire was joking. His smile immediately disappeared when the look on his master's face convinced him he was not. Straight away he tried to change the subject.

'Why do you hate this Wayland fella so much then?'

The Squire's expression darkened making the constable feel uneasy.

'Suffice to say, he knows what he has done. Tomorrow he will pay with his life.' His voice became louder, 'And you will join them too, if you don't improve your behaviour towards my daughter, 'cos I'll fucking kill you myself.'

CHAPTER 17.

The two men had been riding since dawn. During the night it had rained, making the track leading out of the deserted village wet and muddy. The horses were making slow progress as they walked up the hill that over looked the dale.

They had spent the night on the floor of the kitchen, laid out in front of the fire, after talking until late.

Charlotte had been a generous host and during the evening Isaiah was sure that he had detected an obvious connection between her and Thomas. When they set off, he had tried to question him about his friendship with the old woman, but he was met with a stony silence.

'What happens now Master?' Isaiah asked, looking across at the other man. Thomas didn't answer, so they travelled on in silence.

After several miles the track led them into dense woods. They slowed their mounts to a walk, both men were now on their guard, watching for any sign of an ambush. After a while Thomas stopped.

'What is it Master?' Isaiah asked reigning in next to him and tightly gripping the basket hilt of his sword.

'Let us rest here for a while, Mr. Cooper. I think we need to talk.'

They dismounted and led their horses to the side of the track. Isaiah tied the reins to some low branches, allowing the horses to graze whilst Thomas sat down against a tree.

The younger man noticed how Thomas had chosen their position well. They had a good view of the track in both directions. He sat down and looked at Thomas,

'You wanted to talk Master?'

'Yes. I think there are a few things we need to discuss.'

Thomas reached into his leather sack and pulled out two lumps of bread. He handed one of them to Isaiah, he then pulled out a stone jar of ale.

Cooper didn't realise how hungry he was until he took his first bite of the bread. Surprisingly it was the best he had tasted for a long time. He reached for the stone jar that was by his boot.

'Isaiah, what did you think of Charlotte?' Thomas asked taking another bite of his bread and glancing at the younger man.

Cooper stopped eating and looked at his companion.

'What do you mean, what do I think of her,

139.

Master?'

'I mean what is your opinion of her?' Thomas took another swig of water.

'Well, apart from being a raving lunatic, I just think she is a bit lonely.' Isaiah smiled and drank a few more mouthfuls of ale. 'Most healers are,' he said wiping his mouth with the back of his hand, 'It comes from living alone in the middle of nowhere.'

Thomas smiled at him. 'She's a witch you know.'

'Eh! She's a witch?' Cooper spluttered, looking stunned. 'Shouldn't we be hanging her now or something, at the least arresting her?'

'Not really.' Thomas paused. He thought about the best way of explaining himself. 'When I say she's a witch, I mean she's a true witch.'

Isaiah still didn't quite understand what was being said.

'Is there a difference? Surely they are still just evil hags.'

'Yes,' Thomas laughed. 'There is a vast difference. For one, true witches or Wiccas as they should be properly called, do not worship Satan.' Thomas glanced up and down the deserted track whilst he spoke. 'They worship Mother Nature, whilst at the same time they also revere the Lord God.'

'So what do we do?' Isaiah asked.

'We do nothing, Mr. Cooper. She and her like are no threat to the church. If she were to be accused of anything, it would be for brewing bad ale.' Thomas smiled, 'You said yourself that she was just a lonely healer.'

'Master, I'm sorry if I have offended you. I recall that you said she was a friend of yours.'

'Not at all, Isaiah. In a way I can see your point. She has adopted a few unusual character traits after her years of solitude.'

Suddenly he stood up and took hold of his quarterstaff.

'I suggest you arm yourself Mr. Cooper. I think we have visitors.'

Isaiah jumped up, drew his sword and spun around. He looked down the track, the way they had come, just as a band of riders came into view, galloping wildly towards them, their horse's hooves sending mud and earth flying in all directions.

'Bloody hell! It's the Squire. What does he want?'

'I believe the Squire still has a score to settle.' Thomas said holding his staff out in front of him, ready to meet an attack from the riders.

Four of the riders quickly dismounted and grabbed sturdy looking crossbows. They all spread out and faced Isaiah and Thomas, all the while pointing their loaded weapons directly at them.

Thomas looked at the men's faces. All seemed capable, none of them looking particularly edgy. 'A worrying prospect.' he thought to himself. He looked beyond their captors to see that Squire Danvers and the constable were still mounted.

'Good morning Robert. A pleasant day, I'm sure you'll agree.'

Danvers urged his horse forward slightly.

'I'm Glad you think so,' he answered in his usual gruff voice. '…because it's your last, you bastard!' His face twisted into a mask of pure hatred.

Martin Richards glanced sideways at the Squire. He still didn't understand why he hated this man so much.

'I have been waiting for this, for a long time.' The Squire said, an evil smile appeared on his face. 'Finally, after all these years, you are going to pay for what you have done.'

'And what have I done Robert?' Thomas asked, his voice getting louder.

Isaiah watched the men whilst the exchange of words took place. Their faces betrayed no visible emotion. 'They seem to be well picked men.' he thought to himself. Obviously the squire had learnt his lesson about what sort of men he employed.

'You know full well what you did. Anyway the time for talking has passed.' Danvers sneered. 'Now, you miserable whoreson, you're going to die.'

Thomas looked warily at the crossbows aimed at him and Isaiah, but then unexpectedly he heard something from behind the men, that caught his attention. He glanced past them, trying to look into the trees. Then he heard the noise again, a quiet, whistling bird call.

Isaiah tightened his fingers around the hilt of his sword, the weight of the blade didn't give him the comfort he wanted. Just then, a loud booming laugh jolted him from his thoughts. When he looked around he saw that it was Thomas.

'Oh shit.' he said under his breath. He had heard about people acting in strange ways when they faced death. Somehow he thought Thomas would have be different.

The squire enjoyed what he was seeing. Finally the arrogant Thomas Wayland was losing his nerve. Suddenly something buzzed past his arm. He spun around in the saddle to see what it was, but the track behind him was deserted. Another burst of Thomas's laughter caused him to turn back.

Immediately, he could see that two of his men were on the ground, one with a short thick arrow embedded in his skull. The other lay next to him, choking loudly with blood bubbling from his mouth and a similar arrow protruding from his throat.

'What the hell is happening? Richards, where are you?' He looked around to see that the constable had turned his horse and was already galloping off down the track.

Thomas had stopped laughing and was now looking intently at the two remaining henchmen. They both looked back at him with worried expressions on their faces.

'If I were you gentlemen I would place your weapons on the ground and go.'

One of the men turned to Danvers, who had drawn his sword.

'Squire, what do we do?'

'Shoot them, damn you!' the squire shouted, 'Shoot them now!'

Isaiah was struggling to take in the events that were unfolding in front of him. He glanced at Thomas who just stood there and grinned.

'Master what's happening?'

'If you trust me Isaiah, you will stand very still and keep quiet.' Thomas answered.

Cooper saw Thomas's face and knew he was being serious. He looked back, when he heard another buzzing sound followed by yelp.

Another of the squire's men had been struck in the throat by one of the wicked looking arrows. His crossbow clattered to the ground as he fell to his knees and toppled over, with blood frothing from his mouth.

At this point the squire had had enough. He turned his mount wildly and galloped off in the direction he had come.

The last man watched forlornly as his master rode off down the track. He turned back to face Thomas before dropping his weapon and falling to his knees.

'Master Wayland, I was only doing what I was told.' He looked from Thomas to Isaiah as he spoke.

Thomas glanced at the man, with a grave expression on his face.

'Leave the weapon and go. Pray nightly that we never meet under these circumstances again.'

The man quickly got to his feet and ran over to his horse.

Isaiah called out to him.

'Leave the horses!'

The man turned around, looking as if he was about to protest. But Cooper shook his head, knowing what was going to be said. The man, quickly realised what his only option was and ran, slipping on the muddy, uneven track as he went.

When the fleeing man had gone Thomas walked into the middle of the track.

'Titus!' he shouted at the top of his voice.

Just then a huge man walked out of the trees, with a wide beaming smile on his face. His cheerful eyes and huge moustache were set above a chiselled jaw line. The wide crimson sash, which he wore around his waist, stood out against a dark green tunic and black breastplate.

Altogether, with a huge hat and the long sword that hung from his belt, he appeared like a giant, conquering hero.

Isaiah thought the man looked like one of the insane, murderous pirates from the tales his mother used to tell him.

With a flourish the man swept off his huge, wide brimmed hat and bowed. He started laughing again as he walked towards the two men.

'Master Wayland!' he bellowed, 'I'd wager my best codpiece that I've never seen you look so relieved to see me. Ha ha!'

CHAPTER 18.

'Damn you, Titus, you cut it fine.' Thomas laughed lifting his eye patch and rubbing the empty socket. He pushed the leather patch back in place and glanced at Isaiah, who had a look of utter astonishment on his face.

Then Titus saw the young man's face.

'The last time I saw a look like that it was on a head, stuck on a spike on London Bridge,' he said loudly.

'Old friend, you have always had that effect on people.' Thomas said cheerfully, as he clapped Isaiah on the shoulder. 'Mr. Cooper I have the…dubious pleasure of introducing Captain Titus Barnard.'

Isaiah stared in bewilderment at the newcomer.

'P...pleased to meet you sir.' he stammered, bowing as low as he could.

'Ha! Get up boy. If you're a companion of Master Wayland's you have no need to bow to me.' Barnard put his hat back on, checking the brim was set at the correct angle. 'Well Master Wayland, what did you think of the men's marksmanship?'

'Same as always, Titus. Faultless.'

'Bollocks! I told them all, I wanted head shots,'

Barnard said loudly. He turned to the tree line he had just appeared from. 'Sergeant Roach!'

'Captain!' answered a loud, rough voice from the trees.

Isaiah watched dumbfounded as a short, bull like figure appeared from the trees.

Sergeant Roach was uniformed much the same as Barnard, with the exception of the crimson sash and the large hat. His weather beaten face was criss crossed with old scars, which spoke of a lifetime spent on numerous distant battlefields. The large horse pistol that was pushed into his belt and the long sword that hung at his side only added to the look of a battled hardened veteran.

'Bartholomew assemble the company please,' Barnard called out calmly.

'Certainly Captain,' Roach answered with a nod before disappearing back into the trees.

'Would you like the cowardly whoreson who scampered off brought back?' Barnard asked as he smoothed his moustache.

Thomas shook his head.

'A kind offer Titus, but no. We'll see the squire again soon enough. I also have a feeling that we are going to need him alive.'

Then Sergeant Roach marched out of the trees, this time stopping in the middle of the track. He was followed by some men similarly uniformed, who all stopped in front of him, lining up into two files. Nobody spoke while they were forming up, until Sergeant Roach's hard edged voice broke the silence.

'That was the worst display of shooting I have ever witnessed,' he suddenly screamed at them. He began pacing along the front rank, 'I now have to go to the Captain and explain why you poxed scum can't hit a barn door at ten paces.' He stopped and faced the men with his powerful arms held out, 'What do I have to do, eh? Next time, go to the nearest inbred collection of hovels and find the local half witted, cross eyed wench and get her to chuck the bolts at them, eh?' Most of the men were trying to stop themselves from grinning as he shouted at them.

Isaiah looked out of the corner of his eye and realised that Captain Barnard was now standing in between him and Thomas.

'Best fighting men you'll ever meet,' Titus said proudly, in a low voice.

'Then why so hard on them, Sir?' Isaiah asked, remembering to sound respectful. The Captain's loud, bombastic behaviour unnerved him.

'That is precisely the reason they are the best. That and one of the finest Sergeants I have ever had the honour to serve with.'

Cooper saw the expression on Barnard's face and knew the man meant every word.

Whilst they were talking Sergeant Roach marched over to them. The assembled company stood on the road, all silent and unmoving. He stopped in front of Barnard and saluted.

'The men are formed up and ready for you to address them Sir.' Roach then saw Thomas and a smiled appeared on his face, softening his hard features. 'Hello Master Wayland, it's been a long time. I'm glad the lord has chosen to keep you safe and well.'

'God bless you, Bartholomew. I'm relieved to see Titus hasn't managed to lead you to certain death yet,' Thomas said warmly, smiling back at him.

'It's not for the want of trying, sir.' replied the Sergeant, grinning.

'What was that Sergeant? I've got ears like a shithouse rat you know,' Titus called out.

'I was just telling Master Wayland how much of an honour it is to serve under you Sir.' Roach answered, bowing slightly.

'You're a lying weasel, Sergeant.'

'Thank you, sir.'

It was plain to all that this was just a regular charade, being played out between two men who had known and respected each other for years.

'Shall I order the company to mount up, Sir?' Titus looked to Thomas.

'Is our work finished here, Master Wayland?'

'Yes I think it is, Titus.' Thomas nodded to Sergeant Roach. 'Thank you, Bartholomew.'

Barnard clapped his hands.

'Ready the company Sergeant. I want scouts on the flanks as well please. I'll speak to the men later and where's my fucking horse!' he bellowed.

CHAPTER 19.

The company galloped into Honeybourne as daylight was disappearing beneath the horizon. They thundered along the village's main street until they reached the end of the row, where they turned into the court yard at the rear of the Black Dog. The chaotic sound of the horse's hooves on the cobbled yard echoed off the back wall of the tavern.

At once the men started to dismount and attend to the horses; none needing to be reminded what tasks had to be carried out. Some were removing saddles from horses, while others were rubbing the sweating beasts down with handfuls of straw.

Stood in the centre of the yard, watching the activity in the yard with an experienced eye, was Sergeant Roach. He had been soldiering for over thirty years and knew every trick there was, but as usual the company got to work with no complaint or any need for him to chivvy them along.

Isaiah was also impressed when he watched the way that the men worked together. He had never seen proper soldiers before. The town guards in Evesham and the militia in Worcester had uniforms but they were old men and youngsters with no trade, nothing like this and there weren't as many either. Then he remembered that on their journey back to the village he had noticed that a few more riders had joined the company. One of the newcomers seemed different from the rest, even though his uniform showed he was a member of the company.

The thing that stood out the most was that he looked exactly like Samuel, with his harsh looking face and intelligent eyes. His beard though was close cropped as opposed to Samuel's wild appearance, but still the similarity was striking.

Thomas urged his horse next to Isaiah.

'Mr. Cooper. The company will stay here in the charge of Sergeant Roach. You will come with me back to the vicarage, along with Captain Barnard and Dr Napier.'

Isaiah looked at the newcomer across the yard.

'Is that Dr Napier there?'

'Why yes. Most observant, Mr. Cooper. A remarkable man and a truly gifted doctor.' Thomas leaned a little closer. 'I advise you, don't seek to anger the man. Can I also assume you have noticed the obvious resemblance to Mr. Bolton.' Thomas held his hand up to stop Isaiah's interruption. 'Yes, they are brothers, but

153.

it is a matter that is not openly discussed.'

'Are you saying they don't get on? That's not that unusual, you know. Me and the other two can come to blows sometimes as well.'

'Samuel and Jonathan haven't spoken for fifteen years.'

Cooper listened to Thomas's words as he watched the doctor, who sat rigidly on his horse.

'Why Master? What happened between them?'

'Samuel has never told me and I've not seen fit to press him on the matter, nor should you. Come now, we must leave for the vicarage. Samuel should already be back there with your two wayward siblings.' They walked their mounts towards the gates of the yard. 'Titus, if you and Jonathan are ready we'll be away.' The four riders then trotted out of the yard.

Barnard turned and shouted back, 'Sergeant Roach, your company!'

The Sergeant replied with a salute, 'On the morrow men!' He kicked his spurs back and galloped out of the yard to catch up with the others.

Not far from the tavern, deep in the bowels of the earth, a very different sort of company were gathered together.

Twelve robed figures stood in a circle around a chamber, waiting in silence. Their faces were hidden by the voluminous hoods of their long black robes. Their long shadows cast by the inadequate, spluttering lanterns danced across the grey stone walls of the chamber.

A shrill voice broke the eerie silence.

'My children! The dark lord has called me to assemble you here tonight.'

A low chant started from the assembled figures as the new arrival walked around the circle and took his position in the space that had been left for him.

'Baphomet, Baphomet, Baphomet.'

The newcomer raised his arms and the chanting stopped.

'My children! The interlopers are still in our midst. He, who we serve, the nameless one, demands another sacrifice, in this time of peril.'

'Baphomet, Baphomet, Baphomet.'

'Between now and our next calling, a suitable candidate is to be chosen. You must seek my children, seek!'

'Baphomet, Baphomet, Baphomet.'

'I must speak to the interlopers. They are to have the chance to see the joy! The rapture! That is to serve the dark lord.'

'Baphomet, Baphomet, Baphomet.'

'Should they choose not to take up service with him, they must be destroyed.' This time when he raised his arms, in his hand he held a large black handled knife. 'The blood must not be wiped from the blade!' the man shouted. 'We serve Lord! We serve!'

'Baphomet, Baphomet, Baphomet, Baphomet...'

CHAPTER 20.

Bartholomew picked up his pot of ale from the bar and walked, through the tables, over to the rowdy group of men that took up almost half of the entire taproom.

'Well lads, the nags are all tucked up. The patrols are out, those of you who are next out, make this your last mug.'

'Will you sit with us Sergeant?' asked Will Spink, his baby face looking expectantly up at Bartholomew. Spink, even though he was nearly twenty and was by no means the youngest in the company, just couldn't grow a beard, much to the amusement of the men. One thing he did have in his favour was his formidable reputation as a scrounger. Titus would boast that Spink could pull a golden egg out of his backside if he ordered him to.

'Thank you Will, yes if I might. God bless you boy.' Bartholomew sat down wearily, 'What's the ale like lads?'

'Horse piss!' answered Billy Gould; the rat faced former game warden. He was one of the best shots with the crossbow and he was also one of the worst tempered men in the company. Over the years though he had proved his worth many a time, showing he would stand with any of the other men when the fighting started.

'Well, looking around, you all seem to be drinking it, so will I.' Bartholomew raised his pot, 'Barnard's Company! To hell and back!'

'The company! To Hell and back!' the men cried out in reply, with mugs raised.

The gathering went quiet for a moment. Will Spink cleared his throat.

'Sergeant, do you think you could give us a tale?'

The men muttered their agreement, before falling silent in anticipation of Bartholomew's answer.

All over Christendom soldiers loved a good story and Bartholomew was a master storyteller. His stories were famous amongst mercenary companies throughout the continent, keeping whole regiments spell bound with his tales. It was well rumoured that some men had lost control over their bladders whilst laughing at some of his funnier stories and cry like babies at the sad ones.

Everyone in the room went quiet, all of them looking at Bartholomew as he drained the last of his ale.

'I've got a tale for you lads,' he said wiping his mouth, 'If someone puts another one in there,' he said pointing to his empty mug.

As the four riders galloped through the quiet village, Isaiah spotted the church spire silhouetted against the leaden sky. The tops of the tall trees that surrounded the ancient building yielded easily to the evening breeze.

The four men rode in silence as dark shadows among the trees made them wary of their approach to the church yard. The only sound they heard was the wind gently whistling through the gravestones. Thomas led his horse through the yard gates first.

'The vicarage is at the rear of the church gentlemen, follow me.' Thomas said to his companions, slowing his horse to a trot.

They rounded the corner of St George's church, the vicarage came into view. A lit candle in the porch window served as a beacon. But when they were closer they could see that something had been attached to the front door.

Thomas held up his hand and they stopped.

'Wait here.' he said, jumping down. Quickly he scanned the immediate area. He pulled a cudgel from his sleeve as he stepped onto the porch. In front of him, hanging from the large brass knocker, was a little figure of a man. He looked closer and saw it was fashioned from wax. Iron nails had been pushed into the head and torso.

'Thomas! What is it?' Titus called out.

'Just a vain attempt to cause alarm, Captain Barnard.' he replied wrenching the doll from the door. 'It is nothing. We should go in now.'

Suddenly the door swung open. Thomas leapt back, with his club out in front of him, ready to strike.

In the doorway was a very frightened looking verger.

'Master Wayland! God be praised you've returned.' he stammered, sounding relieved.

'Don't be alarmed Mr. Mathews. I've brought some companions back with me.'

Justin looked past him at the mounted men. 'Do you have Mr. Cooper with you?'

'Of course, Isaiah has been very helpful.' he stopped when Justin's face didn't change. 'Mr. Mathews is anything the matter?'

'I'm afraid I have some very bad news for Isaiah. His brother Eli is dead. He's been murdered.'

Bartholomew glanced at the eager faces and closed his eyes.

'First I need you all to try and picture a castle. A huge white stoned castle, nestling amongst the tall trees of a great forest.' He opened one eye and saw that some of the men had their eyes closed. Some of the others just looked off into the distance, mesmerised as if they were standing on some rocky out crop, actually staring down at the high turrets and crenellated walls of a huge fairytale castle, rising out of the lush green canopy of a vast forest.

He continued, 'The bright sunlight glints off the tall spires. Banners and gaily coloured pennants fly from every spire and hang from every battlement. The courtyards and the great halls are all decked out with vast displays of flowers and colourful ribbons. Cheerful music and laughter echo through the corridors and halls. The bells of the great abbey chime loudly while a wedding procession parades through the cheering crowds.'

He saw that the whole of the taproom was silent, everyone was engrossed in the tale. 'At the altar stands a young handsome prince. The future king, nervously waiting for his future queen. Then the abbey's great organ starts to play and the bride is led down the aisle by her proud father. The prince turns to see his bride for the first time. Instantly, he is gripped by the vision of the most beautiful girl he has ever seen, walking down the aisle to be his wife.' Bartholomew paused for a moment to take a few swigs of ale. He winced at the sour taste.

'Well, the ceremony went perfectly, the

161.

congregation could see immediately that the prince and princess were deeply in love with each other. After the ceremony the wedding feast was a grand affair. Long tables filled the banqueting hall and food of every kind was spread out in front of the guests.

All sat merrily as they were entertained by nimble dancers, deft acrobats and hilarious fools, who juggled with all manner of items. Minstrels began to play jaunty tunes and the dancing started. Everyone danced and laughed, all seemed to be having a wonderful time.

As the evening went on the musicians had to stop for a rest, so the bride suggested they all play some games. The guests liked the idea and agreed, all were completely captivated by the lively young princess. One of the guests had the idea of playing a game of hide and seek. The prince thought it was a wonderful idea and he suggested his bride was to be the first to hide. Well, off she went laughing with joy as she ran through the corridors of the castle, eagerly trying to find the perfect hiding place.

After a while the prince set off with the other wedding guests to search for his bride. But no one could find the hidden princess. As the hours went by the prince and the other guests were becoming concerned about the princess's whereabouts.

By the end of the day the guests had been sent away and the castle was turned upside down by the guards, as they searched. Days went by with neither hide nor hair of the princess being found. The prince even suspected that she had been kidnapped and spirited away. Broken hearted he sent his troops all over the kingdom to search for his bride. He even offered a massive reward for her safe return, but alas nothing. Years later the prince became king and he ruled the land, alone, until he was an old man. It's said he died of a broken heart.'

Bartholomew stopped and drained the last of his ale. He stood up and stretched his back. 'Well it's time for me to turn in lads.'

'What happened, Samuel?' Thomas asked his companion, who was seated in the minister's office. Isaiah had gone directly up to the guest room where Saul had been since returning to the vicarage.

'The boy was dead when we got there, Master. They laid out his clothes in the bush where he had been hiding to make it seem like he was still there watching. They tricked us. They had pegged him out on the floor of the cottage, splayed open like a carcass in a butcher's shop.'

'Be calm, Samuel,' Thomas soothed.

'The boy shouldn't have to see that. God in heaven, but I tried to stop him seeing it.'

'My friend, you did all you could have done.'

At that moment Titus and Dr Napier walked in. Napier went straight over to the window and sat down on the seat.

'Samuel, good to see you again. I trust you are well,' Titus asked.

'Titus,' Samuel answered, nodding to Barnard, 'God sees fit to preserve me as I see he does you.' He looked back to Thomas and ignored Napier entirely.

Thomas glanced briefly to Titus who gave an imperceptible shake of his head. Thomas sat down at the table and looked around the room.

'Now your company is present, Titus, we can try to find Baphomet's lair.' Thomas lifted his eye patch and rubbed the empty socket. 'These people seem to think they can lead us a merry dance my friends. Well, I think it is time they were rooted out and punished.'

The taproom instantly erupted into shouts of protest. Cries of 'No' and men banging the tables.

'What happened to her?' someone called out.

'Alright! Alright! Quieten down and I'll tell you,' Bartholomew shouted smiling at them all.

Once the taproom was quiet again he carried on with the tale.

'A year after the king died the new ruler of the kingdom decided to repair parts of the old castle that had fallen into disrepair. He walked around the castle with his advisors taking note of what was going to need repairing. At the end of one of the long corridors he came to a locked door. None of his advisors knew what lay beyond and none had any key to open it. Some of the king's guards were summoned and the door was broken down.

Well, to everyone's surprise the doorway opened up a whole wing of the castle that had been disused for years. They looked through the various rooms to see what lay within. Most of the dusty, deserted rooms were empty, but inside one of them was a large trunk.

They tried to open it, but it was locked. One of the palace guards was ordered to smash the lock and the trunk was opened. Inside...were the bones of a young woman wearing a wedding dress, peacefully curled up and hidden from the world. It seemed that the princess had climbed into the trunk to hide and the lid had locked, cutting off the air. The poor girl fell asleep and never woke up.

The new ruler was so touched by the tale, he saw to it that the princess was buried with her dead husband. The young lovers were reunited at last.'

Isaiah walked along the passage that led to their room. He felt numb, the realisation of what he had been told had not hit him yet. They were brothers, all that was left of the Cooper family. He couldn't be, surely Eli couldn't be … He didn't want to think it let alone say it.

He pushed open the door. The room was dark, except for the wan moonlight that shone through the open window. The few items of furniture that were in the room were outlined by the pale glow. Outside everything seemed still and quiet. It was as if the usual night sounds were being stifled out of silent respect.

'Saul?' Isaiah called out, looking around the room.

'He's gone, Izzy,' came the weak reply. 'They killed him.'

Isaiah frowned at the use of his childhood nickname. He could just make out Saul's outline, sat on the floor next to his bed. He was leaning against the wall with his knees drawn up to his chest. Isaiah had never seen Saul like this before. When their mother died he and Eli were too young to realise what had happened. Of course he had been upset before, but not like this.

'They killed him and then gutted him like an animal. I called out to him but he wouldn't answer, he wouldn't answer Izzy.' Saul's voice trailed off.

Isaiah went and sat on the bed next to his brother. He noticed on the floor, by Saul's foot, was a sword, drawn and shining in the moonlight.

'We're going to kill them for this, for Eli.'

Saul reached down and gripped the hilt of the sword.

'We're going to kill them all.' he said raising the blade into the pale light.

CHAPTER 21.

The next morning Isaiah woke with a start. Dawn's first light was just starting to show through the window. He sat up and tried to stretch the stiffness from his shoulders. He looked over and saw that Saul was still curled up on the floor next to the bed, holding the sword. Reaching over, he pulled the blanket off the other bed and laid it over his brother. He watched him sleeping for a moment, briefly seeing one of the innocent little boys that he had been forced to bring up, when he was still a boy himself.

He left the room, closing the door quietly behind him, and wandered downstairs. He realised he hadn't eaten since the previous morning and he was famished. In the kitchen on the large table in the centre of the room was a tray of bread and cheese. He grabbed a few chunks of the hard bread, a lump of the pale cheese and then poured himself a mug of ale before walking out of the back door to eat his breakfast in solitude.

In the back yard his plans of a quiet breakfast were foiled when he was greeted by the sight of Titus and Dr Napier, in their shirt sleeves, engaging in a bout of early morning sword play.

Both men looked the epitome of the gallant, dashing warriors of many a young maiden's tale.

He sat down to watch and was immediately shocked to see Titus lunge at Napier's mid section, a long thrusting movement that almost disembowelled him. Napier parried the move easily and back swung his blade in a scything arc, causing Barnard to duck.

'Damn and blast your eyes Napier!' Titus spat bringing his sword up ready for the next attack.

'Ha! You're getting slow, sir.' Jonathan laughed.

'Only readying for the final blow, you cock sure whelp,' he answered before advancing on the doctor with a series of brutal swings, laughing and screaming as he made the assault, driving Napier backwards.

The doctor tried in vain to parry the wild attack, but he was desperately losing ground. The last blow caught the doctor's sword just under the basket hilt. The weapon flew out of his hand and he watched open mouthed as the blade sailed over his head to land behind him, in the ground point first.

'I submit sir.' He held his hands up in defeat.

'Ah ha! Napier you cocky bastard. There's life in the old dog yet eh?' Barnard shouted with a triumphant smile on his face. He looked over

169.

and saw Isaiah, who had finished his breakfast. He had watched the whole exchange with awe. 'How about it Cooper? How's your sword arm?'

'I've never fought with a sword before, Sir.'

'Well, Doctor I think it's time someone taught him, eh? I seen you carry a blade, so now's the time to learn how to use it.' Titus held his sword out and Isaiah took hold of the hilt. 'Guard yourself then boy, and widen you stance. You're no good to man nor beast on your arse.'

Cooper stood with his feet apart and the weapon held out in front. The doctor stood opposite and took up the guard position as well.

'Now boy, the doctor is going to swing over the top and try to slice you in half. What are you going to do?' He took a pace back and looked at Cooper's confused face.

Isaiah raised the blade above his head horizontally and looked at Titus.

'No, no, no!' Titus responded shaking his head. 'The only way you're going to stop getting cut in half is to move. Rule number one, the way to avoid a blow is to not be there when it arrives.' He looked at Cooper, trying to gauge whether the information was sinking in. 'Understand?'

Isaiah nodded and stepped to one side as the doctor slowly swung his blade over his head to emphasise the point.

'Now! As your opponent's sword sails past you, he is off balance. That is your opportunity to bury your blade in the bastard's guts. Making him wish he'd never been born.' Titus explained, exploding into raucous laughter.

'The captain can get carried away with himself,' the doctor said, with a wink, 'But you do get used to his insanity, after a while.'

'What was that Napier, you weasel?'

'I was just asking Mr. Cooper if he would like to try the whole move again, sir.'

Isaiah tried to hide his smile. He was starting to realise that Barnard was a complete madman who had to be placated whenever possible.

'Of course, good man! Raise your guard Cooper. Doctor if you please!' Titus waved Isaiah back to his starting place while the doctor took up his position. 'Doctor a little more power to your stroke this time, if you would.'

This time Isaiah was ready to side step the blow, although he hoped he could bring his blade up, at the right time, to make a convincing counter attack on the doctors mid section. He watched Napier make a few practice swings as he readied himself for the attack. Suddenly a loud voice caused all the men turn towards the door of the vicarage.

'Titus! Thomas would like to see you in the

minister's office,' Samuel called out, 'I think it's important!' He added when he saw that Barnard was about to protest.

'Alas, I fear the lesson is at an end gentlemen. More pressing matters are at hand.' He nodded to the doctor and Isaiah, who both bowed. The men made their way inside to hear some very strange news.

'The bastard wants to meet with you!' Titus cried out, struggling to believe what he was hearing. 'I trust he is aware that we're going to kill him and the rest of his devil worshiping scum?'

'Who gave you the note?' Isaiah asked, directing the question to Simon Hawkins, who had arrived early that morning with the note.

'It was on the bar in the taproom when I came down stairs this morning.' Simon answered warily. He still seemed a little taken back by Titus's out burst.

Thomas looked at the landlord suspiciously.

'So you didn't see who had left it there, Mr. Hawkins?'

'I fear not, Master Wayland. It was very busy in the tavern last night. On account of all the soldiers taking over the taproom.'

'Are you complaining about my men landlord?' Titus asked.

'No captain! No, I was just saying there was a lot of them.' Simon answered

'I'm sure Sergeant Roach was in complete control, Titus.' Thomas interrupted, attempting to curb Barnard's rising temper. He was acutely aware how Barnard reacted when negative comments were made about his company.

'Mr. Hawkins, may the lord bless you for bringing this to our attention. Mr. Mathews would you be so kind as to show Mr. Hawkins to the door.'

Once the Verger had led the chubby landlord from the room the men all looked at each other.

Thomas glanced back at the note again.

'It says I'm to meet him at the Whispering Knights, two nights from now. And he wants me to come alone.'

'Bugger him! My men will be in position around these Whispering Knights, where ever they are, and I'll have the bastard's head.' Titus could feel his anger, welling up inside him.

'Titus please.' Thomas held his hands up to try and calm his friend down. 'I will allow one patrol to shadow me. I know they won't be seen.' He was glad that one of the company's strengths was that they could melt in to the surrounding countryside, living off the land for days at a time. One of the many reasons the company was held in such high regard and always in great demand.

'What are the Whispering Knights?' asked Dr.Napier.

'They are some ancient stones, about ten or so miles from here,' Isaiah answered.

'I will pass it on to Sergeant Roach,' Barnard replied, 'And a patrol will be waiting, out of sight of course, ready for your meeting with this Baphomet whoreson.'

'Thank you, Titus. Can I also assume that you have men watching the village?'

Barnard smiled proudly.

'Thomas, old friend, I've had men hidden in this area days before you saw me.'

'Then one of those men should have seen whether anyone entered or left the tavern during the evening, would they not?' Thomas asked.

'I will have sergeant Roach question the sentries,' he answered nodding.

Titus and Dr Napier left the vicarage and returned to the Black Dog. Saul had gone for a walk with Samuel and Isaiah found that he was the only one left, apart from the minister sitting at his desk, busy working on his sermons. Earlier he had heard the minister and Justin talking together, saying that since Thomas and Samuel had been lodging in the village, the Sunday service had started become a popular affair again.

At the back of the vicarage he took his sword outside with him and decided to work off some of his anger, by practicing some the moves he had seen during the morning. He planted his feet firmly and started to swing the large blade in wide arcs. As he swung, the blade felt heavy and cumbersome. How ever did they use their swords so easily? He found the faster he swung the harder it was to control. At this rate, he thought, the only person that was going to die by his blade was him.

'You'll find that it's a lot easier when someone is trying to kill you.'

Isaiah turned to see Thomas standing in the door way.

'Captain Barnard said the best way to avoid an enemies strike is not to be there when it arrives.'

'He is correct. Titus may be completely insane, but he is one of the finest soldiers I have ever met.'

'How is it that you know a man like Captain Barnard, Master?'

'Barnard's Company are members of our Order,' Thomas answered, walking over to where Isaiah stood.

'What does the Order actually do, master?'

'The Order of St Michael is a martial order,' Thomas replied. 'We carry out the bidding of our superiors. Which could mean travelling to any part of Christendom.'

'I want to kill them for what they did to Eli,' Isaiah said after a while.

Thomas looked at the young man. He had become fond of him recently and he was well aware of the pain of a family member's death.

'I know Isaiah, I know.'

CHAPTER 22.

Morning the next day brought the sound of frantic banging on the front door. Justin ran down the passageway towards the noise.

'Lord save us! I'm here.' he called, feeling a little apprehensive at the urgency of the banging. Just when he was about to pull the latch and open the door he heard, behind him, the rasping sound of a sword being drawn. Slowly he turned around.

Samuel stood in one of the doorways along the passage. Holding his sword low, he put his finger to his lips. Justin relaxed slightly seeing this. The nervous verger was starting to get used to Samuel.

'Open it slowly and see who it is,' Samuel ordered, 'Do not let them in until I say.'

Justin turned back to the door and took a deep breath.

'Who is it?' he called out.

'It's me, Sarah Hawkins, Mr. Mathews, from the Black Dog.'

He looked around for guidance, Samuel nodded. He pulled the door open and gave Sarah a relieved smile.

'What seems to be the matter my dear?'

Sarah was still panting from her hurried journey to the vicarage. 'I'm sorry… to disturb… you so early…Mr. Mathews,' She paused to take a breath. 'I need to speak to Isaiah Cooper. My father said he's here.'

'Calm down Sarah and catch your breath. Now tell me, what is this about?' He looked at the heavy set girl. She really shouldn't be charging around, being the size she is, he thought to himself.

'I need to see Isaiah Mr. Mathews, it's about Old Lottie. He was asking about her the other day.'

Suddenly the door was yanked open and Samuel appeared.

'What's happened girl?' He growled at her, 'Speak!'

He saw the fright on her face and sheathed his sword.

'Don't be afraid Miss Hawkins.' he said. 'Just tell us what has happened.'

'It's Old Lottie sir, she's been arrested by the magistrate.'

Cold, dirty water hit her in the face, instantly waking her from her exhausted half sleep.

'Wake up, you filthy evil whore!'

Charlotte could just see the gaoler's boots, in front of her. She readied herself for another kick. She was cold, wet and hungry. The two sadistic gaolers had been chucking buckets of shit and piss at her all night. At first she had gagged at the stench, but after a night of repeated kicks and slaps, along with the buckets of filth thrown over her when it looked like she was about to fall asleep, it didn't bother her any more.

Diggory Brabazon did enjoy his job. He and his oldest friend, Faithful Whitlocke had been gaolers at Evesham lock up for more that fifteen years now.

'You know something, Faithful?' he asked quite theatrically.

'I know a lot of things, Diggory. But I beg you please enlighten me.'

'I'm going to use my senior man's sense and say the this piece of devil scum is nearly ready to tell Mr. Ramsbotham all about her awful 'hereticalness'.' He smiled, revealing a row of broken, discoloured teeth. He frowned when Faithful didn't smile back. 'What's wrong with you?'

'Since when have you been senior man?' Whitlocke's right eye started twitching, the nervous condition that always started when he became anxious.

'Sheep's arse said I was,' he lied.

'Did he, by fuck!' He threw the bucket he was holding across the cramped cell, hitting the wall. 'We've been here the same years as each other, how can he make you senior man, it's not right.'

'Listen, old chum. Sheep's arse is our gaffer and he has a good eye.' Diggory loved baiting his colleague. He enjoyed it almost as much as causing pain to the prisoners in their charge. 'He knows when a man deserves a bit of promotion.' He knew that any time now Faithful would catch on and reward him with a punch in the ribs.

Faithful's mouth dropped open, 'Since when have you deserv…' He stopped suddenly realising that he was, again, falling for one of Diggory's jokes. 'You bastard! You had me there.' He grinned at his companion. 'And now, I'm going to break your nose.'

'Good morning Mr. Ramsbotham!' Diggory called out loudly, tugging his forelock.

Faithful spun round. Stood in the door way was the diminutive, but upright figure of Mr. Peregrine Ramsbotham, the high constable of Evesham. Their employer.

'Good morning to you Master Brabazon, and to you Master Whitlocke.' Ramsbotham hated the stench and the two brutal looking gaolers.

'Well? Has the witch decided to confess?' Ramsbotham's nose twitched when he talked, giving his face a hawk like appearance. A look that matched his astute manner and keen mind.

'I'm afraid Sir, the prisoner didn't sleep much last night.' Diggory tried to sound contrite. He knew very well that it was illegal to actually torture prisoners, but he and Faithful had always agreed there were 'ways and means' of getting them to talk. 'We even tried to give her some breakfast Sir, to try and perk her up, but she spilt it up the back wall of the cell.'

Ramsbotham could guess exactly what had happened. He sighed with annoyance.

'Bring her to the press room gentlemen, if you please.' He sniffed a small bag of herbs to try and mask the overpowering smell.

The two gaolers grabbed her under the arms and lifted her off the ground. The filthy woollen dress she wore hung from her willowy frame, stained and damp from her night time drenching. Then they half carried, half dragged her from the cell and along the dingy, stone flagged corridor.

The end of the corridor opened out into a large room, where in years past prisoners, who were required to confess all, were laid out. Heavy stones were then piled on top of them,

181.

crushing them slowly until they complied with their questioners, a process known as pressing.

The only furnishing in the room now though, was a small stool in the centre of the floor. There were a few barred windows high up in the walls, that reluctantly allowed in thin shafts of light, dividing the room into quarters.

Ramsbotham watched as Charlotte was dumped roughly down on the stool. She started to whimper and her shoulders slumped, her head hanging low.

'You are a witch Charlotte,' he said calmly, 'I know that you are and now you will confess it so, before God.'

Thomas stared out of the window of the minister's office.

'Who arrested her?' he asked without turning around.

Sarah felt nervous as she stood in the dark office. The only friendly face was Isaiah's and even he looked more serious than normal.

'It was the magistrate, Sir Nicholas Dickinson. He's supposed to have said that someone had accused her of casting spells on folk.'

Isaiah leaned forward and looked at Sarah.

'Where did they take her?' he asked. He could

see she was scared witless. She still cowered away every time Samuel went near her.

'I think they took her to Evesham gaol,' she answered timidly.

'Bugger, we've got to get her out of there, Master.' Isaiah said. 'The two bastards who work in there will be able to get her to confess to anything.'

Samuel sat at the table.

'We also have to find out who has accused her and why.'

'The king has allowed us some measure of authority,' Thomas said thoughtfully, 'But we now run the risk of offending the local church, a matter that may well cause him to rethink his decision.' He paused for a few moments, to collect his thoughts. He then turned and looked at the men in the room. 'We go to Evesham.'

CHAPTER 23.

'Have you ever attended a sabbat?'
Ramsbotham asked Charlotte. He watched her
shiver as she sat in the cold damp room.

'No.' she whispered the reply.

'I know that you have my dear.' he said
ignoring her answer. 'I also know that you have
made a pact with Satan himself. Do you deny
this?'

There was a long pause.

'Yes.' came the weak reply.

He tried a change of tactics.

'Have you ever made a potion to cure a man,
woman or child of a disease?' He straightened
up when he saw her head raise slightly.

'Yes, I am a healer by trade.' she rasped, her
head drooped down again.

'Ah, at last a simple answer to a simple
question.' He started to pace around the outside
of the room, his steps echoed off the bare stone
walls. 'From where or from whom did you learn
this...Trade?' He made no attempt to hide the
derision in his voice.

'My mother taught me,' she paused sensing a
trap, 'When I was a little girl.'

Diggory and Faithful looked at each other and

grinned. They had seen Ramsbotham interrogate prisoners before and although they mainly saw him as a figure of fun, he did on occasion impress them. The way that he asked the questions, which sometimes caused the prisoner incriminate himself, before he even knew what he had said.

'Can I ask,' he asked matter of factly, 'what happened to your mother?'

'May I have some water please, Sir?' Her voice was a whisper.

'Of course my dear, as soon as you have answered some more questions,' he said. 'Now tell me, what happened to your mother?'

There was silence. The sounds of the town could be heard from outside. People laughing, the clattering of a cart being pulled through the street, a dog barking, all reminders that outside there were ordinary folk carrying on with their normal lives, all blissfully unaware of what was taking place in the dimly lit room.

'She was accused of being a witch.' Charlotte eventually answered, sighing. She knew it was what they wanted to hear, it was also true, she knew it and they knew it.

'Ah ha! So your mother was a witch!' Ramsbotham said, triumphantly.

'No sir, I said she was accused of being a

185.

witch.' She knew it was useless to argue but she could feel her antagonistic side starting to emerge.

'Forgive me. She was accused of witchcraft. But please tell me, what happened to her?'

'You know what happened,' she hissed.

'Remind me please.' He was starting to enjoy himself, he always did like gaining the upper hand.

Charlotte felt trapped and helpless, just the way her mother must have felt when she had been caught. She remembered seeing her mother hang. At that time she was still too young to know what was going on, but now it was happening to her and she still didn't understand.

'She was hanged,' she answered finally.

'So, she was found guilty of practising witchcraft, and when you were a child she taught you how to make these… potions and medicines. Yes?'

She turned her head slightly, trying to see where he was standing.

'As I've told you, I'm a healer.'

'So you say my dear, so you say,' he answered dismissively. 'Tell me, do you acknowledge Jesus Christ as your lord and saviour?' He crossed himself piously.

The two gaolers quickly looked at each other

186.

and then copied him realising he was watching them.

She stiffened slightly and her heart sank. Finally the question she had been dreading.

'No,' she replied defiantly.

'Forgive me, Charlotte, could you say that again?' He stopped behind her and waited for the answer.

'I said no!' she replied, her voice failing her as she realised she was beaten.

'Woman! Do you know what you are saying?' his voice rising to a shriek, 'Your words condemn you. You are confessing to heresy!'

'You misunderstand me Sir.' she said calmly, now resigned to her fate. 'I love god the creator, but Mother Nature is my saviour.'

'Silence harlot!' he cried with a look of horror on his face. He pointed at her, spittle flying as he spoke. 'You will burn for your blasphemy.'

Thomas and Samuel waited in a booth in the back of the Red Horse Inn in Evesham. They sat in silence whilst the noisy town pub carried on about them as normal. When they had entered there were the usual hushed voices and quiet mutterings, but that subsided after a while and they now sat forgotten, whilst most of the

187.

drunken patrons continued on their journey to oblivion.

Then there was a loud bang. Thomas, who sat with a clear line of sight to the front door, watched Isaiah enter the pub and push his way through the crowd. He reached their booth and sat down next to Samuel.

'She's in the gaol alright.' Cooper said, trying to rub the chill from his hands. 'They said she's been questioned by the high constable all morning.'

Thomas frowned.

'Who is the high constable?' He had dealt with these petty local officials before and at best they were a nuisance, but it was always best to try and know who they were.

'Mr. Peregrine Ramsbotham. A right, rat faced bastard he is. He thinks he's clever because he makes people talk.' He looked around to see if anyone was listening. 'What he doesn't know is that the only reason people talk is because of Diggory and Faithful.'

'Who?' Samuel asked irritably, he had always disliked busy towns.

'The two gaolers. Evil bastards the pair of them. They've been there for years.'

'We shall have to talk to Mr. Ramsbotham, I think.' Thomas said. He only hoped Charlotte hadn't confessed to anything yet. The trouble was, that with a couple of malicious gaolers and a high constable with delusions of grandeur, the situation didn't look good.

'Mr. Ramsbotham has gone to fetch the High Sheriff.' The guard outside the gaol said, in answer to Thomas's question. 'There's going to be a trial in the morning.'

'Who for?' Isaiah asked guardedly.

'Not for you Isaiah Cooper, not yet anyway.' The guard saw the surprise on the young man's face. 'That's right. I know who you are, boy!'

'It doesn't matter who he is,' snapped Samuel, 'Who is the trial for?'

The guard blinked at the abrupt out burst, before quickly regaining his composure. He was not a timid man, but he knew when to be cautious and even though he was well aware of Cooper's reputation, his two fierce looking companions were another matter.

'The old woman who was arrested yesterday. She's to be tried for heresy.'

Thomas stepped closer to the guard. His anger was starting to well up inside him and he was fighting desperately to control it.

'Where will the trial be held?' His acid tone unsettling the man even more, 'As far as I remember, there is no session house in the town.'

'They're held in the town hall Sir. All trials are held in the town hall.' His nerves finally got the better of him and he started to talk too quickly. 'That's why Mr. Ramsbotham has gone to fetch the High Sheriff.'

'Thank you Mr.?' Thomas looked at the man expectantly, his rising temper now in check.

'Edward Lane, Sir'

'Thank you Mr. Lane for your kind help.' Thomas nodded his head slightly.

Edward watched as the three men turned and walked back across the market square, disappearing into the crowd. He was glad they were gone, especially the wild bear like one. They may have been dressed like clergymen, with their black cloaks, but they certainly didn't act like them. We'll see how they behave at the trial in the morning, he thought to himself.

CHAPTER 24.

The next morning the atmosphere inside the town hall was one of barely contained excitement. The pews at the back of the room, the aisles and the balcony were all full of town's folk, most standing, but all eager to witness the trial of a suspected witch. The long seats towards the front, which had been left empty as the room was filling up, had now been taken up by the wealthier people and town officials.

At one end of the hall, on a raised platform was a long table, where the High Sheriff, Sir Richard Walsh was seated. To his left was the canon of St. Lawrence's, Dr. Troilus Plummer, and to his right the town clerk, Mr. Peter Rawlins.

Sir Richard was regarded as a heroic figure by the people of Worcestershire. A few years previously he had led an assault on Holbeach House to try and arrest a gang of conspirators, who had plotted to blow up the king, as he sat in parliament. The fugitives had barricaded themselves inside the house, but after a short but bloody battle the felons had all been either killed or captured.

The short, portly canon, Dr. Plummer, was a

different person altogether. A quarrelsome man who enjoyed provoking confrontation, whether it be religious or corporeal. The smile on his broad face revealed to all the fact that he was looking forward to the hearing.

The same fact couldn't be extended to the other member of the bench, the town clerk, Peter Rawlins.

He was a young man who had worked hard to gain the position he now held. Over worked and unappreciated was the way he saw it, nobody really understood what his job entailed. So a trial like this was a big obstacle for him, urgent civic matters would have to be postponed.

A sudden, loud banging on the table called the proceedings to order. The conversation eventually died down to a dull murmur, the curiosity at the impending trial still causing some fascination for the spectators.

Thomas stood with Samuel in the aisle on one side of the hall. They both kept as close to the wall as possible, so as not to draw attention to themselves by obstructing anyone's view. Whilst looking around the room he still found it amazing how people gained enjoyment from the misfortune of others, 'shadenfreude' the Germans called it. He knew that death and hardship were commonplace. The pestilence itself had destroyed whole communities, with some villages being wiped out altogether. He returned his attention to the trial, inwardly despairing at the situation.

Isaiah was stood at the back of the hall, near the main doors. He was still a notorious rogue and even though he hadn't actually committed any crimes recently, he still wanted to know that he could make a quick getaway if he had to. Old habits die hard, he thought. From where he was positioned he made sure that could see the whole room. Thomas and Samuel had told him they wanted to be nearer the front of the hall so that they could witness the hearing close up.

'Bring in the accused Master Bailiff, if you please!' Sir Richard suddenly called out, his voice bringing the room to order.

A door at the side of the hall opened and a sober looking man in a black robe and starched ruff strode into the room. Behind him Charlotte was escorted out, burly guards holding each of her arms.

The congregation gasped in unison at her dishevelled state. Her lank grey hair hung like rats tails over her face, obscuring her features. The dirty brown dress was soiled and only added to her filthy unkempt appearance.

The chains around her ankles rattled along the floor, whilst she was dragged around to the front of the hall to the chair positioned facing the bench. The guards forced her to sit down and then one stood either side of her.

'You are Charlotte Perry, a former resident of the village of Poden.' Sir Richard asked in a commanding tone. The murmur of the crowd swelled momentarily at the mention of the abandoned village.

'Answer your name my child.' Dr. Plummer said calmly.

'Yes sir.' Charlotte replied.

'You are brought before this court charged with maleficia, the making of a pact with Satan and denying the Lord Jesus Christ.' Sir Richard banged the gavel loudly on the table, trying to quell the sudden uproar in the hall. 'Order! Order!' The clamour slowly started to subside and the room finally went quiet. 'What say you of these charges?'

She looked up at him, 'I have not made a pact with anyone, Sir.' She said in an even tone.

'You will answer the charges woman! Guilty or not guilty?' Sir Richard demanded.

'Not guilty,' she replied.

'String her up!' someone said from the crowd, which again caused the room to erupt into more shouting and stamping of feet, drowning out any attempts by the High Sheriff to call the room to order.

Samuel leaned close to Thomas's ear, 'She doesn't stand a chance, Master.'

'I know.' He replied, the sick feeling of helplessness heavy in his stomach. He knew that, now he had heard the charges, it was a matter of how she would be punished. The result of being found guilty of witchcraft in England was hanging, but a guilty heretic was burned at the stake.

'Can the High Constable please step forward.'

Ramsbotham stood up proudly, he appeared resplendent in his best doublet and hose, more suited to an appearance at the royal court, rather than a trial in a market town. He approached the bench and bowed smartly to the High Sheriff.

'Good morning Sir Richard.'

'Good morning Peregrine. Shall we continue?' The latter was said to stop Ramsbotham entering into one of his fawning complements that always made Sir Richard's stomach turn.

'Of course Sir.' He turned and addressed the room. 'Gentlemen of the bench,' he announced in his high pitched voice, 'I have brought this woman before you, charged with these heinous crimes, but it is the one matter that I would like to bring to your attention above all.' The hall was quiet. He was now in his element, the entire congregation waiting with baited breath for his next word. 'Yesterday I asked Miss Perry if she recognised the Lord Jesus Christ as her saviour.' He bowed his head and crossed himself. The rest of the hall did the same, all except Charlotte.

Thomas watched her and his heart sunk when he heard the High Constable's last question. Even though he was not in the gaol cell yesterday, when she was first asked that question, he knew full well what her answer would have been.

Suddenly he was again standing on that hot German plain, the citizens of Treves crying out in torment as the flames climbed higher. The smell of burning flesh was rancid in the air. Thick black smoke billowed up into the sky, blocking out the sunlight. The heat on his face was searing his skin. Chanting priests every where, their monotone mumbling reverberating in his head.

'…guilty, without benefit of clergy.' The High Sheriff said looking down at Charlotte, his face neutral. 'Do you have anything to say?'

She looked up at him mutely.

'If you wish to make a plea for mercy woman, your moment is now.'

Still, she gave no answer, she just continued to look up at him.

Sir Richard lent back in his chair and sighed.

'Very well, the sentence of this court is that you will be taken from this place to whence you came, and from there, tomorrow morning, to a place of lawful execution, there to be burned at the stake till you be dead, and may the Lord have mercy on your soul.' The words echoed around the quiet court room.

Once the proceedings had ended the townsfolk started to file out of the hall. The prospect of a public burning was a rare thing. It meant a public holiday for most and a chance for the local traders to sell their wares to a wider crowd.

Thomas and Samuel waited until most of the people had left the hall before they moved. Suddenly a voice called out from behind them.

'Master Wayland!?' It was Sir Nicholas Dickinson. 'I had no idea you were here at the hearing. I trust you are well?'

'Quite well thank you, Sir Nicholas.' He looked at the fat magistrate with disgust, 'Had I noticed you were here I would have approached you sooner. May I ask you a question, Sir?'

197.

'Of course dear fellow, if there's anything I can do to assist.'

'Who made the accusation against Charlotte Perry?'

'Hmm, to be quite honest I don't know. I will speak to Murray though, when I return tomorrow and I will send a message to you.' The magistrate answered helpfully with a smile. 'Now, can I invite you to dine with me? Mistress Wyatt at the Swann Inn does excellent devilled kidneys. You must try them.'

'Please forgive me, Sir Nicholas. I'm afraid Mr. Bolton and myself are otherwise engaged.' He replied.

'I quite forgot about Mr. Bolton. Please excuse me Sir, God preserves you, I hope?' he said looking at Samuel. 'Did you enjoy the proceedings,' he asked, not waiting for a reply, 'Justice was done here today don't you think?'

'It was enlightening, Sir Nicholas.' Samuel answered sounding bored.

'Well! I'll see you at the execution tomorrow gentlemen.' He tapped the thick chain around his shoulders, 'Official duty you understand.'

'Mr. Lane?' a voice called through the gaol's front gate.

Edward Lane wandered out of the guard's watch room to see who it was and Standing there was Isaiah Cooper.

'What do you want, Cooper?' He felt a little apprehensive as he walked towards the gate. 'You are going to get me into trouble lad, do you know that!'

'I need you to do me a good turn, Mr. Lane.' Isaiah asked in the most convivial voice he could manage.

'What do mean good turn? God save me Cooper, you shouldn't be here.' Then he stopped, 'Are you alone? Your two companions aren't here as well are they?'

'That's just it Mr. Lane, we need to come in and see the old woman.' He looked at the worried guard. 'We only want to talk to her. We'll be out in two shakes, as God is my witness.' he said sincerely, with a hand on his heart.

'Good morning Edward.' Thomas said stepping into view. 'My young companion is right. It's important we get to see Charlotte, before her execution.' He saw the uncertainty in the man's face. 'Please forgive me for asking this boon of you.'

After a few moments the guard reluctantly started to rummage around inside the leather pouch that hung from his belt, becoming more fraught by the minute. Finally he pulled out a large key.

'Please Sir don't take too long. I beg you, or it's my job.'

'Thank you Edward and don't fret' Thomas said, patting him on the shoulder as he and Isaiah slipped past him.

Samuel watched from the other side of the market square, as they disappeared inside the gaol. Thomas suggested that he wait outside, mainly because he unsettled the guard and they didn't want to scare him witless. He looked back to the activity going on in the centre of the market place.

A stout post now stood in the centre of the square. Lines of men were passing along faggots of wood and piling them around the base of the pole. The whole operation was being overseen by the broad-shouldered, shaven headed executioner, who quietly hoped he could remember how to do it properly.

It had been a long time since there had been a burning in Evesham. When he thought back he was pretty sure that the last one was a woman who had killed her old husband. What he did remember though, was that it was important that the right equipment was supplied.

The High Constable seemed to think that it was just a matter of setting the prisoner alight and watching them burn, a subject he had tried to enlighten him on. That morning he had presented the bill for expenses to Ramsbotham in his office, he still remembered his reaction.

'Eleven pounds!' he cried when he read the list.

'And five shillings Sir.' The executioner calmly added.

'Eleven pounds and five shillings! How in the name of God am I going to pay this?' he said still sounding shocked.

'You don't Sir.' was the reply.

Ramsbotham was still reading the itemized list and didn't fully hear what the man said.

'I don't? What do you mean? Who pays it then?'

'Exactly the same as when they're hanged, Sir.' The executioner answered, he waited while Ramsbotham studied the bill.

'What is a hurden robe?' The constable asked pointing to the parchment, a note of suspicion in his voice.

The man sounded bored when he answered.

'It's what the condemned wears whilst they

are burned. Look Sir, I know this bill is more than usual but that is because burning is more costly than hanging.' The other man still looked dubious, 'If you look at the bill Sir, you'll see that when somebody is sentenced to death by burning you need to first find a stake and then dress it. You then need to lay coal for the base of the fire. You need tar to cover the twenty bundles of faggots,' He could feel his anger building at the man's ignorance. 'You need iron hoops to secure the condemned to the stake...'

Ramsbotham held his hands up in weary submission.

'Please forgive me, I meant no offence.' he said trying to sound penitent. 'I respect and also acknowledge the fact, Sir, that you are a master of your craft. I was just momentarily taken aback by the size of the bill.'

'As I said sir,' the executioner continued, 'you merely present the bill to the condemned for payment as usual.'

'I assure you she does not have the means to settle this bill.' he sighed wearily, 'I shall have to present it to the town clerk instead and I know Master Rawlins will not be pleased at the prospect.'

'Bugger Master bloody Rawlins,' the executioner said to himself, stood back in the

202.

square. He looked at the stake and the bundles of wood now piled up. There were still lots more work to do before the site of the afternoons execution would be ready and he still hadn't seen any barrels of tar being delivered yet.

Thomas recoiled at the stench of the gaol as he walked along a barred corridor. The rank odour violently assaulted the senses, causing tears to roll down his cheeks.

Isaiah was also struggling to keep hold of his composure. He held his scarf over his nose and mouth in a vain attempt to block out some of the rancid smell.

'We use the cell at the end of this corridor for the condemned's last night Sir.' Diggory chirped. He was still amused by the visitors reaction to the gaols condition. It wasn't unusual for people to want to see the condemned. But he thought these two, especially, were a bit peculiar. Neither of them wanted to give their names and the gentleman with the one eye, looked a right nasty piece of work.

When they reached the cell the gaoler, with a clumsy flourish and a maniacal grin produced a large set of keys. He unlocked the door noisily and stood to one side.

Thomas glared at the obnoxious man, resisting the urge to attack him.

'We don't want to be disturbed.' he said curtly and entered the cell without waiting for an answer.

Isaiah followed him in and pulled the heavy door shut.

'I told you they were horrible bastards, Master.' he said, but when he looked at Thomas, the big man was standing there just staring at the crumpled figure, sitting huddled in the corner of the cell.

After a few moments Charlotte pushed herself upright. She forced a painful smile when she looked up at them.

'At least the beatings have stopped,' she said. 'You know, they actually left me alone long enough to get some sleep last night.' She suddenly winced as she shifted her position, her hand held tentatively to her ribs.

'What happened Charlotte?' Thomas asked.

She opened her eyes again.

'I had a dream last night Thomas. We lived in a lovely cottage, Mary had a pony …' her voice trailed off.

'You had all of that once, if you remember?'

Cooper looked from Charlotte to Thomas, he was definitely missing something. He walked to the back of the cell and sank down against the wall, which he thought seemed a little less damp than in the rest of the gaol.

Charlotte lowered her eyes.

'Yes I had that,' she answered eventually, 'But not with Mary's father.'

'Mr. Cooper would you please step out. I need to talk to Charlotte alone.' He asked without looking around. He waited whilst Cooper stood up, without question and walked out of the cell. 'Why didn't you tell me?' he asked sadly.

'You were a corruptible rogue back then Thomas, not the man you are now. Robert offered me a better life.' She looked apologetically into his watery eyes. 'I thought you would have been killed a long time ago. Then one day I start to hear tales of Master Wayland, this great warrior and how he is riding across Christendom, punishing the enemies of the church.'

'The day I left was the day I gave up earthly love, you saw to that!' he said the last few words a little too sharply and instantly regretted it. 'Forgive me. I came to find out who made the accusation against you and I discover that I am a father. A little disconcerting wouldn't you agree?'

'Well I didn't ask you to come!' she answered,

her voice faltering.

'Who accused you Charlotte?' Thomas had
regained control and his question sounded cold.

Charlotte heard the official tone in his voice
and realised that their conversation was drawing
to a close.

'The magistrate wouldn't tell me. He just said
it was someone in the village.'

Thomas straightened up and turned to leave
the cell.

'Mary doesn't know about you.' she said
behind him.

He paused, fighting back tears.

'May God forgive you.' he said quietly and
walked out of the cell.

Isaiah, who was standing out side the cell
door, was feeling extremely uneasy. The two
gaolers had been staring at him all the while he
had been there. He felt like a defenceless
woodland animal, who was being stalked by
two brutal predators. He then saw their hideous
grins disappear as Thomas strode out of the cell,
with a look of thunder on his face.

Diggory and Faithful stood up respectfully.
The tall, one eyed gentleman did not look
happy, they thought. The gentleman started to
walk towards them, but Diggory had already
thought of something amusing he could say to

him, which was bound to make him smile.

Thomas quickened his pace as he neared the two gaolers. One of them opened his mouth to say something, but before he could get a word out Thomas drove his gloved fist into the man's stomach, dropping him like a stone. Quickly, the other man moved in to help his companion.

Thomas saw the movement and immediately stepped closer, easily batting away a clumsily aimed blow. He gripped the front of the man's tunic. The gaoler knew instantly was going to happen, but before he could react Thomas pulled him forward and head butted him right in the centre of his face.

Faithful's nose immediately exploded, turning his features into a mass of blood and snot, and he fell back against the wall.

Isaiah just stared, open mouthed while he watched the sudden, unprovoked attack on the two gaolers.

Thomas nonchalantly brushed at the front of his tunic, before stepping over the two fallen gaolers.

'Thank you gentlemen, you have been most helpful.' he said and then walked out of the gaol followed by Isaiah.

CHAPTER 25.

When the afternoon arrived the crowds, which were gathered in the market square seemed subdued, as they all avidly watched the activity around the execution site.

In the centre of the square there was a tall wooden stake rising from the ground. Piled around it, forming a crude platform, were bundles of tar covered wood. More bundles of wood were piled next to the platform, ready to be laid around the condemned prisoner once they had been secured to the post.

The executioner was standing motionless next to the platform. In one of his hands he held three long iron strips, which had been specifically forged for the execution that morning. In his other hand he held a large hammer, borrowed for the afternoon from the same smithy.

The bell of St. Lawrence's church started ringing at one o'clock. The ominous sound of the solitary bell reduced the noise of the crowd to a dull murmur. For the townsfolk it would normally have been a happy, jovial occasion, when presented with the opportunity to finish work early and witness the sentence of the court being carried out. This time though the mood of the people was one of quiet contemplation. During the trial some of the spectators had sympathised with the condemned woman and over night that belief had spread to others.

The town militia knew that on that cold October afternoon public opinion was firmly divided. Sensing this they had ringed the execution site, keeping the onlookers at a respectful distance, armed with their long poleaxes. Usually they would fight to keep the people back, but today there was a feeling of disapproval and a real reluctance in the crowd to get too close.

Thomas stood some way from Isaiah and Samuel, at the back of the crowd. For once Cooper saw fit not to question what Thomas was doing, he just followed Samuel to another position in the square.

Suddenly the gates of the gaol opened and all heads turned to watch the keeper march out. For a moment he seemed surprised when there was no cheering or applause from the crowd.

Waiting for him outside the gates were the High Sheriff and the Canon of St. Lawrence's. Just then two town guards, one either side of Charlotte, walked out into the daylight. They stopped when they drew near to where the keeper stood. The keeper then bowed and handed a rolled up parchment to Sir Richard.

Once the Sheriff was satisfied with the documentation he bowed to the keeper, who stood to one side. Two militia guards marched forward and took charge of the prisoner.

Thomas watched the hand over from the back of the square.

Charlotte was dressed in a brown robe and bonnet, both made of the same rough hemp like material. Her face looked pale and drawn, with hollow eyes that looked dispassionately into the faces in the crowd.

Sir Richard led the small procession along the path, that had been made through the towns folk. There were no jeers, no shouts of abuse, just an uncomfortable silence. When they reached the platform the executioner bowed to Sir Richard, who responded with a curt nod. The two escorting guards were then instructed to lead Charlotte up to the platform. Some of the bundled wood shifted under their feet as they climbed up to the stake and pushed Charlotte into position. The executioner then looped one of the iron straps around her waist and pulled her tight against the post. She winced slightly as the hoop tightened. He took an iron rivet from his belt and started to hammer the two ends of the hoop together, into the back of the post.

Thomas wanted to leave. He just wanted to get on his horse and ride away. All he could do though was stand by and watch, as Charlotte burned for no other reason than she didn't believe. Deep down he knew that Charlotte's old ways made her a natural target and somehow Baphomet had discovered this and had engineered this whole matter in an attempt to weaken him.

Charlotte was now secured to the post by her feet as well. Dr Plummer had also climbed up onto the platform and was reading a passage from a small bible. His muttering voice was the only sound to be heard, except the hammering of the rivets into the back of the post. The executioner placed the remaining bundles of wood into position, leaning them against Charlotte's legs. The two guards helped until her entire lower half was obscured by the tarred wood.

Sir Richard was then seen to call something out to the executioner, who nodded and fetched a length of thin rope from a barrel by the platform. He climbed back up and tied one end of the rope around Charlotte's neck, making a slipknot at the back of the post. The crowd started to mutter its approval when they realised that the Sheriff had decided, that as a last minute act of mercy, Charlotte was to be strangled before she was burned.

Dr Plummer finished his reading and closed the bible. He raised his hand and said a prayer, crossing himself when he had finished. Two guards helped him down just as the executioner was holding a burning torch to the base of the platform.

The crowd gasped as flames started to rise almost immediately, thanks to the use of the tar soaked wood. Charlotte closed her eyes and raised her face to the sky. Some people could have been forgiven for thinking she was asking forgiveness, it was more a matter of the thick oily smoke stinging her eyes.

Thomas watched the Sheriff point to the back of the platform. Large flames had already started to rise from the piled faggots, the wood snapping and cracking in the bright orange heat. The executioner realised he had forgotten the thin rope tied around Charlotte's throat. He ran to the rear of the platform and began to frantically look for the end of the rope. As he moved closer clouds of thick black smoke were rising from the burning bundles of wood making it almost impossible for him to see.

The guards that ringed the site and the townsfolk, who stood the closest to the platform, could feel the heat of the fierce flames on their faces. As they watched Charlotte raised her arms above her head and held on to the post. Her sobs had now changed to loud screams as the bottom of her hemp gown was now alight. The dancing flames were starting to work their way up her body.

All of a sudden the executioner spotted the rope; he leaned nearer and quickly snatched the end out of the flames. The crowd saw that the rope was charred in places and when he pulled it back to take up the slack it snapped. Several people cried out in alarm, while others just stared in horror as the end of the rope dropped back into the roaring flames.

The thin noose that had been tied around Charlotte's throat then loosened and fell away into the fire. She suddenly realised what was happening and her screams became hysterical.

'No!' Thomas cried out when he saw what was happening. He quickly started to force his way through the crowd towards the fire, Charlotte's screams of torment stabbed at his heart. He reached the front of the crowd to see the town officials standing helpless and unwilling to get involved any further.

At first only a few people noticed the tall, shaven headed man with the black eye patch, calmly walk out of the crowd and stand in front of the pyre. By then Charlotte's screams of agony were echoing loudly around the square causing some of the gathering to avert their eyes in distress. But then more and more people started to notice the stranger as he stood there. None of the guards attempted to apprehend the cloaked figure, they just stood and watched as he bowed his head in prayer.

'Bless this soul.' Thomas said in prayer, 'May God forgive me.' He crossed himself then reached into the sleeve of his robe and pulled out his dagger. The entire crowd watched dumbfounded while he kissed the blade. Nobody breathed as he quickly drew his arm back and launched the knife at the burning woman. The screaming stopped instantly.

The crowd strained to see the heat blurred shape of Charlotte through the flames. A few could see that her head had dropped forward, and that the handle of a knife was now protruding from her smouldering breast. She then disappeared from view as a gust of wind caused the fire to flare up violently and engulf the whole platform in roar of flames.

The townsfolk stood in awed silence as Thomas turned away from the fire and walked out of the square.

CHAPTER 26.

The next day Titus was standing outside the back door of the vicarage. He was feeling extremely uncomfortable at the prospect of having to go in and talk to Thomas. Since the events of the previous day in Evesham, his old friend had been somewhat subdued. Titus wasn't good at coping with delicate situations, he had Bartholomew for that.

He remembered what the shrewd sergeant had said when he was about to leave the tavern, to walk up to the vicarage.

'Perhaps a subtle approach might be prudent, Sir,' the sergeant said respectfully.

'Hells teeth, Bartholomew,' he was happy to use the sergeants Christian name when out of earshot of the men, 'You really do think I'm incapable of being tactful. Don't you?'

Bartholomew raised his eyebrows and looked into Barnard's eyes. He let out a sigh.

'I just think a humorous tale, offensive or not would be inappropriate at the present time, Sir.'

Titus opened his mouth in mock disgust.

'I'm merely going to inform Thomas of what has been happening around here over the past few days.'

'Its how you deliver that information that concerns me,' Titus's ignorance annoyed him sometimes, but he had learned over the years that it was futile to attempt to change his character. Making helpful suggestions seemed to be the best he could do.

Titus held his hands up in surrender.

'Alright Bartholomew, I will use the utmost discretion, not even the amusing tale about the two bathing nuns. One of yours I might hasten to add.' he said, giving the sergeant a mock look of disapproval. 'No. I assure you, I will tread carefully.'

He was now stood by the back door feeling completely disarmed. After a few moments he straightened his sash, gripped the basket hilt of his sword and walked in.

Thomas heard the heavy foot steps in the passage before the door was knocked.

'Come in Titus, old friend.' he called out. After a brief pause the door swung open and Barnard strode in. Thomas immediately stood up and grasped his friends hand in greeting, he then gestured to one of the chairs at the table, 'Sit down, Please.'

Titus sat down and placed his hat on the table next to him.

'I have information from my sentries.' he said

shifting in his seat, still feeling awkward.

Thomas noticed his friend's discomfort.

'It's alright Titus. I am not saddened by yesterday's events.' he reassured his friend. 'There's no need to be cautious. We have known each other too long for that. Anyway, over the years, we have both seen our fair share of needless death. Have we not?'

'I am sorry Thomas. My sergeant seemed to think that a little consideration was in order.'

'I will thank Bartholomew for his thoughts.' Thomas smiled, guessing what sort of things the sergeant might have suggested 'So Titus, what news have you?'

Barnard smiled; feeling more relaxed, now everything was out in the open.

'Firstly my sentries situated around Bretforton Manor are reporting all manner of activity.'

Thomas looked interested.

'For instance?'

'Well it seems that the Magistrate does have several companies of troops, stationed in the grounds of the manor.'

Thomas nodded.

'Samuel and I did meet some of his guards when we called on Sir Nicholas a few days ago,' he looked doubtful. 'The amount we saw hardly constituted one company, let alone two.'

217.

'Bartholomew sent Tom Allen into the grounds of the manor house last night.' Titus said smugly.

'How is Tom?' Thomas asked, he had always been amazed by the young trooper. He did have some unusual abilities.

'Still an odd little bastard!' Titus replied, 'The boy doesn't seem to sleep, bloody good trooper though.'

'What did he see then?' Thomas asked, trying to change the subject before Titus started reeling off endless anecdotes about the young man.

'Of course! Well, it seems that the magistrate has at his disposal an infantry company of about fifty men, muskets and pikes, and he can put thirty mounted dragoons into the field as well, all of them Landsknechts.' Titus looked at the other man and waited for a reaction.

'What does a country magistrate want with all those men?' he said quietly to himself looking past Titus. He glanced back to Barnard, 'How does their moral appear?'

'Apparently they look like they know what they are doing. They have good equipment. The uniform is a bit gaudy but serviceable, that's the Swiss though. Matchlocks, that they seem to know how to use and they can protect themselves with pikes as well.'

'The cavalry?'

'Good mounts. Bartholomew thought they weren't heavy enough though. We've watched them train in the grounds and outside the manor. They form well enough, I suppose, but they carry no fire arms. They've got no punch. They're probably just for chasing cowards.'

'What about officers?'

'None have been seen for the infantry yet but the commander of their horsemen is a different matter.' Titus cleared his throat, something he only did when he was being serious. 'Do you remember, a number of years back in Bavaria, when King William gave up his crown and his son Maximillian took over?'

Thomas nodded at the memory.

'A very disturbed young man, yes I do remember.'

'Indeed. Anyway King Maximillian employed some of those garish Swiss bastards, with their big hand an a half swords, and one of the companies were led by a blood thirsty whoreson called…'

'Baader!'

'That's the fellow. Well he now commands Dickinson's horsemen. A curious state of affairs I think?' Barnard said casually.

'So it would seem Titus.' Thomas recalled only

219.

too well how bad it had been in the state of Bavaria, all those years ago. He and Samuel had almost lost their lives and yet again Titus's company had to come to their rescue. Baader had indeed been a cruel and brutal man, but why had he appeared in an English village?

'They go on regular patrols around the estate, but can I tell you Thomas, they're useless. They couldn't find their own backsides with either of their expensively gloved hands,' Barnard laughed at his quip. 'I wanted to know how good their patrols were. So I had Tom Allen lay a few markers. The blind bastards haven't discovered any of them yet!'

'We need to keep a close eye on Sir Nicholas from now on I think. There is definitely some questionable activity going on at the manor.' Thomas stood up, bringing the meeting to a close. 'We must discover what he is doing.'

Barnard nodded as he picked his hat up from the table and they walked out to the back door. When they stepped into the daylight they heard the sound of approaching horses.

Around the corner of the vicarage appeared four of Titus's Troopers. They stopped in front of their commander. Will Spink saluted and then smiled at Barnard, over his saddle was a body of a man tied up with a sack over his head.

'Sergeant Roach sent us up here with a present for you and Master Wayland, Sir.'

He pulled the sack from the captive's head revealing a very frightened Robert Danvers.

He looked up and when he saw Thomas's face.

'Thomas, they've taken Mary!' he called out.

'Who has taken her, Robert?' Thomas asked the anxious Squire, who was now sitting in the minister's office flanked by two of Barnard's men. His normally broad shoulders were dwarfed by the troopers. He stared at Thomas with hatred in his eyes.

'How in God's name am I supposed to know that?' He banged the table with his fist. 'If I knew who took her I would be there taking her back, wouldn't I?'

Thomas started to laugh. Danvers gave him a look of disgust.

'I find it ironic, Robert!' The last word was said with undisguised bitterness. 'The other day you tried, unsuccessfully, to have me killed and now you come to me for help.'

Robert's shoulders slumped and he leaned forward, he had tears in his eyes.

'She's your daughter.' he said quietly.

'I know.' Thomas replied after a few moments. Robert looked up. 'Her mother told me just before she died,' he then stood up. 'Thank you gentlemen, I would be alone with the Squire. You may wait outside.'

'Did she suffer?' Danvers asked once the troopers had left the room.

'She burned in the fires of hell! Of course she suffered.' Thomas snapped.

'She hated me. Did you know that?' Robert said calmly. 'A few years after you left, she told me that she hated me and then left. She agreed to leave Mary with me though, she said that I could give her a better life.'

'Did you ever tell Mary about me?'

Robert shook his head.

'You were supposed to be dead. It was only years later that we heard stories that you were still alive.'

'What do you know of Baphomet?' Thomas suddenly asked.

'Who? Is that who might have taken Mary?' Danvers asked eagerly.

'If it was Baphomet, then she will die…' he let the words hang in the air, '…unless we can find his lair. He wants to meet with me; it seems he also wants me dead.'

'Can't blame him for that,' Robert mused. 'When are you meeting him?'

'Tonight!'

'I'm coming with you.' Robert said bluntly.

'No you will not! You will return home and wait for me to send for you.' He held his hand up halting Roberts protest. 'If you try and interfere or if Baphomet finds out her connection to me she will surly die. Do you understand that Robert?'

After a few moments Danvers reluctantly nodded his agreement.

'Gentlemen,' he called out. The two troopers entered the room, 'Could you please escort the Squire out?' Once they had left the room Thomas stood up and walked over to the window. He looked out over the countryside and he could just see where the narrow track disappeared into the distance. Somewhere at the end of that road he knew the Whispering Knights were waiting. 'Tonight!'

CHAPTER 25.

That night a full moon shone in the cloudless sky, covering the countryside in a silvery sheen.

Thomas quickly doused the candle when he heard the light knock. Tom Allen nodded to him when he slipped out of the back door of the vicarage.

Allen was the first to move and quietly jogged across the yard. He stopped and silently waited for Thomas, in the shadow of the garden wall.

Thomas didn't try to talk to his guide, he knew Allen wouldn't answer him. For the rest of the night all communication between the two men, either on the move or in hiding would be done by hand signals.

Tom Allen was by far the best night scout in the company. Titus firmly believed that the man could disappear into thin air, walk through walls and see in the dark. There were other skills that Titus mentioned but Thomas was just contented to know that Tom was a capable man, who was at home in the dark.

He briefly allowed himself to think about how the evening was going to turn out. Titus had made sure that there had been some men in hiding, around the meeting site for the last couple of days and was confident that Baphomet could easily be followed back to his lair, once the meet had finished.

Thomas reached where Allen was positioned. There they waited, listening for any sounds or signs of pursuit. After a while Allen climbed through the gap in the wall and disappeared into the night, closely followed by Thomas.

They moved along the tree line next to the track. Allen was wearing his soft leather boots, which allowed him to move soundlessly, made climbing obstacles easier and generally aided him in all matters of stealth.

Thomas wore his old riding boots, but he'd wrapped sackcloth around them, to dull the sound. Both men wore long dark riding cloaks, with black scarves tied around their heads. They had armed themselves with short swords and crossbows, which had been wrapped in black cloth to stop them rattling as they moved and also to stop the bright moonlight glinting off any exposed metallic parts.

When they reached the end of the wood they stopped. Thomas looked out across the open ground to the next wooded area, about three hundred paces he guessed.

Allen gestured to him that they should walk about twenty paces apart whilst moving over open ground. Thomas nodded and then waited while the younger man set off first. When he got far enough away he turned and waved him forward.

The night was cold enough for Thomas to see his own breath and with the moisture in the air everything was starting to feel damp. He watched, as every so often, Allen would stop and cock his head to one side with his mouth open, listening. The usual sounds of the night seemed a lot louder in the open space of the field.

A distance behind him a fox screamed, making him smile. The tormented cry of the fox was one of those night noises that had startled many a young trooper whilst on campaign. But if the animal was confident enough to stand around in the open and call out to the moon, then there was a good chance that they were not being tracked by anybody yet.

As soon as they had reached the trees, on the far side of the open ground, they stopped and crouched down. Thomas felt a light tap on his arm and saw that Tom was pointing back in the direction they had come. He looked, but he saw nothing. Just then something caught his eye. So they were being pursued after all, he thought as he watched the lean shape of the fox trot out from a patch of gorse. It suddenly spotted them watching him and darted off in the other direction, disappearing into the bushes.

They walked along the next tree line until they came to the track that led through the woods. It was well worn and rutted by the heavily laden carts used by the foresters. The moon glinted off the water that had collected in the deep cart tracks. Thomas was grateful that apart from the damp of the woods, the recent dry weather had ensured them of a relatively mud free journey.

They followed the track through the woods, keeping out of the moonlight by staying just inside the trees. Thomas tried to shift the weight of the crossbow he had slung over his shoulder, the brass trigger guard was starting to dig into his spine. A few more miles of that and he would be in agony. He also had a leather bag filled with short, bodkin headed arrows that hung from his belt.

The crossbow would not normally be his weapon of choice, he was better with blades. He was a competent crossbowman though and he supposed due to the nature of their journey it was the sensible choice.

His skill as a swordsman was second only to Titus, but he was a master of the throwing knife.

Titus said that his skill with a knife was just some kind of fairground trick. The usual weapon that the company used when mounted, apart from the sword, was the long horse pistol. Titus had insisted that they use the more expensive wheel locks instead of the more common match lock. 'You can fire in the bloody rain man!' he used to shout when ever Bartholomew tried to change his mind.

Ahead of him Allen had stopped to listen again. When he was satisfied he turned around and pointed to the ground, the signal for them to stop and rest. He walked a few paces further into the trees and sat down.

Thomas caught up and sat down next to him, leaning back against a tree. Tom passed him a leather flask of honeyed water. He pulled out the stopper and took a long gulp, the sweet liquid instantly perked him up. It wasn't what he would normally have drunk, but he was glad of its kick. Tom then shoved a hunk of bread into his hand. He took a few bites, immediately realising how hungry he was.

Tom took the flask from Thomas and pushed it back into his satchel. He then got up and crept to the edge of the track. He listened for a few moments and then looked in both directions before stepping out of the trees. He stopped and stared into the distance, his hands shading the moonlight from his eyes.

Thomas looked at the man stood on the track. His long riding cloak reached to the ground and apart from his scarf covered head he provided no human shape. In fact with the trees behind him there was no silhouette at all, rendering him almost invisible. Thomas admired the younger man's understanding of camouflage and stealth, it was obvious why Titus boasted about him. All he had done was master a skill that most fighting men overlooked. All of a sudden Tom beckoned him over.

When he reached him, the younger man pointed down the track. Ahead of them was the end of the wood and beyond that, in the open, a bridge.

Minutes later they were crouched at the end of the wood with a clear view of the foot bridge. Thomas remembered that in the note from Baphomet it said he was to wait for a guide.

The area around the bridge seemed clear of any obstructions. No bushes, no walls, no obvious hiding places of any sort. On the other side of the river, about ten or so paces from the bank there were more woods.

Whilst they were planning the night's journey, Samuel, quite rightly, pointed out that if there was going to be an ambush it would be here. Looking at the other side of the river he was inclined to agree with his friend. They're probably watching us right now, he thought.

They waited in the cover of the trees for what seemed like hours. Tom had silently removed their cross bows and loaded them. He laid the weapons down next to each other ready to use if needed.

Thomas was amazed; the younger man hadn't made a sound carrying out the whole task. Obviously the time they had spent during the afternoon oiling the catches on their weapons hadn't been wasted. He returned his gaze back to the bridge when, on the other side of the river, a figure walked out of the trees.

Tom slowly picked up one of the crossbows and pulled it into his shoulder, taking aim. He watched the figure walk to the bridge, who ever it was they weren't very big. Then it dawned on him, it was a child.

Both men watched as the little boy stepped onto the bridge, his breath blowing out into the cold air. He was wearing a long white gown, almost like a night dress. He had his arms wrapped around his thin body in a vain attempt to keep warm. When he started to cross the foot bridge they could see him shaking, as he took tentative steps across the narrow boards. Thomas wasn't sure whether it was fear or the cold. When he reached their side of the river he stood still and waited.

Thomas looked around for any sign of Baphomet. He could feel his anger rising every time he looked at the small child, an innocent pawn in an evil game. He then stood up and walked slowly out of the trees.

When he stepped into the moonlight he stopped and waited. Tom gave two light, almost inaudible, taps on the stock of his weapon. Thomas, hearing the signal that it was safe to proceed, walked towards the bridge.

The wet grass had soaked the sackcloth covering his boots and he could feel the added weight each time he moved his legs. As he neared the bridge he saw that the boy was staring at him, a look of pure fright etched on his young face.

'You have no need to fear me boy,' he said gently, the child's expression softened slightly, 'What is your name?'

'D...Daniel Sir,' he answered.

'Are you leading me into the lions den, young Daniel?' He said to the child smiling.

'I'm sorry Sir?' Daniel replied, too young to understand the irony of the question.

'Where are you to lead me Daniel? The Whispering Knights?'

'My master told me to tell you to wait here, Sir.' He answered, his teeth almost chattering from the cold.

'So, where are these Whispering Knights Daniel?' Thomas asked after a few moments, 'And where is your master?' He started to suspect that he knew the answers to at least one of his questions.

'He's here.' the boy said. 'Wait here please Sir.' He then walked back across the bridge. When he got to the other side he stepped off the board, turned around and waited.

It was then that a figure, wearing a long dark robe, appeared out of the trees behind Daniel. When he started to walk towards them Thomas could see that his face was hidden under a large hood. He soon reached Daniel and stopped behind him, placing a hand on the boy's narrow shoulder.

Thomas looked at the man. He was a head and a half taller than the boy and seemed quite portly, although his shape was mostly obscured by the folds of his robe.

'Hiding behind children now, are we scum?' Thomas asked acidly.

'Please, Master Wayland.' Baphomet hissed.

'We don't want to upset Daniel now, do we?'

'I see you have changed the location.' Thomas's hand rested on the hilt of his sword. 'Why?'

'I think you know why,' came the reply. 'I thought this place would be a lot quieter. Just you, me and Daniel.'

'What do you want?' he asked, pleased that Baphomet was unaware that Tom was hidden in the trees across the river.

'I want you, Thomas.'

'I'm here,' Thomas said raising his arms. 'Now, what do you want of me? And where is Mary Danvers?'

'Mary is safe, but as I said, I want you Master Wayland. To be more exact I want your blood.' Baphomet chuckled, a low guttural sound.

'Ha! Well you only have to come and take it.'

'No, no, no. You have to give your blood to me,' he paused 'All of it.'

'You want me, to give my life to you?' he asked calmly.

'There, I knew you would understand,' Baphomet rasped. 'You must realize, the nameless one will have a sacrifice and the most powerful sacrifice is…'

'…the blood of a willing adversary.' Thomas finished for him. He looked at Daniel, the boy just stared back at him, his hollow eyes gazing straight through him.

'Exactly! So you see how important you are to me? All I have at the moment is virgin blood. Good, but not as good.'

'Release Mary Danvers first, you dog!'

'I think not! What if you change your mind Thomas? No, I think I will keep Mary and after you have been sent in offering to the dark Lord, she will be released.'

'How do I know you will keep your word?'

'I find it ironic, Thomas, that you are questioning my word. You were supposed to appear alone, tonight, yet you bring a scout who is concealed in the woods and you also arrange an ambush at the original meeting site.'

Thomas was annoyed at the discovery of the night's plans. He turned around and shouted towards the trees, 'Tom, you can come out.'

'Tell him to leave any weapons behind.' Baphomet added.

Thomas was about to deny the existence of the crossbows when Baphomet raised his other arm. Out of the sleeve his hand appeared, holding a long curved knife. He then pressed the blade against Daniel's throat.

'Leave the weapons there!' Thomas shouted, seething with anger as he realised that

Baphomet now had the upper hand.

As he stared at the robed figure across the bridge, the feeling of helplessness gripped him. Tom silently appeared at his side.

'Good evening Trooper!' Baphomet called to Tom cheerfully, Allen looked at him, impassively, giving no reply.

'You do know that as soon as you cut that boy's throat, I am going to come over there and kill you!' Thomas said coldly.

The other man chuckled.

'Daniel, would you pick up that bit of rope, on the grass there please?' The boy bent forward and picked up a length of rope. 'Now give it a pull, there's a good lad.'

When Daniel pulled the rope, Thomas heard a loud snap from under the bridge.
Suddenly he felt the wood shift under his feet. He just managed jumped off the end in time, landing on the grass. The bridge collapsed into the river with a splash.

'Now, I hope you will dispose of any ideas of heroism and listen. You will be sacrificed to the nameless one on sahiman, or Mary Danvers will be!'

Thomas felt for his knife in the back of his belt, he wondered if the river was too wide.

Baphomet took Thomas's silence for

indecision.

'You would be saving an innocent life, Thomas. After all you have done, I hope you still don't regard your self as innocent?' He shook his head, 'I don't think the villagers of Treves would agree with you, if you did.'

Thomas was still looking at Daniel as the knife was slashed across his throat. Blood instantly sprayed from the wound, soaking the front of his gown. The boy's eyes slowly rolled back into his head and his mouth dropped open.

Baphomet let his arm fall away and the boy collapsed to the ground. The last threads of life trembling from his body.

'How many more lives, Thomas? The children from the village, the Cooper boy and now poor Daniel. Who next? Mary? You can stop it all, you know.'

Thomas reached around his back and grasped the handle of his knife. He drew it back swiftly and flung his arm forward, sending the knife over the river.

Baphomet didn't flinch as the knife flew towards him and landed between his feet.

Tom had already sprinted off to fetch the crossbows. Thomas stared at the other man as he turned and walked back towards the trees.

'Sahiman, Thomas! I will send word of where,

closer to the time.' he called back just as he disappeared into the trees.

CHAPTER 28.

Billy Gould lay motionless whilst he watched the gates of Bretforton Manor. He was in the sentry post that had been hidden in the bushes opposite the gates.

'Gould, you moody bastard! Tell me what you've seen then.' Titus whispered as he crawled along the carefully cleared path that led into the bush.

'Nothing, Sir.' he whispered back.

'What do you mean nothing?' Titus said looking at the gates. It was a good position he thought and well hidden too.

'No movement since me an' Spink took over from the last two, Sir.' He liked Barnard, even though he was a lunatic. Some of the men were worried sometimes that their flamboyant commander might get them all killed in some pointless, suicidal assault, in some far way part of Christendom. Billy accepted that this was a distinct possibility, he also knew that any one of them would follow Barnard, to certain death, without complaint.

'Good lad! Where's Spink now?' The other man should have been in the position, so news could be sent if anything happened.

'He's gone for a piss, Sir.'

'God help us! That boys innards will be the death of him.' he patted Billy on the shoulder and crawled out.

A few moments later Spink crawled back into the hide and slumped down quietly next to Billy. He noticed that Will's face had a pained expression on it.

'What's wrong with you?' Will just let out a low groan. Billy smiled to himself, half guessing what was wrong. 'I take it you saw Titus then?'

Will nodded, not looking up.

'Not soon enough though.'

'Gut punch?'

'Yeah, the bastard got me before I knew he was there.' He breathed out, wincing slightly. 'I bet I start pissing blood.'

Billy laughed quietly.

'I told you that you should have pissed here.'

'I can't piss lying down, you know that!' Then he stopped when he saw that Billy wasn't listening any more. Instead he was staring at the manor house gates.

Four riders had just galloped down the road and stopped at the gates. All were dressed in the uniform of the magistrate's personal guard. One of the riders carried a long, heavy looking bundle that he had in front of him, draped over his saddle.

Billy saw that one end of the bundle seemed to be twitching. The rider looked down and thumped the other end. The bundle twitched again and went limp.

When the gates swung open two guards ran out, both were armed with long, heavy bladed billhooks, ready to ward off any potential attackers. The horsemen trotted through the open gates.

Once the riders had vanished inside, one of the guards stood sentinel, watching the road, while the other started to pull the gates shut. At the last moment they both disappeared back inside. The loud metallic clang echoed across the road as the iron latch fell into place.

'They look like they know what they're doing, don't they?' Spink whispered.

Billy frowned.

'I know one of those riders from somewhere?' He whispered glancing at Will. 'I've seen his face before.'

'Baader!' Cawthorne called out when the four riders rode into the yard, at the back of the manor house. The Magistrate's aide looked immaculate as usual, in his black tunic and breeches, the starched white collar prominent against the dark cloth.

'What d'you want, servant!' sneered the scarred horseman, his long blonde hair appearing from under his hat. 'And you will refer to me as Captain Baader, servant!'

Cawthorne ignored the insult.

'Take the girl inside. Sir Nicholas is waiting.' He turned his back without waiting for a response, knowing the effect it would have on the other man. When he started to walk away he heard a snort from behind.

'One day servant, you will turn your back on me from the last time!' his voice, rising to a shout, echoed across the yard, Baader despised Cawthorne. He was aware of the man's reputation for being intelligent and shrewd, but his arrogance almost drove him into fits of rage. After years of soldiering he was reduced to taking orders from this poxed scum of a servant. He looked forward to the day when he would simply hack the man's feeble body to pieces.

'Captain?' one of his men called.

He looked down, still smiling at the thought of murdering the arrogant manservant, one of his men was stood there with the long bundle in his arms.

'Yes Karl? Ah yes! Take her into the house.

241.

That bastard Cawthorne will show you where to put her.'

The man smirked.

'Yes, captain.' The men were well aware of their commander's dislike for the magistrate's aide. As he made his way to the door at the back of the house, he felt the bundle begin to struggle again. You'll struggle soon enough girl he thought.

'I'm sure it's that fancy Swiss bugger, Sir. I'm sure of it!' Billy was convinced. He looked at Titus waiting for an answer.

They were knelt in a thicket, to the rear of the forward sentry posts, hidden from view.

'It is him, Gould.' Barnard answered sounding apologetic, he didn't like keeping things from his men. 'It's Baader. Tom Allen identified him the other night. I suppose the rest of the Company should know now.'

'What are we going to do, Sir? I mean are we going to kill the bastard or not?' Billy could feel himself getting angry.

Titus looked at Billy and saw in his eyes that the memories of their last meeting with Swiss mercenaries were still fresh. 'Billy, I give you my oath. Baader will die before the Company has finished here.'

Gould nodded, happy with his commander's response. He then turned and hurried back to his post.

Bartholomew appeared at Barnard's side.

'Shall I inform the rest of the men, Sir?'

'Thank you, Sergeant.' He waited until Bartholomew had gone before sitting back against a tree. He took his hat off and wiped his brow. The memories of Bavaria still stung him. Baader had almost succeeded in having Thomas and Samuel arrested for heresy. Eventually, they managed to flee over the border. He stared through the trees at the walls of Bretforton Manor. He would have his revenge, he thought to himself, Baader would die.

'Up there please.' Cawthorne said, pointing up a wide staircase.

Karl grunted his response and hefted the girl onto his shoulder. She whimpered as he manhandled her. He then started to climb the oak panelled staircase, his heavy riding boots echoing on the hard wood.

Cawthorne followed him up the stairs. The Swiss mercenaries irritated him with their rude coarse manner and their morose attitude. He had tried to convince Sir Nicholas to employ other mercenary companies. The landsknechts did have a brutal, efficient reputation overseas, but they had been known to turn on their employer if they disagreed at all. Sir Nicholas, though, wouldn't listen to his aide's advice and had been thrilled at the Swiss commander's acceptance at his offer of employment.

Cawthorne bridled at the slight, he had even suggested to the magistrate, the possibility of propositioning Barnard's Company. Unfortunately after all his searching they couldn't be found. Later he had heard that Titus and his company had been recruited by the church.

'Which room?' the guard asked abruptly, standing at the top of the stairs.

Cawthorne stepped past him.

'Follow me please.' He led them along the dark corridor to another flight of stairs.

This time the narrow stone steps climbed upwards in a tight spiral. At the top, the stairs opened out into a large round room.

Cawthorne waited in the centre of the dimly lit room, while the guard struggled up the narrow steps. He smiled with satisfaction as he listened to the grunts of effort and Germanic curses at the lack of space and the weight of the bound girl.

'Surely it would have been better to have let her walk up the stairs.' Cawthorne offered in his most condescending tone. The guard appeared at the top of the stairs and growled something he could only assume was an insult. 'Place her on the bed please.' he said.

The guard marched over to the large four poster bed and heaved the girl off his shoulder. She landed heavily on the mattress, still semi conscious, wrapped in her cloak with her hands tied behind her back.

Cawthorne waited until the guard had stomped out of the room, turning to give a last murderous stare before disappearing down the stairs. He then went over to the bed and gently unwrapped the cloak from around the girl's narrow shoulders.

'Very nice, Sir Nicholas will be pleased.' he said when he saw her face.

The small amount of light, let in by the shuttered windows, gently illuminated her delicate features. He untied her hands and laid her out onto the bed. He looked down at her unconscious form. He then started to feel that familiar warm tingling in his groin. He looked round in the direction of the staircase and listened for sounds of any possible interruptions.

There were only the noises of the men outside, dealing with their horses.

Satisfied he was alone; he turned back to the comatose girl. Sir Nicholas had never minded him taking liberties, probably to ensure his loyalty and silence, he mused undoing his breeches. She won't wake up yet anyway, he thought, as he sat on the bed.

The girl lay there motionless, unaware of what was about to happen to her.

CHAPTER 29.

'Oh fud! Oh fud!' Guy mumbled before ducking back behind the wall. He wasn't sure what to do, as he waited behind the wall in the tanner's yard. Guy was alone, he knew that because the only other person that was ever in the yard was Duncan and he was with the squire. That morning he needed to tell Saul something, but sat next to him on the pillory was the big scar faced man. He started to panic, he had to tell Saul.

Guy liked Saul and he had liked Eli as well. He felt sad at the thought of Saul's murdered brother. They had always been good to him, even Isaiah, who people said was nasty. He trusted the Cooper brothers and he knew they would listen to him. Not like Duncan and the others who went in the Black dog, they called him names. Guy remembered how Toby always said that he didn't know someone could be that stupid with just one head. All of them would then laugh at him.

He slowly peered out from behind the edge of the wall again. He didn't want the big scar faced man to see him. Ever since he had seen him pick Duncan up with one hand, in the tavern that night, he had felt scared of him. Him and the one eyed man. From then on he had been watching out for the two frightening men. The village lads said they were churchmen. That was just daft, he was sure they couldn't be churchmen. Proper churchmen are supposed to help people, scar face and one eye had done nothing but hurt people since they'd arrived. He looked again at the two men sitting on the platform of the newly repaired village pillory. He had to speak to Saul; he had to tell him what he'd seen.

Saul sat and watched the traders putting away their market stalls. The village green had always been a hive of activity on market days and today had been no exception. He had been sitting there all day, watching the buying and selling, the cutpurses, the thieves, the farmers auctioning off their cattle, the drunken farmhands fighting for the affections of the cross-eyed girl from the baker's yard. But even with all that activity, even with the busy atmosphere of the crowded market, he felt lost and alone.

Sometime during the afternoon Samuel had appeared from nowhere and just sat down next to him, saying nothing. But what could he say? Eli was dead.

Then something interrupted his thoughts.

'Did you say something Mr. Bolton?' he asked.

'I said, I think we are being watched.' Samuel answered. 'Don't look,' he snapped as Saul started to turn his head. 'The tanner's place. By the look of it it's the hunch back who works there.'

Saul glanced out of the corner of his eye to see Guy's moon face disappear back behind the wall of the tanner's yard.

'It's just Guy acting the fool.'

'He's a determined little fellow,' Samuel muttered. 'He's been there all afternoon, spying on us. He always runs away when he sees me, so I can only assume he wants to see you.'

'If he's here to ask me about Eli then he can bugger off.' He said looking away, 'I don't want to speak to any body at the moment. I don't want to do anything any more.'

Samuel could hear the grief in the young man's voice.

'Eli is with god now.' he said softly. Out of the corner of his eye he saw that the young man had tears in his eyes.

'Thank you.'

'What for?'

Saul wiped his face.

'You have no cause to be here with me, you're

249.

not my family. But still you're here and for that I thank you.'

Samuel could still conjure up the image of Eli's mutilated body, sprawled on the floor of the abandoned cottage. He could still remember Saul's cries of anguish and the anger in himself that he failed to keep him from seeing his brother's tortured corpse. He knew, from his own experience, that sights like that could never be erased from memory. He waited for a while, content to just sit and watch the slow activity of the village.

'What will you and Isaiah do now?'

Saul thought for a while as a cart noisily clattered past.

'We're thinking of joining Captain Barnard's company.'

Samuel looked at him and nodded.

'It's a good life. A hard life, but a good one.' He sat up and stretched his back, 'From what I have seen you can both ride well enough and you are both used to living on the road. You can be taught to fight with a sword and fire the cross bow and pistol, but I feel it only fair to tell you… Titus is completely insane and at some time you will be killed.' He winced at his last choice of words. 'What I'm trying to say is, you should think carefully before making any decisions.'

The light started to fade and the village green had become deserted. The windows of the Black Dog were starting to glow brightly against the dusk.

Saul jumped down from pillory's platform.

'I think I need some ale,' he said looking at Samuel, who had also jumped down and was now stood next to him. 'Will you join me Mr. Bolton?'

The burly man patted him on the shoulder, his scarred face showed a trace of a smile.

'I will Saul, come.'

The two men walked across the green towards the tavern. The sounds of the busy taproom already starting to carry across the village.

'I've never seen you smile before.' Saul said.

'You're still young. There's a lot you haven't seen yet.' Samuel looked up to see a face disappear behind the wall of the tanner's yard. 'He's still there you know,' he said and stopped.

'What's that?' The younger man asked.

'The hunchback, Guy, he's still there watching us. I think you should at least see what he has to say.' He saw the expression on Saul's face. 'I will follow you, but I'll have to keep out of sight, or he'll just run off.'

Saul sighed wearily and stepped off in the direction of the tanner's yard.

When they got closer to the yard they saw Guy look out again. This time his crooked form appeared from behind the gate post and beckoned them over.

'We're coming you bloody idiot.' Saul said under his breath, but as he reached him he was struck by the look of utter terror on his face. 'Guy, what is it? What's wrong?' He glanced round to see if it was Samuel's large shape that was spooking him, but he was hidden from view.

Guy couldn't stand still. His mind raced as his eyes searched the area to see if anyone could overhear him. He had waited all afternoon to speak to Saul and now he was here he couldn't say anything.

'She's gone!' he hissed.

'Who's gone Guy?' Saul asked him, now aware that this could be serious. 'Who's she?'

The cripple stared at him.

'They took her,' He frowned when he saw the confused look on Saul's face. 'Mary! They took her!'

CHAPTER 30.

'Sir Nicholas will not be receiving visitors today.' The guard stated through the gates of Bretforton Manor. He tried not to sound nervous as he looked at the three mounted figures glaring down at him.

Thomas could feel his calm mood ebbing away at the response from the obstinate sentry. They had arrived with every intention of just asking the magistrate for an explanation into the occurrences around the manor. But when they had attempted to gain entry to see Sir Nicholas they had been met with blunt refusal.

Titus had already lost his composure, but he remained silent, knowing full well how Thomas reacted to interruptions. After a while he realised they were at an impasse and urged his horse forward until he was along side Thomas. He leaned close to his companion.

'Thomas, may I try?'

Thomas looked at his friend and nodded, unable to hide his reluctance.

Titus slid out of his saddle and landed calmly, laughing to himself. He marched up to the gate with a huge smile on his face.

Isaiah, who had been sat on his horse silently

watching events unfold, noticed that Thomas had his eyes closed and seemed to be mouthing a silent prayer to himself. He looked back to Titus, who was making his way over to the gate. It then dawned on him that he might know what was coming next.

Titus was now stood at the gate, towering over the sentry.

'Now, my boy! Do you know who I am?' He saw the blank look on the man's face. 'Well, my name is Captain Titus Barnard!' He saw a brief flicker of recognition on the man's face. 'I see you've heard of me, might I know your name, my boy?' The guard just stared at Titus, seemingly unable to react to his enthusiastic manner. 'It's naught but a common courtesy,' he bellowed, 'I can't keep calling you 'boy' now can I?'

'Trooper Kemper.' he said flatly.

'Kemper eh! One of those Swiss lot I expect,' he paused and stepped closer to the gate. He looked at the young trooper's appearance and noticed that by the state of his uniform, the ill fitting tunic, the dented, rusty helm and worn boots, he was probably new to his company. There was a good chance that he was still being treated with the contempt that all new recruits had to suffer when they joined companies. The endless sentry duty, having to clean the kit of the longer serving men. In short he would be the company dogsbody until the next lot of recruits joined. The other thing Titus noted was that the man had a set of large keys, hanging from his belt. 'Landsknechts! That's what you fellows are called, aren't you?'

The trooper opened his mouth to answer the question. But suddenly, with the speed of a striking snake, Titus's gloved fist lunged through the bars of the gate, and smashed into Kemper's jaw, dropping him like a stone. Titus quickly glanced around to see if he had been spotted. Luckily the area around the gate was deserted. He squatted down, grabbed the unconscious troopers boot and dragged him closer to the bars of the gate.

Thomas and Isaiah watched as Titus had reached through the bars and started fumbling with the trooper's inert body. Their hands instinctively dropped to the hilts of their swords as Titus stood up with a large set of keys in his hand and started to unlock the gates.

Titus turned the key one last time and was rewarded with a dull click. He stood back and drew his sword before slowly pushing the gates open. He then stepped through with his blade held low, ready for any possible attack.

Thomas urged his horse forward as Titus disappeared through the gate.

'Be ready Mr. Cooper, today's visit will not be a friendly one.'

Suddenly Titus reappeared with a wide grin on his face. He sheathed his sword, removed his hat with a flourish and bowed to the two mounted men.

'The gates are open, my friends.'

Thomas smiled.

'Thank you Titus. I trust the welcoming party are on their way?'

'Not as yet, but there was some shouting and fuss starting up at the house,' he answered leaping on to his horse and taking the reins from Thomas. 'I'm sure they will all be along in a moment to receive us cordially.' He laughed loudly and followed Thomas through the open, unguarded gates.

Once inside they could see soldiers running towards them. Some of them had drawn swords in their hands, but most were armed with long billhooks.

'Sheath your swords gentlemen we're not here for a fight.' Thomas called over his shoulder.

Titus snorted.

'Not yet!'

Three soldiers stopped in front of them, two of

them holding their weapons out to bar their path. A third man, holding a sword glared at them.

'You will all leave, now!' he barked. More soldiers were appearing, all with grim expressions on their faces, clearly caught off guard with the intrusion.

'Come now gentlemen,' Thomas said, holding his hands out, 'We are here to speak to Sir Nicholas.'

The soldier armed with the sword was one of the officers in charge. He stepped closer to them, still holding his blade out.

'How did you gain entry?'

Titus laughed.

'Through the gate of course. You don't think we jumped the wall do you?'

Isaiah looked at the armed men that were threatening them and suddenly he felt vulnerable. His hand gripped the basket hilt of his sword, even though he thought by the time he had drawn it he would have been pulled from his saddle and butchered. He risked a glance at Thomas and Titus, both men seemed calm. In fact Barnard had one of his wide smiles on his face, eyeing their would be captors with amusement.

The officer glared at them.

'Get down from your horses now!'

'Bollocks!' Titus said, 'Why should we?'

Thomas noticed out the corner of his eye that they were now surrounded.

'Your last chance. Get down, now!' The officer stepped towards Titus's horse and reached for the reins.

Titus grinned menacingly and slowly started to draw is sword.

'Thank you officer!' a loud voice called out behind them, breaking the tension. All eyes turned to look at the newcomer.

The officer spun round and saw the dour figure of Cawthorne, stood behind his men. He glared at him, still slighted at the fact that his men had failed to prevent a breach in the Manor's security.

Cawthorne's hawk like features and grey eyes stared back impassively.

'That will be all.'

'They are to be escorted from the premises, buy the order of Captain Baader.' the officer growled, staring at the magistrate's aide.

Titus snorted.

'Captain Baader eh? I remember a snotty little weasel called Baader, from years back. He used to wear those frilly Swiss garments that the mercenaries out there used to wear, like you bunch. Bavaria I think it was.' He turned to Thomas and chuckled, 'Do you remember the fellow Master Wayland?'

'It does ring a bell, Captain yes.' He answered flatly, his eyes still watching for any movements from the guards.

Cawthorne saw that Barnard's insult had not gone unnoticed. But before the officer could reply, he stepped forward.

'Officer, if you would be so kind as to give Captain Baader my complements, but Sir Nicholas has decided to receive our…' he paused, half smiling, '…unexpected guests.'

Isaiah stifled a grin as the officer angrily rammed his sword back into his scabbard. He turned to his men and barked a few words of command, in his own language. The guards dispersed, some of them going back towards the manor house, while others made their way towards the gate.

Cawthorne watched as the three men dismounted. He inclined his head respectfully.

'Master Wayland, it is a pleasure to see you again, with Captain Barnard and Mr. Cooper this time, I see. Sir Nicholas will see you all now.' He raised his arm and ushered them towards the house. 'I will have one of the stable hands attend to your horses.'

Once inside the manor house they were shown into the library. It was a vast room that overlooked the grounds at the front of the house. The three inner walls of the room were obscured, floor to sealing, by shelves filled with rows of books.

Isaiah stared, open mouthed, at the sight of so many books. He remembered hearing stories about the huge libraries that the monks had had hidden away in their monasteries. But he had never seen anything like this before.

Thomas quickly scanned the room. There were two doors, the one they had entered through and another on the far side of the room. A large table was positioned at one end, with a high backed chair behind it. Near the large mullioned windows there was a leather arm chair, turned to face the glass. He placed his hand on the seat of the chair, it was still warm.

'We were being watched, gentlemen.' he said looking out of the window and seeing the path from the gate, where their brief exchange with the guards had just taken place.

'I hope he was proud of the spineless worms he has employed to protect this grand property.'

A door closed behind them causing them all to turn.

'I think proud is hardly the word I would use,

Captain Barnard.' Sir Nicholas answered, striding into the room with an amused glint in his eye. 'Embarrassed would be more appropriate, I think. But I do thank you for highlighting my poor security arrangements.' His fleshy features creased as he smiled. 'Now gentlemen, how may I be of service to you?' When he raised his arms the voluminous velvet robe he was wearing caught the light, making it appear like he filled the room.

Thomas looked at the rotund figure standing before them.

'I wonder if you would be kind enough to answer a few more questions, Sir Nicholas?'

'Sounds a bit ominous, Master Wayland.' The Magistrate's face brightened. 'As I have already stated, if there is 'anything' I can do to assist…'

Thomas caught the brief mocking tone in the other man's voice.

'I am grateful Sir Nicholas for your kind offer, after all we do need to sort out this unfortunate matter.'

The magistrate waddled across the room to the table.

'And that matter is?' he said sitting down in the high backed chair.

Isaiah felt the tension in the room growing. He glanced at Titus and noticed the look of perpetual amusement had been replaced by one of cold calm. He saw that Thomas was standing to the side of the table, with a hand on his sword hilt.

Thomas Smiled and then casually started to remove his gloves.

'It has come to my attention that some of your men were seen bringing a person, bound and gagged I believe, into the manor.'

Sir Nicholas looked shocked.

'Who, might I ask has made such a foul accusation?' he said, now standing up.

Thomas ignored the question and continued.

'It has also been observed, that your personal guard, which I might add are numerous, have been engaging in rigorous and quite aggressive training sessions, in and around the grounds of the manor. I am obliged to ask for an explanation on these matters.' He watched as the magistrate sat down again.

'Firstly, Master Wayland,' he said with undisguised scorn, 'I have no knowledge of a…captive…being brought onto the grounds and secondly the actions of my personal guard are in the hands of the guard commander, Captain Baader.' The fat man banged his fist on the table as he leaned forward, 'Frankly Sir I am offended by your accusations about the goings on around 'my' house and I would also like to know on whose authority you are acting?... By God Sir, the King shall here about this!'

Thomas reached into his cloak and withdrew a roll of parchment. He leaned closer to Sir Nicholas and placed it on the table in front of him.

The magistrate regarded Thomas with suspicion whilst he picked up the roll. He unwound it and started to read. His face instantly blanched.

'This…is…signed by the…' he slumped back down onto the chair.

'You can see by the royal seal, that His Majesty the King 'shall' hear about this.' A slight smile turned up the corners of Thomas's mouth. 'So Sir Nicholas, I ask again. Who and where is this captive, that was seen being brought into this house?'

The magistrate stared blankly across the room. After a brief moment he sat up.

'Cawthorne!' he called out. Almost immediately the door at the far end of the room swung open and the magistrate's aide appeared, offering a slight bow. 'Call the guard and have these gentlemen escorted from my house.'

Cawthorne casually stepped aside and some of the Swiss guards entered the room.

'Efficient little bastard aren't you.' growled Titus.

'Stay your arms!' Thomas shouted, stopping Titus and Isaiah from drawing their swords. He turned to Sir Nicholas, 'What madness is this, man! You dare defy the name of the King!?'

Sir Nicholas ignored the accusation and calmly glanced at Cawthorne.

'Is Captain Baader there?'

'Yah!' a deep, rough voice answered from outside the room.

All of them turned to the door. The three of them were each flanked by two armed guards. Then they watched as a squat, barrel-chested man appeared. His heavy cavalry boots echoed loudly on the wood floor as he walked into the room. His weather beaten face was clean shaven except for a huge drooping moustache, which twitched when he smiled at them, revealing a row of discoloured, broken teeth.

'You called, Sir Nicholas?' Baader answered.

'Captain could you please escort our guests from the grounds and if they try to gain entry again, uninvited, you have my permission to deal with them as you see fit.'

Baader nodded his head.

'Of course, Sir.' He looked at one of the guards, 'Sergeant, take them out!'

Thomas felt a dig in his back. He looked back at Sir Nicholas as he was pushed across the room.

'We will be back tomorrow, to look for the girl. Mark my words, you will regret this.' he snarled.

Titus laughed as he was pushed past the grinning Captain Baader.

'Next time we meet, dung breath, I'll have your fat head on a spike.'

'I look forward to it, Barnard.' Baader answered, with a strong German accent.

The three of them were marched out of the manor house and over to their waiting horses. They were then escorted to the gate, surrounded by guards.

Once they were out of the grounds the gates were slammed behind them and locked.

'I thought that went very well.' Titus chuckled as they mounted up.

Isaiah stared at him in disbelief.

'I don't see how that went well.' he said.

'Think about it!' Titus said looking at him, 'We now know his intentions.' he could see by Isaiah's expression that he still didn't quite understand.

'I think Captain Barnard is right. We now know that Sir Nicholas has dropped his air of respectability, that he has something to hide, and

265.

all those armed men he has employed are going to try and stop us finding out.'

'We'll move at dawn.' Titus said looking at the gates.

'Won't that take a while to get ready?' Isaiah asked. 'I mean, they know we are coming, we can hardly surprise them, can we?' Titus started laughing loudly.

Thomas smiled at him.

'Titus's men have been in position, ready to assault Bretforton Manor, for the last two days.'

CHAPTER 31.

'So you have men hidden inside the walls of the manor as well?' Isaiah asked, sounding impressed.

'That's how my company works, Cooper!' Titus answered whilst the three of them trotted back to the tavern. 'My men aren't just a band of rouges and brawlers, God in heaven, no! The men in 'my company' are the best at what they do, or they wouldn't be in 'my company'.'

'I'm afraid the Captain is right Mr. Cooper. Barnard's company are famed across Europe. If they were not now part of our order, they would be being sought after by all and sundry for employment.'

'Master Wayland, please! You honour me too highly,' Titus cried, feigning surprise and causing the other two men to laugh, 'Although you do speak the truth.'

They rode in silence for a while, until Isaiah spoke.

'I want to take part in the attack.'

Titus shot a quick glance at Thomas, before turning to Isaiah.

'You can't Cooper. You're not in the company.'

'Then Captain, may I have your permission to join the company?'

'Why?' Barnard asked, flatly.

Thomas slowed his horse until he was next to Isaiah.

'Do not make rash decisions, Isaiah.'

Cooper looked up, he was not used to hearing his Christian from Thomas.

'Me and Saul have talked about it. We're sick of living rough, robbing people... being alone,' the last two words were said quietly.

'So, it's not just about revenge for Eli's death?' Thomas asked.

'No.' Isaiah lied.

'What makes you think I want you in my company, eh Cooper?' Barnard called out from behind. He pulled his horse in beside the other two men. 'You can't just wander in and join up, you know!'

'You have to have a skill, Mr. Cooper, other wise you have to join by trial.' Thomas said.

Isaiah chilled at Thomas's words.

'What do you mean 'by trial', Master?'

'Well Cooper, what can you do?' Titus asked.

Isaiah went quiet for a while.

'I can ride.'

'I can see that, you ass! I mean a proper skill.'

'I don't know?' he looked at the men, confused.

'Please captain! Just give me and Saul a chance to prove ourselves.' he said sounding desperate.

Thomas looked at Barnard who nodded and then turned to Isaiah. 'I will talk to Sergeant Roach when we get back.'

'Thank you captain.' He answered excitedly, 'You will not regret your decision.'

'No boy! But you might!' Titus answered.

That night in the Black Dog, the taproom was quiet.

'What about the girl?' Samuel asked sounding concerned. He looked across the table at the other men.

Thomas drained the mug of ale and placed it back on the table. He winced at the bitter taste.

'We don't even know if she is still alive. I hope for her sake that she is dead.'

'After hearing what has happened to the others I'm inclined to agree.' Titus frowned at the thought of the other mutilated children.
'Anyway, my men are positioned around the manor and all gates are covered. Tom Allen even found a hidden gate. It's only wide enough for one man at a time. They had tried to obscure it with ivy.' He sounded like a proud father

when he talked about his men. All of a sudden he spun around in his chair, 'Sergeant!'

Bartholomew, who was sat a few tables away from Titus, stood up.

'Yes Captain!' he answered walking over to Barnard's table.

'Where's Allen tonight?' Titus bellowed cheerfully, 'I promised him a hogshead for finding that gate.'

Bartholomew stopped by the table.

'You know where he is sir.' he answered calmly, he was used to replying to Titus's sudden, abrupt questions.

'Damn and blast the man! Well when he's back give him the ale.'

'He won't drink it sir, he only drinks water.' Bartholomew answered, he then stood and patiently waited for Barnard's response.

'Christ on his cross! Am I in command of a bunch of fairies?' he looked around the room at the amused faces that were clearly enjoying the show. 'Give him the ale anyway, he can share it with the other men.' he said, throwing his hands up in the air.

'Before you go Bartholomew would you please take a seat.' Thomas called out as the sergeant was about to turn away.

'Of course, Sir,' the sergeant answered. He sat

down and watched as the other men huddled around the table conspiratorially. Thomas looked at him.

'Now Bartholomew, did any of the sentries see who delivered the letter the other night?'

'No Master. After you entered the tavern, nobody came or went until you left after midnight.'

Thomas paused.

'What about the back of the building?' he asked expectantly.

Bartholomew glanced at Titus, who grinned at him. He then looked back to Thomas.

'Sir, the sentries are positioned around the village in such a way, that no one can enter or leave a building without being seen.'

Thomas saw the hurt look on the Sergeant's, rough, weather-beaten face.

'Please, accept my apologies Bartholomew, I meant no offence. I should know not to doubt the abilities of the men.'

Titus's eyes widened.

'So that means that if no one delivered the note...'

'...It was already here.' Samuel finished for him.

'Exactly!' Thomas said quietly to himself.

'The landlord, Hawkins, said that a man came

in and delivered it.' Titus paused, 'The bastard was lying. Sergeant!' Thomas raised his hand and stopped Titus before he started to issue the order.

'Wait Titus, this could mean something. Bartholomew?' he looked at the Sergeant again. 'How well do you know Mr. Hawkins?'

'We speak Master, he seems friendly enough.' he answered. 'And he's happy enough to provide the company with provisions.'

Thomas lowered his voice.

'Bartholomew, I need you to become Mr. Hawkins's best friend. You must become his confidante, his shoulder to cry on. In short you must watch him like a hawk and report anything that you believe is unusual.'

'You suspect Simon of being involved in this murderous business?' the sergeant asked in disbelief. 'He doesn't seem the sort, Sir'

Thomas smiled and raised his hands in mock surrender.

'Bartholomew, please be calm. I won't be asking Mr. Bolton to hoist our portly landlord up to the rafters just yet.'

Titus snorted with laughter.

'Sounds like you're holding a torch for the fat bastard, Sergeant! You do know it is his daughter you should be trying to roger not him?'

Bartholomew looked a bit embarrassed.

'Thank you Captain,' he glanced at Thomas, 'Please, forgive my out burst, Master.'

Thomas clapped the Sergeant on the back.

'Pay no attention to your rowdy commander, Bartholomew, there's nothing to forgive.' He had to raise his voice so he could be heard over Titus's hysterical laughter. 'Samuel? Would you be so kind as to pat Captain Barnard on the back, before he chokes himself to death.'

After a lot of coughing and spluttering, Titus quietened himself down and the table returned to normality.

Sarah brought over another tray of ale. They thanked her and waited until she was out of earshot.

Thomas glanced at Barnard.

'Titus I think it is time to mention the other matter.'

Titus looked blank and then smiled.

'Ahh yes! Sergeant Roach, we have a couple of potential recruits.'

It was Bartholomew's turn to smile.

'Could they be the Cooper boys Captain? I have heard a rumour from some of the men.'

Barnard looked at him seriously.

'Well Sergeant, your comments?'

'From what I have seen so far, Sir, they're good lads. They can ride well enough, they both seem to have a bit of pluck about them. I haven't seen them fight yet, but that can be seen to later.' he sounded thoughtful as he spoke. 'They don't seem to have any skills to offer to the company either Sir, so they will have to suffer the trial.'

Barnard nodded.

'That's what I thought. What do the men think of them?'

'The lads like them Sir. If it goes well they'll fit in nicely.'

Titus clapped his hands together loudly.

'Good! That's what I thought. We'll have to do it soon Sergeant. I will of course leave it in your capable hands.'

Later that evening Isaiah and Saul got up from their table. The three other men, all from the company, were still sitting down.

Will Spink laughed out loud.

'There's no way you'll be able to join the company if you can't drink lads.'

'It don't look like we're going to join anyway, no one's said anything to us yet.' Isaiah said sounding hurt.

'Dr. Napier told me that you have to have a

skill to bring to the company or they won't even look at you.' Saul muttered.

'What about the tr…..' Will stopped when he felt a sharp dig in his side from Billy Gould.'

'It'll be a bloody shame lads,' Gould said grinning, 'You two would have done well.'

'Oh bollocks to it,' Isaiah said wearily. 'It don't matter anyway.'

'We'll see you lads in the morning.' Saul said. He then followed Isaiah up to their room.

They climbed wearily to the top of the narrow staircase, and along the dingy corridor that led to their room. When they got to the door, Isaiah turned to Saul, his expression was grim.

'We don't have to be in the company to kill the bastards who murdered Eli, you know?' his voice sounded cold, 'Ok?'

Saul nodded.

'I want to kill them too, though.' he answered quietly.

Isaiah turned the door handle and pushed the door open.

'You will brother, I promise.' he said stepping into the dark room. Straight away he heard a noise to his left, causing the hairs on the back of his neck stand up. He stared into the shadows to try and see where it had come from. 'Who's that?' he called into the dark. Suddenly strong

275.

hands grabbed his arms and yanked them painfully behind his back. 'Bastards!' he cried out. A cloth sack was then pulled over his head. Behind him there were more sounds of struggling and cursing.

'Fuck off you poxed scum!' Saul shouted, trying to fight off the grasping hands that had reached for him out of the dark. He felt the thin cord being looped over his wrists, pulling his hands together. He winced as it bit into the skin. He tried desperately to pull away as a stale smelling cloth bag was pulled over his head. Then without warning one of his captors punched him several times in the stomach. He doubled over in pain

Isaiah heard the punches being thrown behind him and he tried to turn around to get to Saul. His captors started to drag him backwards. Up to now their attackers hadn't said a word to them, the only voice he had heard was Saul's, shouting and cursing.

He then felt himself being dragged along the narrow upstairs corridor, his captor's grunted with the effort of moving along the cramped space. After a few moments he knew they must be nearing the top of the stairs. That would be the best time to try and alert some of the men drinking in the taproom. He could hear Saul's voice again.

'Lads! Lads! They ...' his warning was cut off when a gloved hand clamped over his mouth. He tried to make himself heard again but his muffled shouts were being drowned out by the noise of the rowdy drinkers downstairs He stopped shouting and listened for any clue as to what was going on. It was then that he could hear another stifled voice and realised it was Isaiah, who was also trying to call for help.

He tried to see through the material of the bag, but the cloth was too thick and dirty, it also stank of rotting straw and piss. The hand that was being held over his mouth had forced him to chew on some of the dirty cloth, making him want to gag.

All of a sudden the two men that held him gripped him tighter under the arms and lifted him off his feet. He tried to shout out but the sudden movement disorientated him. He tried to struggle again, but his renewed efforts were rewarded with a sharp blow to the side of the head.

'Poxed scum!' he cried out. One of them thumped him again, causing bright flashes to jump before his eyes. Behind him there were sounds of struggling and he guessed that Isaiah was being bundled down the stairs as well.

After all the blows to the head he'd received, Saul felt disoriented. He couldn't work out where they were going. But then he felt himself being dragged through a narrow doorway, when he felt the chill night air, he realised he was in the stable yard.

Isaiah tried to kick his legs out, knowing that the men who were carrying him were finding it difficult on the cramped stairway. He felt a heavy jolt and realised they had reached the bottom of the stairs. He knew the corridor leading to the taproom was on his left and to his right was the door that led to the stables. He tried to call out again but the hand over his mouth clamped tighter, forcing him to taste the filthy sack cloth. Then he was pushed outside.

He felt the hand that had been covering his mouth drop away.

'Where we going? Where are you taking us, you bastards?' A gloved fist smashed into his face, causing pain to suddenly explode across his eyes.

Isaiah shook his captor's hand away from his mouth.

'Saul! Saul! Are you alright?' A heavy blow landed in his stomach, knocking the wind out of him. He groaned with the pain, coughing uncontrollably. Then strong hands lifted him upright, before picking him up and throwing him over the saddle of a horse. His arms were then untied from behind his back and retied in front. He was still reeling in pain from the last blow, when he felt his ankles being tied.

When their horses set off Isaiah heard Saul moaning.

'Keep silent, until we know where we are going.' he said as loud as he dared.

Saul grunted in response.

The silent captors then rode off into the muddy lane behind the tavern, with the bound Cooper brothers.

Isaiah listened as they trotted along the lane. He still hadn't heard any talk from their kidnappers. He felt the horse lean to the left slightly and realised, because of the short time they had been travelling, he might know where they were in the lane. He decided that if they were going to try and escape, it was best to do it as soon as they could, before they were too far away from the tavern.

He wriggled slightly to make sure that they hadn't tied him to the horse. He felt relieved when he found he wasn't.

'Saul?' he hissed.

'Yeah?'

'We go now.'

'Yeah.'

He took a deep breath, in anticipation of the fall.

'Now!' He flung his arms back and slid from the horse. He landed heavily. Saul landed nearby him.

He immediately rolled over and started to untie his ankles. There was a commotion on the track and he realised the kidnappers were turning around to look for them.

The rope around his ankles eventually fell away and he pulled the sack from his head. Saul appeared at his side.

'Come on.' He whispered.

They got to their feet and ran further into the trees. The darkness made it almost impossible to see where they were going. Behind them their captors crashed through woods in pursuit.

'Who the fucking hell are they?' Saul puffed as they ran. When he looked back over his shoulder, he could just about see the dark shapes chasing them. He turned back and patted Isaiah on the arm, 'This way.' He darted left towards the track and after twenty or so paces dived to the ground, pulling Isaiah with him. They crawled into the under growth and stopped.

Isaiah kept his head down and listened. He could still hear his heart thumping in his ears.

He held his hands over his mouth, to try and dull the sound of his heavy breathing. He knew Saul would be doing the same, it was something they used to do when they would lie at the side of the road, waiting to rob unsuspecting travellers.

All around them they could hear their pursuers running through the trees, searching for them. Isaiah nudged Saul's elbow. A few yards in front of them one of their captors had stopped.

Saul could feel his heart beating faster now. Every muscle in his body had tightened in anticipation. Suddenly he realised the woods had gone silent. The crafty bastards were listening for them, he thought.

Isaiah watched the shape in front of them. It stood immobile, its head turned slightly to one side, listening. Then a twig snapped to his right. Out of the corner of his eye another shape had appeared. It seemed still, but he watched it take another, very slow, pace closer. 'Bollocks!' he thought to himself. He lightly nudged Saul's arm and just as he was about to move a loud, metallic click sounded in his ear. He instantly froze when he felt hard, cold metal being pushed into his ear.

'Shit!' he said out loud. A low harsh chuckle

281.

came from one of the shapes. 'Come on then you bastards!' he shouted and he went to jump to his feet. Before he could react there was a sudden movement behind him, followed by a solid blow to the back of his head, sparks flashed in front of his eyes, then darkness.

Isaiah blinked as he regained consciousness and he started to panic. He twisted around to try and see where he was. Then he stopped, realising the sack was back over his head. He blinked again, still feeling groggy from being knocked unconscious.

'Saul? You there?'

'Yeah, I'm alright.' he answered, 'They've left us alone for a while, I think. I've been listening and I can't hear anyone.'

'Are your hand's tied?'

'Yeah. Who are they, d'you think?'

'I don't know, but I tell you what! I've had enough of this.' Isaiah took a deep breath, 'Where are you, you bastards!?' he shouted. Suddenly, they jumped as a voice answered them.

'You can shout all you like Mr. Cooper, no one will help you.'

'Who are you?' Saul demanded, feeling angry and nervous at the same time.

'You will know soon enough, young Saul. Suffice to say, you know me from your nightmares.' the cold voice laughed.

'Untie me and I'll show you nightmares, you fucking whoreson.' Saul spat, and he pulled at his bonds. The voice laughed at him. 'Fuck off!' he shouted back.

Isaiah listened to the voice as it responded to Saul's angry threats.

'What do you want?' he asked calmly.

'What I want, Mr. Cooper is for you and your spirited brother to serve my master.'

Isaiah heard the voice move around in front of him.

'And why would we serve your master, whoever he is?' he answered loudly stopping another one of Saul's outbursts. He relaxed when he heard Saul remain silent.

'The question is, Mr. Cooper, why wouldn't you?' the voice paused for an answer. When he realised Isaiah was not so easily baited he carried on. 'What lives do you Cooper brothers have, eh? The elusive highwaymen… How long till you are elusive no more?'

Isaiah listened as the voice moved behind them. Then he heard some thing to their front, a soft noise. It sounded very faint, like cloth moving. Then he realised, their were others in the room, staying quiet, watching. He now started wondering if they were going to live through this, what ever this was? So far the voice had made no mention of where they were or who he was.

'I'm touched you are so concerned about our welfare, but why have we been kidnapped and who is your master...Mr...?'

The voice laughed menacingly.

'Very cleaver Mr. Cooper. All you need to know about me is that I am a friend, as to why you are here and who my master is, all will become apparent.'

'Friend, eh? Our friends don't tie us up.' Saul replied sourly.

'I'm glad to see you have calmed down, young Saul. Now gentlemen, my master will only make this offer to someone he deems worthy, rest assured if he did not your corpses would be rotting in the woods as we speak. This offer will not be repeated. What is your answer?'

'I've got an answer for...!'

'Quiet Saul!' Isaiah snapped, stopping his younger brother's sudden response. 'Well sir, we have heard your offer and so far you have mentioned no benefit to us. Now if you would be so kind as to untie my brother and me, allow us to leave, I give you my word I will not kill you. I will not repeat my offer. Now, what is 'your' answer?'

Saul shivered at the cold tone of his brother's voice. He had only heard it a few times before, but he knew full well what it meant. Then he blinked when a sudden movement startled him. Some thing big and heavy landed on his lap, he assumed the same had happened to Isaiah.

'What the fucks going on?'

Isaiah felt a weight land on his lap as well. He tried struggling but his legs were tied to the chair. Then a sound stopped him. The unmistakeable metallic rasp of a blade being unsheathed.

'I'm afraid gentlemen you will not be allowed to leave.' said the voice calmly.

Isaiah pulled at his bonds. The old anger that he had always tried to keep under control, bubbled to the surface.

'Come on then, you bastards!' he shouted.

All of a sudden loud raucous laughter broke out all around them. He turned his head from side to side trying to ready himself for the first blow or the slice of the blade that would finally end the ordeal.

Both the Cooper brothers flinched as the sacks were suddenly yanked off their heads. At first they just blinked at the bright lights. But then they saw that they were back in the taproom of the Black Dog, surrounded by most of the men from Barnard's company, all in fits of laughter.

'What the fucks going on?' Saul shouted.

'What the fucks going on… Captain!' bellowed an unmistakable voice. Titus grinned at the two brothers when they noticed him. 'Cut the bonds Sergeant Roach!'

Bartholomew smiled broadly as he cut the rope from their wrists.

'Well done lads,' he said, patting them on the back.

Isaiah looked around the room at the faces of the men gathered. He felt confused at first but then it dawned on him what had taken place. He looked down. In his lap was a folded green tunic and on top was a long, wheel lock horse pistol. He looked over and saw the same on Saul's lap and the wide smile on his brother's face confirmed his thoughts.

Titus walked up to them and held his hands up for silence. The men slowly quietened down, and wide grins turned into proud smiles.

'I am pleased to announce the addition of two new members to the company!' The room exploded into cheers and applause, drowning out Titus's words. 'Quiet you rogues!' he shouted. 'Now, let's welcome Trooper Isaiah

286.

Cooper and Trooper Saul Cooper to the company. You belong to me now, boys!' Applause erupted from the men. 'Stand up lads!'

Isaiah stood up, his face was a mix of embarrassment and pride as he grinned uncontrollably. He glanced at Saul, who looked back at him, they both burst out laughing. Fountains of ale sprayed into the air drenching them and everyone else in the room. They both raised the mugs that had been thrust into their hands and drained the contents, causing another round of cheers.

Saul looked over to the other side of the taproom where Thomas and Samuel sat. The large man stood and raised his mug, a broad smile on his scarred face. Thomas too was applauding, whilst being careful not to get covered in the ale that was being sprayed everywhere.

Bartholomew wandered over and sat down at Thomas and Samuel's table. Those two are going to have sore heads tomorrow.' he slurred, the ale affecting him slightly.

'Will they get the day off, Sergeant?' Thomas asked wryly.

The sergeant started laughing.

'Will they bollocks! Tomorrow they will sorely regret being a member of the company, I can tell you.' He took a long drink and then slammed his mug down on the table, a bit harder than he wanted to. 'Sorry Master Wayland… Samuel.' The two men grinned. 'No…their good lads those two, the men like them as well. Lets just hope they stay alive long enough to do well.'

'Let's hope so.' Samuel said quietly.

CHAPTER 32.

The next morning Sergeant Roach stood in the centre of the stable yard and smiled. The yard was a hive of activity, horses were being rubbed down, and saddles were being fitted. Everywhere, there were men checking and re-checking equipment. Some of the men, who were adjusting their breast plates, were laughing at Saul, who was leaning against the stable wall being violently sick.

Isaiah, who was sitting on his horse, frowned when the smell of the vomit eventually reached him. He fidgeted in his saddle, trying to make his riding position more comfortable. It didn't help that his tunic was too tight. Sergeant Roach said it would fit better after he had lost some weight during training. He worked his fingers under the rim of his breastplate and lifted it up a bit, taking the pressure off his shoulders. The relief was instant. He had always wanted to know what it was like to wear armour and now he knew, bloody uncomfortable. Even the weight of his new sword was bothering him.

'How are we feeling on this fine morning, young Cooper?' Titus bellowed, slapping Isaiah's horse on the rump, making the animal flinch in surprise.

Isaiah struggled to gain control.

'Fine thank you, Sir.'

'Excellent!' Titus replied. He then looked over and spotted Saul throwing his stomach contents up against the stable wall, 'Christ on his cross! Sergeant Roach!'

Bartholomew heard the call and noticed the grins on the faces of the men. He turned around and saw Saul. Straight away he knew what was coming.

'Sir!' he answered loudly as he marched over to where Barnard standing, with a look of amused horror on his face.

'Sergeant Roach! Why is Cooper being sick on my stable wall?'

'Nerves, Sir! Cooper can't wait to begin training this morning, Sir!' Bartholomew answered in his clear Sergeant's voice. He knew exactly what Titus was about to say next and also knew that it was a good training point for the two new recruits.

'Thank the lord for that!' Barnard replied, 'Because if it was anything to do with the copious amounts of fermented horse piss, the landlord calls ale, Cooper drunk last night, then I would have a days pay off him, and he would be scrubbing the stable yard from now until sparrow's fart tomorrow!'

Roach struggled to hide his smile.

'Thank the Lord, that won't be necessary, Sir! Although I will have him clear the mess away with a few buckets of water, when he finally gains control his excitement, sir.'

'Good idea, Sergeant!' Titus raised his voice again, 'A man who can't control his ale is guilty of self inflicted wounds and I will not have it!' As if nothing had happened he clapped his hands together enthusiastically, 'Mount them up Sergeant! Let's go and do some training on the manor field, so those Swiss bastards can have a good gawp at us, eh?'

Twenty miles away a lone rider entered a waking city. As he rode sound of his horse's hooves echoed off the walls of the tightly packed buildings. Samuel had left the vicarage just after midnight and was pleased that his journey had gone without any difficulty. When he looked around, he saw that the grey dawn had done little to light Worcester's deserted streets. Sturdy, dark timbered houses and shops lined his route, a stark reminder of the city's medieval past.

As he urged his horse through the grim streets

he remembered Thomas's words, the previous night.

'Something concerns me, Samuel.' he sat back and stared into the fire. 'Where did Baphomet come from? William said these murders have been happening on and off for the last ten years. So where was he before that?'

'And each year they have always occurred in the run up to samhain.' the Minister added.

Samuel nodded.

'So, there is a good chance that it's the same man. It's also possible he has done the same thing elsewhere?'

William sat up.

'The bishop!' he said excitedly.

Thomas looked at his friend's suddenly animated face.

'What about the Bishop, William?'

'He would know if it had occurred in the shire before. Henry Philpott is a very knowledgeable man. It is said that he is aware of everything that happens in Worcester.' William sat back in his chair, satisfied that he had actually offered something useful to the conversation. When he glanced at Thomas, the lack of a response unnerved him. 'He may be able to help, you know.'

'Henry Philpott.' Thomas said quietly.

'Do you know him?' William asked, hearing Thomas's recognition at the name.

'A name from our past minister.' Samuel answered for him.

'I trust I have not dredged up any bad memories, gentlemen.' William chuckled uncomfortably, wishing he had not said anything.

Thomas smiled at him.

'On the contrary William, you have helped us more than you know.' He turned to Samuel, 'You must leave for Worcester tonight, my friend!' Samuel nodded and left the room.

His thoughts returned to the present as he turned his horse into a wide street. He caught sight of two of the city watchmen, stood on the street corner leaning on their pikes. He stopped by them and asked directions to the cathedral. One of the men told him to follow the street through an area called Sidbury and the cathedral would be in front of him. He thanked the man and tossed him a coin.

Sure enough, once through Sidbury the gigantic stone structure of Worcester cathedral rose up in front of him, easily dwarfing the rest of the city. When he eventually turned the last corner he was impressed at the sight of the immense archway that greeted him.

The gateway of the old castle yawned in front of him like the gaping maw of a tired monstrous beast. He couldn't help looking up as he rode through the arch, noticing that the portcullis was still visible at the top of the opening.

Once through the gate he saw a wide expanse of grass spread out in front of him. When he looked around he noticed that the large solid looking buildings, that skirted the green, appeared to have been built up against the old castle walls.

The grand façade of the largest building certainly left him in no doubt at where the bishop lived. He dismounted stiffly and stretched the long journey from his limbs. Just then a distant voice attracted his attention and he turned round.

'You there! Yes, I said you! Who are you? And what do you want?'

Samuel watched the pale, skinny man that had appeared from one of the side doors of the largest building, hurry across the manicured lawns towards him. He wore long black clerical robes that were immaculately clean and pressed. To further display his vanity he was lifting the hem of his robe off the grass as he ran.

'What are you doing here? You must leave at once!' the cleric cried out in a reedy, high

294.

pitched tone. 'You are trespassing on His Grace the Bishop of Worcester's private property. I will call the militia, you know!' he added when Samuel didn't move.

Samuel cleared his throat, which sounded more like a growl, causing the highly strung cleric to step back in alarm.

'Who am I?' he asked calmly.

The cleric blinked in surprise, clearly taken back by the innocent question.

'I'm sorry?' he stammered.

'Who am I?' Samuel repeated.

'I don't know?' the younger mans voice regained some composure, but still wavered slightly. 'Why do you ask?'

'Well, I'm struggling to understand how you have come to the conclusion that I am a trespasser, who shouldn't be here.' Samuel kept his voice level and calm, 'You asked me who I was, but you didn't wait for an answer.' He flicked the edge of his cloak over his shoulder and patted his horse's nose.

The cleric stared wide eyed at Samuel's sword.

'I…I'm sorry if I have caused offence Sir.'

'That's better,' Samuel said smiling. 'My name is Mr. Samuel Bolton and I wish to speak to His Grace.' He quickly held up his hand, anticipating the cleric's response,' No I don't have an appointment, but if you mention that I am a companion of Master Wayland I'm sure he will see me.'

The younger man blanched.

'F...Follow me please.' he replied and without waiting for a response he turned on his heel and hurried off in the direction of the large house he had appeared from.

Samuel followed, hoping he had not had a wasted journey.

Barnard's company trotted in silence, along the muddy track, that led through Cowley Woods. They were making their way to Manor fields to do some training. Well that's what Isaiah thought they were doing.

He looked around at the faces of the men and there was some thing wrong. Most of them looked worried and unsettled.

'What's wrong with every one?' he muttered to Will Spink, who rode next to him.

'What do mean?' Will answered, without looking at him.

'Every one looks nervous.'

'I know.'

'I don't understand?' Isaiah said.

'We're being watched.'

'Who by?' Isaiah asked, starting to turn his head.

'Don't look round,' Will snapped quietly. 'Keep quiet and ride. You and Saul will be with Billy 'n me. Just do as you're told and keep close.'

Isaiah rode the rest of the journey in silence, straining to look into the trees without turning his head.

After a few more miles the road opened out into some open scrubland. Sergeant Roach galloped past the company and stopped in the middle of a clear area of ground. Titus turned his horse and faced the men as they approached.

'Form up on Sergeant Roach!' he ordered loudly. 'Smartly now!'

Four men rode straight past the company and into the trees on the other side of the field.

'Right you two, come with me!' Gould cried out as they crashed through the trees, 'Will! Take the horses.' he slid out of the saddle and jogged back towards the edge of the wood. Isaiah and Saul both dismounted and followed after him.

The two brothers caught up with Billy, who was kneeling down just inside the tree line.

'What's happening?' Saul asked, as they squatted down next to him.

The older man held his finger up to his lips

and pointed to the field, where the company was.

'Just watch,' he whispered.

The Coopers sat in stunned silence whilst they watched the company form up in the open ground.

Isaiah looked on in disbelief.

'What in God's name are they doing?'

The young cleric held open the door of the antechamber.

'You can wait for His Grace in here Sir.'
Samuel nodded his thanks and walked in.

The room looked immaculately clean, if not a little spartan in appearance, with its white washed walls and highly polished wood floor. The only visible items of decoration were a wide pewter bowl, filled with dried lavender flowers, on a trestle table by one of the walls. There was also a large silver crucifix, which hung on the wall above the hearth.

He walked over to the window and sat down on one of the benches. For a while he watched the shiny, black ravens hop about on the wide lawn, digging for worms. His thoughts drifted as he remembered the young girl's body, tied to the tree. The suffering she would have gone through must have been unbearable. He only hoped that his visit to the Bishop would not be a wasted one. Then a knock at the door startled him out of his thoughts. He checked his hand as it unconsciously sought the hilt of his sword.

'This way please, Sir,' the young cleric said standing to one side and directing Samuel to the office across the hall. The young man lightly knocked the door and walked in. 'Mr. Samuel Bolton, your Grace.'

The Bishop glanced up from his parchment.

'It's a might early for my appointments, Owen, I think?'

'I'm afraid Mr. Bolton has no appointment, your Grace.'

'Then why the interruption, boy?' the Bishop replied, matter of factly.

Owen started to fidget with his hands.

'I…I'm sorry your Grace…I… just…'

'You just what?' Henry snapped as he placed his quill down. The curate stared back, open mouthed, 'Just return to the sacristy and continue with your duties Owen.'

The young cleric nodded and quickly left the office. Both men regarded each other in silence. There was a light bang as the main door shut. The Bishop glanced out of the window and watched Owen jog back across the lawn, towards the cathedral. He looked back to the other man and smiled.

'Hello Samuel, it's been a long time.'

Samuel walked up to the desk and gripped the old man's hand in greeting.

'Henry, you are a sight to warm my soul.' He nodded to the window as Henry sat down, 'You don't like him do you?'

'Young Owen is an acquired taste, I'm afraid, one that I am yet to acquire.'

Samuel patted the dagger hanging from his belt.

'I could murder him for you, if you like, Henry? It's no trouble!'

The Bishop chuckled.

'Thank you old friend, another time may be. Oh! How is Thomas?'

The big man's smile faded.

'Henry we need your help.'

'Quiet and watch,' Gould snapped.

Isaiah couldn't believe what he was witnessing. Up until now he had believed that Barnard's company were the most feared and respected mercenary troops in Europe. But here he was, watching a group of clumsy, chaotic and ill disciplined men on horse back.

Two of the men, in their attempt to form a line, had collided with Sergeant Roach, knocking him off his horse. Another group of men had missed the line completely and were wandering around the field, seemingly unable to control their mounts.

Saul watched, open mouthed, as some of them swigged from brown ale bottles, which they had hidden in their knapsacks.

Then a fight broke out when one trooper tried to pass the queue and push in at the front of the line. Throughout the whole shambles the one thing that remained constant, was the sound of Titus, bellowing with laughter. At one point he nearly fell off his own horse.

'What the bloody hell is going on?' Saul muttered.

'Just watch,' Gould repeated, grinning.

After a while the company started to sort themselves out. Two ragged lines of horses and riders began to emerge from the chaos.

'Please lads!' Sergeant Roach cried out, holding his arms out, 'Calm down and straighten the line, would you!'

'What did he just say?' Saul asked incredulously, looking at Gould. It was then that

Isaiah started to laugh. He stared at his older brother in disbelief, 'What are you laughing at? This is embarrassing!' He then turned back to the company as he heard an order being shouted.

The calamitous sound of scraping metal echoed across the field, as the company drew their swords. Three men immediately dropped their weapons, whilst another hit his horse on the head, startling the beast so much it bolted and took off across the field. The mood of the company deteriorated further into excited amusement, as they sat and watched. Sergeant Roach galloped after the man, shouting for him to stop, with one hand on top of his head to stop his hat flying off.

The rest of the mornings training was taken up with several disastrous attempts to manoeuvre the company as a whole. Horses bumped their neighbour, some men fell from their saddles. At odd times a few of the company would jump down from their horses and run over to the bushes to be sick.

After a while Saul couldn't sit and watch any more, so he got up and walked back into the trees a few paces and slumped down against the base of a tree. He took his hat off and ran his hands through his coppery hair.

'What have we done Issy?'

Isaiah said nothing and looked at Billy.

The older man nodded.

'What do you think of the company then, young Cooper?' he asked cheerfully.

'What do I think?' he replied, in amazement, 'After watching all that, I'm not sure what to think.'

'And what, did you watch?' Billy asked him calmly.

Just then Will Spink appeared and squatted down next to Isaiah. He opened his mouth to say something, but Billy held his hand up, silencing him.

'Come on boy! What did you watch?' The older man repeated.

Saul shook his head.

'Well firstly, most of them can't ride,' he counted off on his fingers, 'half of them can't even grip their swords properly, Sergeant Roach doesn't seem to be able to control them and Captain Barnard couldn't care less.'

'So, what do you think would happen if Baader and his men attacked us?'

Saul couldn't believe what he was being asked. He glanced at Isaiah and Will for support, they just looked back at him with blank expressions on their faces.

303.

'Come on! By the look of them out there, what do you think would happen?' Billy repeated.

'They would be slaughtered of course!' Saul cried out in disbelief, 'Anyone seeing that display out there wouldn't think twice about attacking.'

'That's the whole idea, shit for brains.' Isaiah said smiling.

Saul looked from one grinning face to another. 'What do you mean? What's going on?'

The older man held his hand out.

'Come on young Cooper, I think it's time to explain something to you,' he hauled Saul to his feet and led him to the edge of the wood. 'Master Wayland wants to search inside the manor house for the girl and he can't do that with Baader and the rest of his frilly Swiss bastards inside, can he?'

Saul slowly started to understand what was happening.

'So they have been acting like fools to try and get the Swiss to attack them?'

'Exactly! And to make it look convincing is no easy task, I can tell you.'

'You mean you've done this before?'

'Of course, plenty of times. I pissed my self laughing, last time we did it, Will was the one who had to hit his horse on the head.'

'He still flinches when we draw swords.' Spink chuckled.

'One of the idea's is that if the enemy thinks your shit, they won't fight as hard and they'll make mistakes.' the older man said, 'That's what Titus says any way.'

'Right you two!' Will said, looking at the Coopers. 'Come with me, it's time you saw something else.'

All four men made their way deeper into the woods. After a while Isaiah thought he could see something moving, through the trees in front of them. He tapped Will on the arm.

'There's someone moving, up ahead.'

Spink turn round and grinned.

'I know, follow me and you'll see what it is.'

After another few minutes they all came to a clearing. Isaiah and Saul shot a glance at each other, both momentarily lost for words. Spread out in front of them were about sixty or so men, all dressed in the uniform of Barnard's Company. Most of them were sleeping, but a few were cleaning muskets or sharpening sword blades.

'Who are this lot, I don't recognise any of them?' Saul asked.

'This bunch of puddle hopping peasants…' Will answered loudly enough for the nearest

305.

men to over hear, '…are the Musketeer platoon.'

'Come here and say that Spink, you donkey walloping, horse shagger,' one of the musketeers called out, as he stood up.

'Watkins! You grunt,' Will said, as he walked towards the man, 'Hiding in the woods as usual?' they both shook hands warmly.

'Just waiting for the order to save you bunch of ladies.'

Will leaned closer to his friend.

'Where's fat face?' he said lowering his voice.

The musketeer grinned.

'Don't worry, he's out checking on the pickets,' it was then that he noticed Billy Gould and gave him a curt nod. The older man nodded back and said nothing. Watkins turned back to his friend and smiled, 'Who are these two then?' he asked.

'This is Isaiah and Saul Cooper, two new lads for the Dragoons,' he placed a hand on the musketeer's shoulder and looked at the Coopers, 'This, you two, is Matt Watkins, one of the few men in the Muskets that don't talk in grunts.'

'Fuck off!' a voice sounded from behind them, both men laughed.

'Right lads,' Will said quickly, 'Let's get back to our lot, before fat face comes back.' Watkins laughed and Will jogged off into the trees, followed by Gould, Isaiah and Saul.

306.

'Who's fat face?' Saul asked as they ran.

'That's Sergeant Broadhead,' Billy answered. 'He's in charge of the Musket platoon and he hates Will's guts.' Spink turned around and frowned.

When they reached the edge of the woods they found that the field was deserted.

Billy nodded to Will.

'You better go and get the horses. It looks like we'll have to make our own way back to the tavern.'

Samuel finished explaining the situation in Honeybourne.

'A terrible business Samuel, a terrible business indeed,' the Bishop said, shaking his head. 'But not a unique one, I fear. Something did happen here, in Worcester, some years ago.'

'Anything you can remember, Henry, would be invaluable,' the big man replied. He knew Henry and was well aware of his propensity to ramble on.

'Of course, of course. Now if I remember rightly, three bodies were found,' he said before crossing his breast, 'And like the bodies you have just mentioned, they too had been

307.

decapitated.'

'Were they also tied to a blood altar?'

The old man rubbed his temples as he thought.

'No, only the last girl was… poor creature,' he paused for a moment, 'The first girl was found about twenty or so years ago, after an outbreak of the pox, the second about a year later. Both of them were discovered in deserted houses, a few yards from each other, down in the city.'

'Are there any of the families still living here?'

'The first girl lived with her father. The poor man took his own life, drowned himself. The second victim's parents still live in the city, Thomas Lovell, a chandler. His wife Margaret, the unfortunate woman, hasn't uttered so much as a word since. The last victim's father moved away with his remaining daughter, after the funeral, his name escapes me.' Henry looked up, his face full of concern, 'Dear friend, I would ask you to tread lightly with these people. What they have seen, done to their daughters, will forever be imprinted on their memories,' the old man crossed himself again. Samuel did the same.

'Henry, I have seen for myself what this mad man can do.' the big man replied, 'I will be sympathetic, you have my word.'

The old man smiled in thanks.

'I will arrange for one of the city watch to be your guide.'

Samuel thanked Henry, who dispatched a servant to fetch a watchman. He left the office, not relishing the task of asking these poor people, to remember the time when their young daughters were brutally murdered. He stood in silence, on the steps of the Bishop's house, waiting for the arrival of his guide. Whilst he waited it started to rain.

CHAPTER 33.

'This way Master.' The watchman called back, over his shoulder, as he pushed through the tightly packed streets. Samuel turned his head away when the man spoke, eager to avoid another blast of his fetid breath.

The first thing that you noticed about Sydnam Porter, a balding, rotund former soldier, was the large weeping sore on the side of his neck. When he smiled, in a vain attempt to be friendly, his tongue flicked through his broken teeth, giving him the appearance of a bloated, demonic toad, getting ready to catch his next meal.

After several minutes of battling their way through the busy cityfolk they approached an old woman, who was stood on a street corner holding a wide basket.

'Knives, combs an' ink horns!' she crowed.

'Still here, Bussey?' Porter shouted to her. He turned to Samuel, ignoring the woman's curt reply. 'Bussey has been selling her bloody rubbish here since I was a kid.' he said laughing, as they walked past.

'Devil take you Syd Porter!' she cried back, spitting on the cobbles.

'I don't do this job to be liked, you know?' he

said, pausing to give Samuel the chance to prompt the conversation further. When no answer came, he quickly continued. 'No! If I wanted to be popular I would have stayed in the army. Have you ever seen service Mr. Bolton?'

'No.' The big man answered reluctantly, doubting weather Porter had ever known popularity amongst his former comrades in arms.

'Oh Sir!' he laughed excitedly, 'You missed out on a truly glorious life. I mean it sir, a truly glorious life!'

'Where did you say Mr. Lovell lived?' Samuel interrupted, trying desperately to change the subject. He could feel his composure weakening.

The watchman's smile instantly disappeared, to be replaced with a look of feigned remorse.

'That was a bad time, Mr. Bolton. I remember because I was there when she was found.' he lied.

Samuel didn't answer; he had already been told the full story by Henry. Thomas Lovell had found his own daughter's body, in the deserted cellar of an empty building. Given the choice he would rather have talked to one of the other victim's families. Unfortunately one of them had drowned himself, the mother previously dying in child birth and the other had moved away, never to be heard of again.

The watchman stopped in front of him and pointed to the door of a chandlers shop.

'This is Tom Lovell's shop. He'll talk to you, but Maggie hasn't said a word since young Beth's body was found.'

'Thank you, Porter. I'll be fine from here on.'

The watchman frowned indignantly, and ignored the snub. He moved to walk towards the front door,

'It's no trouble Mr. Bolton; I don't mind showing you in.'

Samuel stepped forward and blocked Porter's path.

'You may go!' he said more forcefully.

The watchman's smile turned into an evil sneer. Without another word he turned and stormed off into the bustling crowd.

When Porter had gone Samuel turned and peered through the shop window. The grimy mullioned glass and the dark interior made it almost impossible to see anything. He ducked his head as he stepped through the narrow doorway and into the shop.

He stood there for a few moments as he looked around the cramped room, the warm shop enveloped him. Every inch of the grey walls were obscured by long lines of candles, hanging from rails, suspended from the ceiling. All the while the heavy odour of wax hung in the air. He waited a few more moments before knocking on the door frame.

'Yes? Hello?' a reedy voice answered from beyond the doorway at the back of the shop.

'Mr. Lovell?' Samuel called out.

A short, fragile looking man appeared through the door, with a cautious look on his face.

'By asking for me as Mr. I would guess you're not a local man, Sir?'

'My name is Samuel Bolton.' he answered respectfully, with a nod.

'You would be the gentleman who has come top ask me about my Beth, then?' the old man said flatly. 'His Grace sent word you were coming.' He saw the flicker of surprise in the big man's eyes. 'Oh don't worry Mr. Bolton, his Grace has always kept in contact with me and Margaret, ever since our Beth was taken from us.'

'His Grace is a compassionate man,' Samuel added wryly.

'If I may ask you Mr. Bolton, why now?' Lovell looked at Samuel, who stared back impassively, 'It's been twenty years and nobody, except for his Grace, has ever shown any interest in our daughters murder. So why now?' the old man's voice started to become shrill, as his emotions took over. 'My Maggie hasn't said a word since I found Beth's body, the shock was too much for her.'

Samuel decided not to prevaricate any longer.

'Sir, recently some bodies have been found, some miles from here.' he watched the reaction in the old man's face.

Lovell shook his head slowly.

'That can't be,' he whispered.

Samuel thought it best to continue.

'Several young girls have disappeared, over the last few years, from a village just outside Evesham,' the old man still shook his head, as if he was dazed. 'Their bodies were found in, shall we say, disturbing circumstances.'

'Impossible.' Lovell muttered. He turned and, without a word, disappeared through the doorway at the back of the shop. Samuel, not waiting for an invitation followed him.

He found the old man sitting on a bench in the back room. A stronger, more oppressive smell of wax was coming from two enormous pans that bubbled away on an iron grate, suspended over a fire.

'Do you know who is responsible?' the old man asked eventually, without looking up.

'Master Wayland,' Lovell shot a glance at

314.

Samuel when he heard the name, '…has reason to believe the murders were carried out by a coven of witches, led by a man calling himself Baphomet.' He watched the old man mouth the name as it was said.' Did you say something?'

'No!' Lovell snapped, standing up abruptly, 'Why do you need me, I can't help you!'

Samuel ignored the hostility.

'I need to see where you found your daughter's body.'

'No!' Lovell answered defiantly, staring at the big man.

Samuel narrowed his eyes; his patience was wearing thin, despite the old man's horrific bereavement.

'Is there something you're not telling me, Thomas?'

'Like what?' he snapped. Then his expression changed, tears appeared at the corners of his eyes and his narrow shoulders dropped. He slumped back on to the bench.

Samuel became aware that someone was standing behind him. He quickly turned round to see an old woman standing in the doorway, calmly watching them. Samuel could see that, at one time, she had been beautiful. But now her hollow eyes showed that any beauty or joy she once possessed had gone, long ago.

315.

'This is Mr. Bolton,' Lovell said, trying to sound cheerful, 'he wants to ask us some questions about Beth,' his voice trailed off into silence.

'Good day to you Mrs. Lovell,' Samuel said, trying to sound polite. The woman turned around and walked off. He looked back to the old man.

'Please forgive me for intruding, but we need your help.'

The old man sighed in defeat.

'There's a house, just off Bridge Street. The windows are boarded over, you can't miss it.' he paused for a moment, 'You'll have to break in, and take a lantern with you. Even in the day it will be too dark for you to see.'

'Thank you Thomas,' Samuel replied. The old man mumbled something as he walked towards the door. 'I'm sorry?' he asked, looking back.

'It's all my fault,' the old man replied.

Samuel regarded Lovell for a few moments, before leaving the shop.

That evening he stood on the corner of Bridge Street, whilst he finished a pie that he had bought from the market. As he ate he realised that he hadn't asked what meat was in the pie, from the strange after taste he didn't want to guess either.

During the afternoon he had borrowed a lantern from the city watchman, who was still smarting from the snub earlier in the day. He glanced down, making sure it was still in the sack by his feet. As the streets became deserted he realised that he was getting used to the pungent smell of the river.

The river Severn flowed from high up in the Welsh mountains and was one of England's main arteries. The woman on the pie stall, when she found out he wasn't a local, regaled him with stories about how the river was named after a princess who, in ancient times, had fallen in and drowned. She then went on to mention that Norse raiders used to sail up the river to pillage the city.

'One time,' she cried enthusiastically, as a crowd started to gather, 'the city folk had a go back. Well, the Norse, after a while had had enough and buggered off,' she held her hands up to calm the cheering and the laughter. 'But! They caught one, didn't they! And do you know what happened to him?' she paused the tale momentarily and looked up at him.

'Go on.' he replied, humouring her, even though he had heard a similar story told to him in York.

'They butchered him and nailed his skin to the Cathedral's back door!' she clapped her hands together and laughed.

He smiled to himself, as he remembered the old woman. The streets around him were almost deserted now and the winter sun had dropped below the roof tops making everything appear very different. Although most of the houses and shops had covered lanterns hanging over their doors, the side streets leading off the main route had been plunged into darkness.

The narrow entry, which led off Bridge Street, was no more than an alleyway. During the day Samuel had noticed that it sloped steeply down, towards the river. He walked past the house several times and saw that it was still boarded up and surprisingly, still in good condition. He had also discovered why it was empty. Part way up the front of the house was a tide mark, evidence of regular flooding.

Now that he stood, staring down the dark street, something puzzled him. How did Lovell know to look for his daughter down there?

Once he had lit the lantern he entered the dark alleyway, his hand unconsciously checked for the hilt of the dagger hidden in is sleeve. As he walked the lantern did little to light the way, the damp, cloying darkness seemed to greedily devour the dull glow.

He stopped when he reached the front of the building, placing the lantern on the step. He noticed that the hinges and the studded ironwork on the front door were heavily rusted. He waited for a few moments to make sure that he wasn't being followed. The narrow street was deserted and the only sound was the lapping of the water against the dock.

The only way in seemed to be through the front door or one of the boarded up windows. He went for the obvious choice, after all the house was supposed to be empty. He had a last cursory look around the front of the house, before me moved.

He gently placed both hands on the door. 'One good shove should be enough,' he thought. But before he had a chance to push, the door swung open, with only a slight moan from the hinges. His hand instinctively reached for his dagger. The muscles in his body tightened, ready for a quick response.

The house remained silent, so he made the decision to continue. He slowly picked up the lantern and stepped inside.

Through the gloom he could see that the room was bare. He also noticed in places, that the

dusty floorboards were pale and warped, more
signs that the river had flooded over the years.
Surprisingly, the usual sounds he expected from
an empty timber house were absent. There was
just the heavy silence that pounded in his ears.

He lifted the lantern up and walked cautiously
over to the doorway on the far side of the room.
The door was already open and he stepped
through.

In the cramped back room, he noticed a small
door on his right. He lifted the latch and pulled
the door open. He held his lantern through the
doorway and saw a damp flight of stone steps,
leading down. He glanced around the deserted
room once more and ducked through the
doorway.

The floor of the cellar was covered with a few
inches of stagnant water that slopped lazily over
the toes of his boots. In the corners of the room
he could hear rats paddling around amongst the
filth. At one end of the chamber there was a long
stone table. He placed the lantern down on the
rough surface and stood back out of the light, to
get a better look.

In the centre of the chamber was a stout
wooden pillar, supporting the ceiling.
Something at the top of the pillar immediately
caught his eye. He picked up the light and

320.

stepped closer.

'Poor child,' he whispered.

At the top of the pillar, nailed to the wood, was a pair of rusty manacles, which hung from the end of two lengths of chain. Part way down the post, he noticed several long horizontal cuts, deep into the wood.

'Baphomet!' he whispered to himself, before crossing his chest and muttering a quiet prayer.

When he climbed back to the top of the stairs the house was still deathly quiet. The only sound he could hear was from the guttering lantern he held out in front of him. The entire time one question still kept bothering him, 'How did the old man know to look for his daughter in that cellar?' He left to try and find out.

When he got back to Lovell's shop it was in darkness. He walked towards the front of the shop and saw that the door was ajar. He pushed it fully open and listened for any signs of life, but the shop was silent. When he walked in he saw that the front room was deserted, so he moved towards the doorway that led through to the back.

'Thomas? It's Samuel Bolton! Are you here?' he

called out. The shop felt cold and the smell of burning wax had gone. Something was wrong?

He stepped through the door and stopped as soon as he saw Maggie sitting in a chair by the stove. Her face was outlined by the flame of the lone candle that stood next to her.

'Good evening Mrs. Lovell,' he said. She stared back at him impassively.

He took a pace closer, trying not to startle her. He immediately noticed that Thomas was sitting where he had left him, on the bench by the wall. His head was leant back and his mouth was open, he seemed to be soundly asleep.

'Sorry to intrude, Mrs. Lovell,' he said, lowering his voice, 'but I have to talk to Thomas again.'

'You can't.' she answered coldly.

Samuel looked at her, surprised that she had just spoken.

'I was told that you were unable to speak?' he asked, still with the feeling that something was wrong.

Maggie just stared back at him with her cold, hollow eyes.

He could see that she had been crying. He looked back to Thomas, his arms hung limply by his sides. Not the most comfortable sleeping position he had ever seen.

A feeling of dread slowly crept up on him. He took another pace closer to the motionless old man, hoping his feeling was wrong. Then something caught his eye. His heart immediately sunk. A knife lay in a congealed pool of blood at the old man's feet.

'Thomas, why?' he muttered. The jagged, glistening cuts across Thomas's wrists confirmed his worst fears.

'Guilt!' the old woman hissed.

'Guilt about what?' he replied, keeping his voice low. He realised that she wanted to tell him something, now that she had broken her silence.

'The innocent life, that he and the others took, that's what!' she continued to stare at him, defiantly for a few moments. Then her shoulders slumped and tears appeared in her eyes. 'Damn foolish old man,' finally she broke down and sobbed uncontrollably.

He looked back to Thomas's body; surely he couldn't have murdered his own daughter? No, that wasn't it, he thought, but something didn't seem right.

'What happened, Maggie?' he asked softly and then waited for her to calm down.

'One night, about a month or so after Beth was found, he came to our door,' she spoke in a distant, monotone voice, '…banging away. Woke the whole street up, he did.'

'Who, Maggie?' he asked, fighting the urge to hurry her along. 'Who came to the door that night?'

'Someone Thomas knew, he was there when they found Beth, I can't recall his name at the moment.' Tears rolled down her cheeks as she remembered, 'He told Thomas, he knew who had killed Beth, he said it was a witch and he knew where he was. Thomas believed him.'

Samuel sat up.

'Maggie, I need to know who the man was?' he realised that he sounded a little more forceful that he wanted.

'I'm getting to it!' she snapped, and then she relaxed, 'I have to tell you it all, so you don't think Thomas was to blame.'

'Go on,' he replied, holding his frustration in check.

She nodded forcing a smile, and carried on.

'Once he had told us that he knew who had done it, folk started to gather with torches,' she brushed at her tears with the back of her hand. 'He led Thomas and the rest of the mob to a house. They broke the door down, went in and dragged the witch out, into the street, bound him and then dragged him down to the river.'

she paused and looked directly at Samuel, 'I told Thomas to stop, but he wouldn't listen, none of them would, they just kept screaming and beating him as they dragged him through the streets. Nobody cared that he wasn't fighting them off, he wasn't even calling for mercy.'

'Go on.'

'It was too late when I finally realised who their 'witch' was, they had already set their minds to ducking him.'

'Who was he Maggie?' he asked, but she had gone quiet. 'Why wasn't he struggling?'

'He was a cripple. He couldn't have fought them off if he wanted to.'

'You said you knew who he was?'

She nodded slowly.

'His name was Roger Bills, the father of the first murdered girl.'

He looked at the old woman in disbelief.

'His Grace said that he drowned himself?'

'He would have had a job, he couldn't walk, the poor man couldn't even feed himself,' she looked away. 'Soon after, folk started to realise that they had drowned an innocent man. After a while someone put a story around that he had drowned himself.'

Samuel looked at her for a few moments, before pressing her further.

'Who was it that came to your door that night, Maggie?' he asked eventually.

'Ah yes, him,' she replied after a while, 'do you know the last girl, that was murdered, was one of his own daughters!' she cried. 'Of course he came under suspicion, like the other fathers had. But this time, though, when the Sheriff's men searched his house they found all manner of evil items, markings on the walls and the floor and such like.' She seemed to drift off into a daze again.

Samuel could feel his irritation building as he regarded the old woman.

'Maggie who was it? What was his name?'

'He disappeared, you know? Took his other daughter with him too, poor child, she's probably dead now as well.'

'Maggie! Who was it?' he asked in earnest. When she finally told him the name he stared at her in utter disbelief. 'Are you sure woman?' he snapped, all thought for her fragile state of mind forgotten.

'I will never forget him, until the day I die,' she answered angrily, tears rolling down her cheeks, 'he took all that I loved.'

Samuel only just caught her last words as he bolted for the door.

CHAPTER 34.

'Oh bollocks!' Will said, sounding annoyed. 'Some bastard's robbed the horses.'

The other three stared at him as he turned to face them.

'Tell me you're jesting.' Gould replied sourly.

'I never joke about stolen horses,' he answered, sitting down heavily. 'Someone's had 'em.'

'Perhaps they've just slipped their reins?' Saul offered, trying to be helpful.

Gould shook his head.

'Not the way we tether 'em, lad.' He glanced back across the deserted field, 'Well! The company has gone now and we've got no mounts. We could always go back to the muskets?'

Will stood up instantly.

'Come on Billy! I can't go back to the puddle hoppers; fat face would make my life hell, wouldn't he!' The panic on his face was plain for all of them to see, 'You know he would.'

'Why can't we just walk back to the tavern from here?' Isaiah asked, puzzled that none of them had suggested it before. 'It's only about six or so miles and me 'n Saul know the way?'

Gould shook his head again.

'We can't, Baader's going to have patrols out. Don't forget he would've had men watching the company acting like a bunch of bumbling fools, so if we're caught sneaking back to the village, he might suspect our ruse.'

Saul grinned to the old soldier.

'Us Coopers have been robbing folk on these roads for years and we've never been caught.'

Gould seemed uncertain as he glanced from Isaiah to Saul.

'Come on Billy! Don't let Fat Face get me?' Will said, appealing to his comrade's good nature. Eventually Gould nodded. Will slapped him on the back, 'I'm in your debt old friend.'

'Alright lads, but we're going to have to watch our step.' Gould said. 'If we get caught and Captain Barnard finds out, he'll bloody fillet us.'

Later, the four of them knelt in the muddy drainage ditch and waited for Isaiah, who had been chosen to lead them, to satisfy himself that the way ahead was clear. After a few more moments he slowly stood up and tapped Will on the shoulder.

Will watched Isaiah scramble up the steep

side of the ditch and hurry across the last open part of the field. He then disappeared into the trees on the other side. One by one they followed, all of them glad that the shadows of the on coming dusk hid their movements.

Once inside the wood they waited again, facing the way they had came and watched for any signs of pursuit. As soon as Isaiah was content that they had not been followed he stood up and led them deeper into the woods.

Some small shafts of light, provided by the new moon, was just enough for Isaiah to realise where they were and pick his route through the trees. He knew these woods like the back of his hand and so he should, the amount of times he and his brothers had had to hide from the Sheriff's men.

Silently the small band followed Isaiah through the gloom. All of a sudden Saul caught a movement out of the corner of his eye. He reached forward and tapped Gould on the shoulder, who passed the movement on. Straight away they all stopped and dropped into a crouch.

Billy slowly turned to see Saul pointing to his left. He looked into the trees to try and see what had caught the younger man's attention. At first there was nothing more than the dark chaotic shadows of the woods. The only sound was the chill breeze, rustling the thick canopy above them. But then a shape rose up from the ground, a hundred or so paces into the woods. He felt Will tap him lightly on the shoulder and he nodded in reply.

Whilst they knelt, Isaiah was sure he could hear the dull murmur of voices, carrying through the trees. He looked at Billy and gestured that he was going to move forward and have a closer look.

The older man looked uncomfortable with the idea, but after a while he saw that Isaiah was readying himself to go anyway. Reluctantly, he nodded his agreement.

Isaiah had started to creep forward when Will leaned close to him and whispered in his ear.

'Billy said keep your head down and don't get too close.' He tugged on Isaiah's arm when he made to move off again, 'He also said keep quiet and watch where you're steppin' and if you get caught, you're buggered.'

Cooper glanced over Will's shoulder. Gould nodded to him and crossed his chest. 'So,' he thought to himself as he looked back into the trees, 'I'm on my own then.'

Silently he moved into a crouch and crept forward into the trees. He knew that the three of them behind him would be watching his every move. Suddenly having a closer look didn't seem such a good idea, silently he chided himself for not keeping his big mouth shut.

He moved forward stealthily in the direction of the voices. He used the broad trunks of the trees to shield his approach. When he got closer, the voices began to get a bit louder. He strained to hear what was being said, but the words were still no more than muffled grunts. Eventually he stopped by the base of a wide tree that was as close as he dared to get. Slowly he peered around the trunk.

Three dark shapes were sat on the other side of a huge log. By their low guttural voices it was obvious they were all men. Once his eyes had become accustomed to their positions he started to notice the ruffled, billowing sleeves of their tunics and the long feather protruding from one man's cap.

'So the bastards have been watching the company all day,' he thought to himself.

After a while he decided he had seen enough and thought it was time to return to his comrades. He cautiously took a step backwards, trying not to step on a twig. But before he could move, he was forced back against the tree. A gloved hand clamped over his mouth.

'Don't move!' a quiet voice hissed in his ear.

Isaiah felt the cold blade of a knife touch his exposed throat.

'Stay still, alright? They've just said that they're going.' the voice whispered again, almost imperceptibly.

Isaiah nodded and he felt the hand move away from his mouth. He realised the knife had gone as well. Without moving, he watched the three Swiss mercenaries stand up. Two of them hefted long hand and a half swords, on to their shoulders, while the other picked up a musket. Together they traipsed out of their hiding place and disappeared into the woods, talking among themselves, all the need for secrecy gone.

When the voices had gone Isaiah quickly spun around to see that he was alone. 'Who the fuck was that?' he said to himself, gripping the hilt of his knife to try and stop his hand from trembling. After a few moments he started to regain his composure, he took a deep breath and set off back towards his waiting companions.

Will was the first to notice Isaiah when he returned.

'He's back.' he whispered to Gould, nudging him. The three of them then stood up as he got nearer.

'They're gone.' Isaiah muttered, still rattled by

his encounter with the mysterious stalker. 'They were Baader's men. It looked like they had been there all day. Watching the Company on the field, by the looks of it.'

'Ha! Good.' Billy said smiling.

'Did you see anything else?' Will asked Grinning.

'Eh? Why do you ask that?' Isaiah replied warily.

'Well, did you?' Gould enquired sounding amused.

'Yes,' Isaiah said after a few moments, 'There was someone else there as well.' By the look on the other men's faces he realised he was missing something. 'Go on then, who was that back there?' he asked finally.

'He was bloody right, the bugger!' Gould said glancing at Will. He then turned to Isaiah and clapped him on the shoulder, 'Well done lad!'

'Who was right?' Saul asked feeling completely confused, 'What's going on Billy?'

Will laughed.

'Tom Allen. He said your brother here,' pointing to Isaiah, 'would be quiet enough to stalk those Swiss idiots and not get caught.'

'So that was Tom Allen back there?' Isaiah asked sounding relieved.

'He's been watching them all day.'

The older man nodded.

'So why did you let Issy go and spy on them then?' Saul put in, still struggling to work out what was going on

'Training, lad.' The older man answered simply.

'So who took the Horses then?' Isaiah asked.

'The Company of course! Horses are bloody pricey, we don't just let folk nick 'em you know.' He rubbed his hand together cheerfully, 'Come on, we've got to get back to the tavern. Will, you lead.'

Just as they stepped off Isaiah leaned close to Gould.

'Would he really have cut my throat?'

The older man looked at him and nodded.

'Yes.'

CHAPTER 35.

Titus bounded down the passageway towards the minister's office, eager to relay the tale of the afternoon's events to Thomas. He couldn't help laughing to himself as he pushed the door open, but the moment he stepped into the room his wide smile disappeared.

Thomas was sitting rigidly at the Minister's desk, looking sternly at the face of the man sat opposite him. The stranger was richly dressed in black velvet, the sleeves of his tunic trimmed with gold thread. A pair of black buck skin gloves lay neatly on the table next to him, the fine cut of the soft leather being another display of the owner's wealth.

Titus immediately felt his anger rising as he stared at the greying, meticulously combed hair on the back of the man's head. Without him having to turn around, he knew exactly who the man was. 'Cecil! You….'

'Captain Barnard!' Thomas cried out in an attempt to distract his angered friend.

Titus instantly flinched at the official way Thomas had addressed him, but his anger surged again. 'Master Wayland!' he bellowed as he drew his sword, 'This scheming dog…'

335.

Thomas jumped to his feet, knocking his chair backwards.

'Stay your hand, Captain Barnard!' he shouted. 'Now!'

Titus shook with anger. He stared wild eyed at the back of the stranger's head. After a few moments he breathed out heavily and rammed his sword back into his scabbard. He briefly shot a glance at Thomas before striding over to the fire, where he began warm his hands.

Thomas sat down, relieved that he had managed to temporarily diffuse his friend's sudden, violent outburst. When he looked across the table he noticed the other man's pale, drawn complexion and smiled.

'By your reaction, Captain Barnard, can I assume you are aware of the identity of our esteemed guest?' Titus replied with a grunt. 'Can I, also, expect you to address our guest by his correct title?'

There was a brief pause after which Titus spun on his heel, swept his hat off with a flourish and bowed.

'Your Grace.' he sneered. Just as he was about to turn away he stopped and smiled evilly, 'May I ask Your Grace, if he is here to investigate and perhaps accuse any more of my men, of being involved in another treasonous plot that he has… discovered?'

Robert Cecil, the Earl of Salisbury, had regained some of his composure. He turned and faced Titus.

'I see, Captain Barnard, that you still have difficulty accepting that one of your men was a Catholic traitor?' he said in an unconcerned voice.

Thomas's heart sunk as he anticipated his friend's reply.

'Fawkes was my best armourer, not a papist plotter!' he stepped forward as he spoke, fighting to control his anger again, 'And I can assure you that he was not going to assassinate the king.'

It was the Earl's turn to smile.

'How so, Captain?'

Titus gripped the hilt of his sword.

'Because, you weasel, I gave him no such order.' he paused, momentarily, 'My men follow my orders and my orders alone.'

Salisbury's smile widened a little as he seized the chance to bait Titus further.

'Ah! Perhaps I should have had you arrested as well then, Captain?'

Before any of them could react, Titus had ripped his sword out of its scabbard and swung the heavy blade violently at Salisbury's head.

The end of the weapon whistled through the air, and missed the top of the terrified Earl's head by a fraction.

Thomas, who had leapt to his feet as soon as he saw Titus reach for his sword, bellowed at his enraged companion.

'Titus! Leave the room, now!'

'Damn and blast your eyes, you miserable cur!' Barnard snapped, and he stormed out of the room, ramming his sword back into its scabbard.

The door slammed loudly, causing chunks of plaster to fall away from the frame. Thomas stood in silence for a while, just staring at the back of the door. After a few moments he looked down at the Earl.

'Your Grace?' he said sitting down.

Salisbury shook his head slowly.

'That mad man nearly killed me.' he replied.

Thomas did start to feel a little sympathy for the other man, when he saw that he was trembling. Quickly though he dismissed the thought when he remembered that the Earl was just as dangerous as Titus was, albeit not physically. It was well known that Salisbury's influence spread far and wide. Couple that with his ruthless nature and it made him a very formidable opponent.

'Might I suggest that Your Grace chooses his words more carefully in future?'

Salisbury was still in deep shock.

'I can't believe that the damn fool almost killed me.' he mumbled to himself.

'Understand this, Your Grace. Titus Barnard is the single best swordsman and military commander on God's green earth. If he had meant to kill you, he would have. Your body would have also disappeared never to be found again, his men would have seen to that, their loyalty to him is absolute.' Thomas sat back, happy that he now had the Earl's full attention, 'No, I fear the only reason that your head is still on your shoulders right now is because of me.' He saw Salisbury's questioning look and continued. 'I would have been a witness and he would had to have killed me too.'

'Well, one day Master Wayland, your luck might run out.' Salisbury sneered, his calm beginning to return.

Thomas smiled coldly, immediately putting the Earl on his guard.

'Fortunately I have no need of luck, Your Grace, Titus Barnard is one of my oldest friends. As I have previously said, every one of his men is loyal and well trained. They would die on his command,' Salisbury stared back mutely, 'even

Fawkes, who I also knew. So you see, I too find it difficult to accept what happened.' The Earl shifted uncomfortably in his seat. Thomas raised his hand, 'Rest assured, Your Grace, unlike my quick-tempered companion, I am able to keep my emotions in check.'

'Well, that as they say is water under the bridge,' he turned away from Thomas's intense gaze. 'His Majesty, however, is keen to know how you plan to solve the matter at hand?'

Thomas looked at the other man and realised that the subject was closed. The demise of the unfortunate Guido was to be forgotten.

Robert Cecil, the Earl of Salisbury, the Kings closest adviser, spy master to some, was a shrewd and calculating man who could answer questions for days and still not reveal the truth.

'And what is the matter at hand, Your Grace?'

'You know quite well Master Wayland, I have already informed you, on several occasions.'

'No Your Grace, you have told me some pigswill about Sir Nicholas falling out of favour with His Majesty and being involved in a treasonous plot.'

Salisbury blinked in surprise.

'You doubt me Sir?' Thomas glanced back at him with out replying. 'Were you anyone else Wayland I would have you arrested for such,

340.

insolence. Fortunately, you and the other members of your order are looked upon favourably by his Majesty and have served him well.'

Thomas held his stare, without blinking.
'And?'

Salisbury sighed.

'Very well. I will not repeat this, but I must have your assurance that you will not either?'

'You have it.'

'Very well.' The Earl Sat back with a cold, smug look on his face. 'Sir Nicholas, in the past has, shall we say, kindly bolstered the treasury in the form of 'gifts'. His Majesty, who was very grateful to Sir Nicholas, insisted the 'gifts' were returned, in part, over a period in time.' Thomas looked away to hide his look of disgust. He had grasped the situation almost instantly. Salisbury continued, 'Sir Nicholas then agreed to accept the return of the 'gifts', in part, over a period of time at an agreed amount.' The Earl was pleased that he was relaying the details of the situation with the right amount of care and discretion. 'Unfortunately, Sir Nicholas has decided to amend the amount His Majesty is to return. An amount His Majesty is hot wholly comfortable with.'

Thomas held his hand up and frowned.

'Thank you Your Grace, I've heard enough. You obviously feel that you can not reveal to me, His Majesty's true situation.'

'Do you doubt my information, Master Wayland?'

'I do indeed.' Thomas replied angrily, 'You can't possibly expect me to believe that this is just a matter of His Majesty wanting to eradicate a greedy creditor?' He watched for any changes in Earl's demeanour, but there was none. 'Now if you had mentioned ...blackmail perhaps?' Suddenly there it was a momentarily narrowing of the eyes and a twisting of the mouth. A very brief, fleeting movement, but Thomas had spotted it. He smiled in triumph.

Salisbury gritted his teeth, as he was temporarily lost for words. The key piece of information, that he sought to conceal, was now discovered.

'It seems, Master Wayland, that you have discovered my ruse. Most clever, I must congratulate you.'

'Please be at your ease Your Grace, I will question you no further. I fear, were I to be in possession of any more of the details, I might be in the same predicament as Sir Nicholas.'

After a few moments Salisbury nodded.

'Your discretion does you credit, Master

Wayland. So, if I may return to my original question, what is your plan?' He started to feel his irritation building when Thomas didn't reply. 'I believe today's deception, by Captain Barnard, was a success?'

'You are well informed Your Grace?' Thomas said. He was confused at the Earl's last comment, then it dawned on him. 'Ah yes! Tom Allen was once in your employ, if I remember rightly?'

'It seems his loyalties have changed somewhat, since joining Captain Barnard. As you have said the good Captain does acquire the loyalty of his men.'

'Indeed.' Thomas replied. 'Well, as for a plan, you may inform His Majesty that the situation will be resolved. However I do feel it only fair that I mention there is another matter.'

Salisbury frowned.

'Continue.'

'Sir Nicholas has a hostage, a girl. Until she is found and moved to safety, I will need to question Sir Nicholas.'

'But after?'

'You will have your conclusion.'

The Earl smiled cheerfully.

'Excellent! His majesty will be pleased.'

'Titus!'

Barnard turned to see Thomas strolling across the lawn towards him.

'I'm going to murder that bastard, you do know that?'

Thomas grinned.

'I know old friend, but not yet.' He then went on to explain why they had to attack Bretforton manor.

'...Because he's pissed the bloody King off!' Titus cried in disbelief, 'My men are disciplined troops, not murderers.' Thomas glanced at him and raised an eyebrow, 'They have always had good reason in the past.' he answered, sounding defensive.

'And they have good reason on this occasion also,' he said, 'they do it for their king.' Titus frowned. He sympathised with his friend's concern, but he also had a concern of his own. Would he be able to free his estranged daughter before the killing started.

CHAPTER 35.

There was a loud knock at the door.

'Come!' Baader answered. He was sitting his desk writing in the company log as the door swung open and one of his men marched in. 'Well?' he snapped, 'Where are they?'

The guard hesitated before answering.

'The patrol has still not returned yet, sir.'

Baader suddenly slammed his meaty hand down the table, causing the guard to flinch.

'They have been gone since first light!' he spat. He then glanced up at the nervous guard, 'When should they have returned?'

'About two hours ago, sir.'

There was another loud knock at the door.

'What!' he shouted.

The door instantly swung open and a flustered Sergeant marched in.

'Captain, there is a messenger at the main gate. He says he knows where Sergeant Heller's patrol is.'

Baader stared at the man for a few moments, his irritation building.

'…Well? Where did he say they were?'

'The messenger said that he would only speak

to you, sir.'

'Did he now?' he stood up slowly and reached for his sword, which was leaning against the edge of the desk. 'Then I shall speak to this…messenger.' He marched out of the office with the two men following behind him.

The sentries, who were stood by the gate, glanced at each other nervously as the bull like form of their captain emerged from the main door of the manor house.

'Where's the whoreson who's seen my patrol?' he bellowed when he reached the gate. His face changed when he noticed the figure, outside the gate, sat astride a huge, bay destrier. 'You did not mention that he was one of Barnard's puppies?' he snarled, looking at the sergeant. He turned back to the gate and stepped forward. 'Where are my men, scum?' he growled.

The messenger, who was dressed in the green and black of Barnard's company, ignored the insult.

'Captain Barnard sends his complements and would like to offer terms for the release of your men.'

'So Titus does have them, eh!' Baader chuckled, 'What's your name boy?'

'Trooper Spink, sir.'

'Well Trooper Spink, let us hear your Captain's

346.

terms.'

Will nodded respectfully, trying not to smile.

'Of course Sir. Captain Barnard requests that you lead your men out of the grounds of Bretforton Manor and make to the nearest port, to then return to your own province. He did also say, Sir, that he would give you and your men permission to carry side arms only. No muskets I'm afraid, Sir.' He stifled a grin as he saw the Swiss Captain's face reddening. 'Your men are to be released once you are at your chosen port, sir.'

Baader glared at Spink's cheerful face.

'Did he say anything else?' he asked.

Will feigned embarrassment, 'Well sir, the Captain did give me another message, but….'

'Go on.' The Swiss Captain urged, becoming more irritated.

'Captain Barnard actually wanted me to call you a 'fat, poxed, German bastard', Sir.'

'Tell him to go and fuck himself!' Baader shouted.

'He said you would say that, sir,' Will laughed. 'I now have to inform you, that your men will be executed on Manor Fields at noon.' he whipped his hat off and bowed his head, 'Good day to you Sir.' He replaced his hat and turned his horse to leave.

It was all too much for Baader. He ran up to the gate and grabbed the railings.

'Tell that bastard Captain of yours that he's dead,' he screamed, spittle flying in all directions, 'his fucking company is dead, you are all dead.' The Sergeant and the other sentries all started to back away from their hysterical commander. 'And tell that bastard that I am not fucking German!'

Spink galloped away, laughing.

'He's coming back sir!' Isaiah shouted. He stood in the tree line and watched Will race across the field towards them.

'How does he look?' Bartholomew shouted back. He was sitting further back inside the trees, sharing a flask of ale with Titus and Billy Gould.

Isaiah squinted as he tried to gauge the expression on Will's face. After a few seconds Will was closer and he could see that his friend was smiling broadly. 'He's alive Sergeant and he's grinning like a fool!'

'Excellent!' Titus cried out.

Bartholomew chuckled.

'It looks like it worked then Sir.'

'Of course it worked Sergeant. Did you doubt

348.

me?'

'Hell would have to freeze over before that happened Sir.'

The men who were sat within earshot smiled to each other, as they listened to the banter between their Captain and his Sergeant.

'Let's just hope, Sir, that Captain Baader waits until the afternoon to attack.' Bartholomew said cautiously, even though he knew that the plan was sound.

'He will. He has to have time to muster his bunch of puffed up fairies before he does anything, you know that.' Titus answered. 'Cooper! Send Spink to me when he gets back.' he shouted.

'Yes Sir.' Isaiah answered as he watched his friend slow his horse to a walk. Will dismounted and he took the reigns from him.

'He's not happy, you know.' Will said cheerfully.

Isaiah laughed and patted his friend on the shoulder.

'The Captain wants to see you, straight away.' Will nodded and hurried into the trees, while Isaiah led the panting horse away.

Will found Barnard almost straight away and jogged over to him.

'Come here Spink, you weasel!' Titus said

when he saw the young trooper. Will took his time to relay all the details of his meeting with the Swiss Captain, even remembering to include the insult he added. 'I didn't tell you to say that?'

'I know Sir.'

'And he's Swiss, not German.'

'I know that as well Sir. When we were in Europe with them, I remembered how they hated being called German, Sir'

Titus smiled craftily.

'How did he react?'

'He was livid Sir.'

'Excellent!' He turned to Bartholomew, 'A flask of ale for this man, Sergeant!'

'After the afternoon's activities, do you mean, sir?' Bartholomew asked.

'Of course! Sergeant, of course!' he turned back to Will, 'Good lad. Now go and get some rest.'

'Thank you, Sir.' Will said and jogged off towards the rest of the company.

'Good man, that Spink.' Titus said bursting with undisguised pride.

Bartholomew passed the flask to Titus.

'When do you want the men in position, sir?'

'As soon as the sentries at the Manor report some activity, I think.' he took a long swig from the flask, wiping his mouth with the back of his hand, 'And when they appear on the field, we'll slaughter the bastards.'

'Have you seen any activity yet?' Thomas asked quietly as he crouched down.

'None as yet, Master, but I can hear the sounds of men and horses in the grounds, lots of them.' Tom Allen was kneeling inside a hawthorn thicket, watching the main gate of Bretforton manor. Further back, hidden in the trees, were men from the company's musket platoon, waiting for the order to follow Tom Allen and Master Wayland into the Manor.

'I think that after witnessing Captain Baader's reaction, there's little doubt that there will be a confrontation on the fields.' Thomas said as he started to back out of the hiding place. 'I'm going to inform Sergeant Broadhead of what's going to happen, when we go in.'

'Master, wait!' Tom said suddenly. Thomas spun around to see the gates of the manor swing open and a rider appear in the gateway.

Baader was sitting bolt upright on his huge black destrier, Woden, the low winter sun glinting off his breastplate. Lined up behind him were file after file of his men, all mounted and dressed in their colourful, ruffled uniforms and highly burnished breastplates.

Thomas opened his mouth to speak, just as the riders galloped off down the road and the gates closed with a loud clang.

'About eighty, Master.' Tom said anticipating his question.

After a few moments the drumming of the hooves on the road disappeared. Thomas tapped the younger man on the arm.

'Time to go, I think.' Both men backed out of their hiding place, ready to play their part in the afternoon's activities.

The same low winter sun warmed the backs of the thirty riders of Barnard's company, who waited at the far, western end of the Manor Field.

Bartholomew was sitting next to Barnard, a few paces in front the company.

'The scouts have estimated that about eighty men rode out of the Manor.' he muttered.

'Fear not, Sergeant.' Titus answered cheerfully. 'We have more that enough men to see off these puffed up mollies. In fact I was considering falling some of them out, so they could they return to the tavern!' he said the words slightly louder, knowing it would amuse the men.

Bartholomew decided to remain silent. He knew full well that Barnard became happier, even euphoric at the prospect of impending battle, it was futile to argue. Then a movement at the other end of the field caught his eye.

'They're here Sir.'

The company, who had also seen the movement, were sitting quietly as they watched a long line of riders gallop on to the far end of the field.

After a few moments two ranks of riders, eighty men in all, were sitting smartly at the eastern end of the field. Barnard chuckled when he saw that their long lines easily out numbered his two puny looking ranks of fifteen.

'With me Sergeant Roach!' he cried out as he kicked his spurs back, sending his horse forward. Bartholomew followed, noticing that two riders were doing the same from the other end of the field.

Both pairs of riders pulled on their reigns when they reached the centre of the field, stopping a sensible distance away from each other.

'May I, Sir?' Bartholomew asked quietly, not taking his eyes off the other two riders.

'Of course, Sergeant.' Titus answered. 'You

know what must be said.'

'Thank you, Sir.' Bartholomew kicked gently, urging his horse forward a few steps. He stopped when he was happy that he had left his adversary enough room to come forward and talk.

'I don't like this Captain.' Sergeant Sturm said in German, 'They only have thirty men and they sit there as if they have three hundred.'

'Quiet, Sturm!' Baader snapped. 'I know this fool. If he had more men, they would be there. His arrogance knows no bounds. Now go and talk, for all the good it will do them.'

Sergeant Sturm urged his horse forward, until he was closer to Bartholomew and saluted.

'My name is Sergeant Sturm.'

'Good afternoon, Sergeant, I am Bartholomew Roach, Sergeant at arms of Barnard's Company.' he smiled warmly as he spoke.

Sturm shifted in his saddle, the English sergeant's friendly nature made him feel uncomfortable.

'My Captain demands that you release our men immediately and leave the field. Failing this we will be forced to attack.'

Bartholomew watched the Swiss Sergeant's face as he spoke. He noted his quick eyes, abrupt tone and the way he kept glancing back over his shoulder. All classic signs of a Sergeant that was being bullied by his commander. He smiled again, relishing the effect it had on his opposite number.

'Sergeant, I believe Trooper Spink informed your captain, this morning, of the terms of release, did he not?'

'He did indeed.' Sturm replied.

'Am I to understand that your captain does not agree to the terms?'

'No Sergeant, he does not!'

'Sergeant?' Titus shouted haughtily from behind, interrupting the Swiss Sergeant.

'Sir?'

'Tell the bastards that I want an apology as well, would you?'

'Certainly, Sir.' Bartholomew answered, watching Sturm bristle at the insult. 'You were saying, Sergeant?'

'You have had our answer, Sergeant.' Sturm replied coldly.

Bartholomew's smile disappeared and he shrugged his shoulders.

'Very well, after Captain Barnard and myself have returned to our company, we will attack. Might I suggest you return to your position and prepare. Good day.'

'How can you possibly attack with so few

men?' Sturm asked as Bartholomew was starting to turn his horse away. 'It will be a massacre!'

'Yes it will,' Bartholomew replied, almost apologetically. 'Good bye Sergeant.' He turned his horse away and trotted back to the company with Titus.

'Well?' Baader said moving his horse along side Sturm.

'They are insane, Sir.' the sergeant said staring at the two Englishmen, as they rode away, 'They said they are going to attack.'

Baader grinned menacingly.

'Good. We will sweep them from the field and then piss on their rotting corpses.' Quickly, he spun his horse around and galloped back to the company.

Sturm was still staring at Barnard's men.

'Something is not right, Captain.' He said, expecting a caustic remark from his commander, but when he turned Baader had already gone.

'May I ask how Mr. Bolton fares, Master?' Sergeant Broadhead asked, as the group of men crept through the woods that surrounded Bretforton Manor.

'He is well, thank you Sergeant.' Thomas replied. 'I did think, though, that he would have returned by now? I sent him on an errand to Worcester yesterday.'

'If I know Samuel, Master, I'm sure he is in good health.'

Thomas nodded in reply. He then remembered that the Sergeant had known Samuel since he was young man and looked upon him, and his estranged brother Nathaniel, as sons even though there was no blood between them.

He turned back and noticed that Tom Allen, who was guiding the motley band through the trees, had stopped. Once they had all halted and gone to ground, he crept forward and knelt down next to him.

'The gate's there, Master,' Tom said pointing at the wall.

All Thomas could see across the wide track was an overgrown bush, seemingly growing out of the wall.

'The bush?' he asked sounding confused. 'How did you find it?'

Tom grinned.

'I saw the Magistrates servant sneak out one night and I followed him. I found out that he was tupping the miller's sister.'

'Ah! Cawthorne, yes I've met him. A sly fellow indeed.'

357.

'It seems quiet enough, we should move now, Master.'

'Yes. If you go first Tom, I will send the men one by one, after you. I'll start with Sergeant Broadhead.'

'Right you are,' Tom said, getting to his feet.

He looked up and down the track one last time before sprinting out of the trees, holding his musket low in one hand as he ran. The other hand gripped the hilt of his sword, stopping it from scraping along the rough ground. After four or five strides he disappeared into the bush.

'You're next Sergeant.' Thomas said patting Broadhead lightly on the shoulder. The aging sergeant immediately broke from the cover of the trees, skipping across the track with the agility of a man half his age. Thomas grinned in surprise.

After a few minutes Thomas was the last one left to cross the track. Just as he was about to move he remembered something and pulled his pistol out of his belt and gripped it by the barrel. The last thing he wanted was to be the one who gave away their position by firing his pistol when he fell. Titus would never let him live it down. He scanned the open ground one last time and dashed out of the trees.

Almost straight away he stumbled on the

358.

uneven, rutted track. He quickly regained his footing before he reached the bush, also relieved that he didn't get his sword tangled between his legs.

When he crashed though the branches of the bush he wondered if he had picked the wrong spot and was actually going to run into the wall. Luckily, strong hands grabbed him and stopped him from colliding with the wall.

'Steady there Master. There's not much room in this gateway.' one of Sergeant Broadhead's men said to him apologetically.

'Thank you Boyle, good man.' Thomas replied, clapping the young trooper on the shoulder. When he peered through the narrow gap in the wall he could see a wide expanse of lawn. In the near distance, was the end of the manor house itself. 'Where are the rest?'

Boyle pointed through the gateway.

'They're all in the shed along there, Master.'

Thomas looked through the gate again and saw that Boyle was pointing to a low wooden shed that was built against the wall, about twenty or so paces away from the gate.

'You go next lad. I'll follow on.' Boyle nodded and then sprinted out of the gateway. He moved in a low crouch, keeping close to the wall. When he got to the shed, the door swung open and he disappeared inside.

While Thomas waited he glanced at the end wall of the Manor house. He noticed, at the base of the wall, there was the top of a set of steps. He assumed they led to a cellar door. From what he could see, that seemed to be the best way in.

He looked once more to make sure that the area was clear. He then ran out of the cramped gateway, towards the shed. Just as he had seen when Boyle had gone, the shed door swung open and he ran inside.

Sergeant Broadhead greeted Thomas once he was inside.

'Tom has gone to see if the way into the Manor house is still clear, Master.' The sergeant said. He saw the look of concern on Thomas's face. 'Not to worry Master, he's a crafty bugger that one.'

'So we just wait, do we?' Thomas snapped. He regretted his tone straight away, realising the sergeant was just being diplomatic. He saw the men glance at each other nervously, when they saw that he wasn't happy with the situation.

'He won't be long, Master.' Broadhead said, still sounding confident.

Thomas just nodded, even though he wasn't fully convinced.

'I'm assuming, Sir, that we wouldn't have actually released the prisoners?' Bartholomew asked Titus, as both men sat on their horses in the centre of the company's front rank.

'You assume correct, Sergeant Roach. The whole idea was to bring them to battle, as you well know.'

Bartholomew detected the hint of menace in Barnard's tone and decided to try and lighten the mood.

'I did like your comment about wanting him to apologise, Sir.'

'Before I kill that whoreson, he will apologise.' Titus growled. Then in the distance there was some movement from the Swiss troops.

Bartholomew spotted it first.

'They're advancing!' he called out.

Titus edged his horse forward. His face a mask of grim determination as he drew his sword.

'Company! Draw swords!' he bellowed. 'Bugler, make ready!'

Thirty swords rasped out of their scabbards. The highly polished, cold steel blades glinted in the afternoon sun as they swept through the air. The men waited in silence for the order to advance. Horses bobbed their heads and scuffed at the earth in anticipation of the coming assault.

After a few moments Titus took a deep breath.

'Company, walk!' As soon as he had shouted the order both ranks of horses stepped off at once. Their riders expertly controlled them with just a squeeze of their knees. Hours of relentless training made every movement instinctive.

By this time Baader's company, who were already advancing, had broken into a steady trot. The gentle drumming of their hooves reverberated across the open ground.

300 yards.

'At their gallop!' Titus shouted.

'Hold your lines!' Bartholomew snapped loudly. He glanced each way along the lines of perfectly straight horsemen.

After an inaudible shout, the gentle drumming of the Swiss cavalry became louder and faster,

250 yards.

'Ha!' Titus laughed. 'Bugler, now!' The bugler instantly put the brass horn to his lips and blew, loudly and clearly, three short, rising blasts. The company, who were advancing as one, broke into a gallop.

200 yards.

It was then that Sergeant Sturm spotted something unusual occurring in the advancing English ranks. He rose up in his stirrups to get a better look and suddenly realised what was

362.

happening.

'Captain! Captain! Look!' he screamed over the thundering hoof beats and rattling bridle chains.

Baader looked to where Sergeant Sturm's sword was pointing. His eyes widened in horror as soon as he saw that Barnard's Company was swelling in size. It was then that the realisation struck, Sturm had been right. Panic gripped him as he started sawing on his reigns, in an attempt to turn his horse.

'Retire! Retire!' he shouted hysterically.

Men and horses screamed at each other as the company descended into a chaotic flurry of stampeding hooves and flying mud.

150 yards.

Titus instantly saw the panic in the Swiss ranks.

'Bugler, sound the charge!' he screamed. He could feel the thrill of battle coursing through his veins, as he heard the three, loud double blasts of the horn. He kicked his heels back and laughed at the sight of Baader's outnumbered men trying to retreat. 'Charge!' he screamed, his sword raised in the air, 'Kill the bastards!'

Sergeant Broadhead looked through the split in the rotten panel, of the shed wall. He watched, anxiously, for any sign of Tom Allen returning. He glanced around briefly and saw that Master Wayland was still pacing the damp floor of the shed. This made the men of the musket platoon very nervous. Apart from Captain Barnard, his men were not used to seeing him look uneasy in another man's presence. Many of them had not met the head of their order before, but they were all aware of his reputation. Suddenly a figure appeared from the cellar steps.

'Master Wayland. Someone's coming, sir!'

Thomas rushed over to where the sergeant stood. He peered through the split in the panel and saw one of the manor's servants, recognisable by his black doublet and hose, high ruff and black cap, casually walk across the lawn towards the shed. He turned to the men stood by the shed door.

'When he comes to the door, seize him. Do not let him cry out!' The two men closest to the door nodded and readied themselves.

After a few moments the door slowly opened. The two waiting men instantly lunged forward and grabbed the startled servant. They wrenched his arms behind his back, which caused his cap to slip down over his eyes. Surprisingly the man didn't struggle.

'It's me, you bloody fools.' said the servant in a familiar voice. He raised his head to look at them all from under the brim of his cap. Tom Allen grinned at them. 'Well I need a disguise if I want to walk around unnoticed, don't I?'

Thomas laughed with relief, as the two men let go of Tom. He felt embarrassed for reacting the way he did, like him they were all on edge. Then he remembered why they were there.

'Is she alive Tom?' he asked grimly.

Tom's smile disappeared.

'I'll not lie to you Master. I only nipped down to the cellar to pick my disguise up, but I think there's something wrong inside the house.'

'How do you mean?'

'Well, it's deserted. There's not a soul about.'

Thomas shot a look at Broadhead.

'Sergeant, we must go. Now!'

The band of men filed out of the shed, led by Tom Allen, who still wore his servant's uniform. Thomas was next, followed by the men from the muskets platoon, with Sergeant Broadhead at the rear.

Tom quickly led them across the wide lawn and down the cellar steps. Without waiting he pushed the door open and disappeared inside. Thomas paused slightly before opening the door, Tom's lack of caution made him feel uneasy.

Once inside they found that the cellar room was dark and oppressive. The rush lights positioned around the walls did little to banish the gloom. Gradually though, their eyes became accustomed to the dark and they noticed the rows of low bunks lining the walls. There was also an overpowering smell of sweat and body odour. It was the usual smell for a room where troops slept, but there was another familiar, more pungent odour that caught their attention.

'These, as you can all see, are the company quarters.' Tom said quietly, 'The rest of the house is through there.' he pointed to a doorway at the end of the room.

Thomas walked across the room without answering, his mind raced as the bitter, coppery smell became stronger. When he reached the doorway he walked through into a long narrow passageway. The end opened out into a wide stair well. He stopped abruptly when he noticed the gruesome scene in front of him. Some of the men behind him, who could see over his shoulder, gasped in horror.

'They were the servants, Master.' Tom said in a hollow voice.

Baader wrenched on his reigns with one hand, whilst slapping the rump of his horse with the flat of his sword. He still smarted at how easily he had been tricked.

'Move, you dogs!' he screamed. When he finally turned his horse he was relieved to see that the rear rank had already turned and were racing for the cover of the trees at the end of the field. He risked a glance behind and saw that the rest of the company were now in flight. Every man and horse were heading for the trees. All the time the constant, thundering hooves, of Barnard's company, were getting louder as they closed the gap.

Baader pulled ahead of the line, kicking his heels back in an attempt to get more speed from his panting horse. All of a sudden the line of riders in front of him started slowing their horses and some were even trying to turn around again.

'What are you doing, you fools?' Sturm shouted. 'To the trees!'

Baader heard the panic in his Sergeant's voice. Normally he would be haranguing the men too, but today wasn't a normal day. He rose up in his stirrups to see what was causing his men to hesitate. His eyes instantly widened in horror as a long line of men stepped out of the trees, all of them were aiming long, heavy muskets at the oncoming cavalry. He opened his mouth to shout the order to retire. He didn't get the chance, because on a shouted order from the trees, every musket fired at once.

Thomas led the men quietly up the wide staircase. The image of the pile of mutilated bodies in the stairwell still fresh in his mind. When he reached the top of the stairs he was in the main foyer of the house. The front door was wide open. He walked over and pushed it shut, shoving the large bolts across, noisily.

He turned around and looked at the men. His face was a mask of undisguised fury.

'Sergeant Broadhead, I want any sentries left at the main gate, brought inside.' he said, 'Leave Tom and two other men here.'

Broadhead nodded and ran back down the stairs with the rest of the men following.

'Mr Allen you may take these two men and search the ground floor.' Tom nodded mutely and set off down one of the corridors followed by the two remaining musketeers.

Thomas, now alone, stood in silence staring up the wide, carved staircase to the upper floor. At the top of the stairs was a huge tapestry, depicting the last temptation of Christ. The grim, sinister form of Satan, mocked Christ as he journeyed through the wilderness. Whilst he stared at the scene it struck him that far more effort seemed to have gone into stitching Satan than it had for Jesus.

He screwed his eye shut as the deafening silence pounded in his ears. Was she alive? Or was she in another pile of butchered corpses hidden in the house somewhere? A wave of helplessness flooded over him, almost causing his legs to buckle. He closed his fists tightly as his anger welled up inside him. After a few moments he could feel the pain of his finger nails digging into the palm of his hands. 'She's gone and it's all my doing.' The hollow words echoed through his mind. Then a noise roused him from his reverie.

Loud voices and heavily booted feet `echoed up the back staircase and Sergeant Broadhead's smiling face appeared.

'We've got one of their officers, Master. The other men are being tied up in the cellar.'

'Well done, Sergeant. Bring him here once the other prisoners are secured in the cellar. Make sure you leave a few of your men to guard them, then bring the rest back upstairs.'

When the sergeant made his way back down

369.

stairs, Tom reappeared with his two companions. 'We found nothing, Master.'

The Sergeant immediately reappeared, closely followed by two musketeers who were holding one of Baader's men. Thomas waited while the prisoner was dragged from the cellar stairs, over to where he stood. He could see that the man had already taken a beating, but his eyes still remained defiant.

'What is your name?' Thomas asked coldly. The prisoner glared back at him, refusing to answer. 'I said, what is your name?' he repeated. This time the man looked away, oozing contempt. Sergeant Broadhead went to step forward, but Thomas held a hand up to stop him. He gripped the man by the chin and wrenched his head back round to face him. He stared into the man's eyes as he started to tighten the grip on his jaw. 'That was the last time I am going to be reasonable. Now where is the girl and Sir Nicholas?'

When the pain started to build in his jaw the prisoner tried to struggle. The musketeers held him firmly. Thomas had now lost his patience.

'Where are they?' he demanded, tightened the hold he had on the man's jaw,

This time the man tried to speak, but it came out as a gargled cry. When the grip didn't loosen he realised that Thomas wasn't going to let go, so he glanced in the direction of the staircase.

Thomas followed his gaze.

'Upstairs?' he asked. He felt the prisoner try to nod and he released his jaw. The man whined in relief. 'Bring him.' he ordered. He walked over to the wide staircase and led them up to the next floor.

'Which way now?' he asked with out turning. There was no answer.

'Master Wayland asked which way,' Sergeant Broadhead snapped, cuffing the man round the head.

'Thank you Sergeant.' Thomas said flatly. He turned his eye on the prisoner, 'Well? Where are they?'

'They're down there.' he said nodding to the corridor that led off to the left. He then grinned wolfishly, 'You're too late though, they're probably dead by now.'

Thomas glared at the man, his face calm and emotionless. The men of the musket platoon all braced themselves for the inevitable burst of rage. Strangely though Thomas seemed to relax.

Baader's man chuckled to himself, safe in the knowledge that the big, one eyed commander was unlikely to harm him. He would probably just send him back to the cellar again.

Just then Thomas's arm suddenly shot forward, sending the heel of his open hand smashing up into the Swiss officer's nose. The man's head snapped back violently, the force of the sudden blow ramming his nasal bone up into his brain, killing him instantly.

There was a look of surprise on the dead man's face as he slumped forward.

'Leave the bastard where he falls,' Thomas growled. He turned and walked down the corridor, 'Tom, come with me.'

Sergeant Broadhead and the other men were in a state of torpor, after witnessing what had just happened.

'Drop him, lads.' the sergeant said eventually.

The two men that were holding the arms instantly let go and the body fall to the floor, blood now freely flowing from its nose.

'Right ladies, let's go. We're not finished yet.' he added and led them away.

In a devastating blast of fire and smoke, a deafening musket volley had completely obliterated the forward line of panicking horsemen.

Baader had only just managed to stay in the saddle and keep a grip on his sword. His ears

372.

were still ringing from the volley as he looked at the carnage around him. The thick smell of rotten egg from the gun smoke assaulted his nostrils and caused large watery tears to obscure his vision. He glanced down at the morass of wounded men and dying horses and recoiled with a feeling of horror and despair. Then he heard a muffled voice shouting from the trees.

'Platoon... reload!'

'Shit, shit! They're going to fire again,' he mumbled to himself, his mind a mass of confusion. But confusion was suddenly replaced by dread as a loud, rhythmic drumming started to vibrate the very air around him.

100 yards.

Titus swung his sword around his head as he howled with laughter.

'Ha! Well done the muskets!' he cried.

'Hold your line!' Bartholomew shouted. 'Hold your line.'

The charging horsemen started to scream their war cries as they raced to the final impact.

50 yards.

'Kill the bastards!' Titus screamed, his voice threatening to drown out the sound of yelling men, as the company crashed into the disorganised Swiss ranks.

They shouted and bawled as they killed, their frenzied bloodlust consuming them entirely. The dazed Landsknechts cowered from their savagery. The slashing and stabbing of the heavy blades and stamping iron shod hooves defeated them entirely.

Titus ripped his sword blade from the abdomen of the Swiss trooper he had just killed. He spun around in his saddle, searching for the next threat. Off to his left he watched one of Baader's men jump down from his horse and hold his hands up in surrender. Billy Gould, who was charging the man, looked as if he was about to let him surrender. Titus readied himself to shout out a reprimand, but as Billy passed the man he swung his sword downwards, the blade slicing into the man's neck, almost decapitating him. He immediately yanked the sword free and the body fell to the ground.

'Good man Gould!' Titus shouted, 'I almost thought you were about to let him go?'

'Lord no, Sir.' Billy shouted back, 'There's only one man in the field who can accept surrender. That's you, Sir.'

'Bloody good man!' Titus replied brimming with pride.

The slaughter was short lived that afternoon.

374.

One murderous volley from the Musket Platoon had crippled the fleeing Landsknechts. It had then been down to the heavy blades of Barnard's horsemen to finish the job.

Now the fighting was over Titus sat on his horse and surveyed the carnage. His violent hatred towards Baader and his men had finally been sated. The feeling of years of unfulfilled revenge had gone. He had always dreamed of wreaking bloody reprisals on the treacherous Swiss mercenaries and he had always expected to experience a feeling of satisfaction or relief when the final moment came. But in truth he felt nothing. All that was left was a dull, hollow void. Sergeant Roach approached him on foot and he quickly pushed his thoughts aside.

'The men are mustered and waiting Sir.' Bartholomew said, standing next to Titus's horse.

'How many, Sergeant?' Titus asked flatly.

'One dead, two wounded, sir.'

'Any prisoners?'

'Only one, Sir. But he is badly injured.'

'Good.' he answered coldly. 'Bury the dead and hold a service over the grave. They may have been perfidious dogs, but they now deserve to rest.'

'Yes, Sir.'

After a few moments Titus realised that Bartholomew was still standing there. 'Yes, Sergeant?'

'The dying prisoner, Sir. It's Captain Baader.'

'Jesus wept!' he spat, causing Bartholomew to wince involuntarily, 'The bastard's still alive?'

Bartholomew nodded.

'Only just, Sir. What ever devil he prays to, has chosen to keep him alive a little while longer.'

Titus swung his leg over the saddle and jumped down to the ground. 'Take me to the dog.'

Thomas wandered along the wide, dimly lit corridor whilst the men searched the rooms. All around him he could hear the sounds of furniture being moved and cupboard doors opening and closing. At the end of the corridor, he noticed that there was a door that was slightly ajar. When he pushed it open he discovered a flight of stone steps, winding upwards.

Then he stopped when an obscure thought flashed into his mind. He didn't actually know what Mary looked like. He had never seen her. Luckily though, he knew Tom Allen had. He thought back to the pile of mutilated bodies they had found, at the bottom of the stairs. Tom had reassured him that Mary had not been one of them. Surely he could only have known that if he knew what she looked like. Small consolation he thought.

Sergeant Broadhead interrupted his thoughts when he walked out of one of the rooms on his right.

'She's not in any of these rooms, Master.' Both men spun round when they heard a voice. 'What was that?'

'Up here!' the voice called again, from the top of the stone steps.

Thomas immediately set off up the stairs, taking them two at a time. His scabbard rattled against the wall as he went.

The top of the stairs opened out into a gloomy attic room. Boyle, the young trooper who had helped him earlier, was standing in front of him, next to the attic room's only window.

'We're too late, Master. They're all dead.'

Thomas quickly glanced around the room, his heart racing. On his first inspection, the room looked deserted. There was a large four poster bed, with a heavy green canopy standing in the centre. A long walnut dresser against one wall and a tall pedestal table, with a wash bowl on the top, next to the window. The room was otherwise bare of furnishings. He turned back to Boyle.

'Where, boy?' he snapped.

'They're on the other side of the bed, Master.'

Thomas slowly walked over to the bed. As he got close enough he could smell the same familiar odour of violent death. The tangy, metallic smell of blood and the rancid stink of bile and shit, from spilt guts.

When he reached the bed he saw blood splattered across the disturbed bedclothes. Reluctantly he walked around the bed.

'God in heaven, no!' he whispered.

'Why aren't you dead you bastard?' Titus snarled, as he stood over Baader's broken body.

'All in good time, Barnard.' came the week reply. 'I'll not be long for this world.'

Titus squatted down next to him.

'You do know that you're going to hell, don't you, you swine?'

Baader coughed, wincing at the pain that lanced through his body. Blood trickled down his chin when he forced a smile.

'Perhaps, but I think one day we will be there together.'

'I have been in hell for the last fifteen years,

you lying, treacherous dog!' He leaned in closer and lowered his voice, 'Because of you, I lost half of my men in those fucking hills.'

Baader chuckled painfully, blood sprayed into the air.

'You're a fool Titus, you always were.' he saw the puzzlement in Barnard's face, 'Your betrayer was one of your own comrades and you couldn't even see it.' He coughed again, but this time the pain caught his breath. He screwed his face up, in agony.

'What do you mean, you bastard. Who?' Titus demanded, raising his voice. Baader, was still coughing when he started to choke on his own blood. 'Who was it?' Titus shouted, grabbing the front of the dying man's tunic.

When the Swiss captain's coughing stopped his chest slowly sagged and a long sigh brought blood bubbling to his lips.

Titus burned with rage as he looked at the body on the ground, the significance of what he had just heard hit him like a lightening bolt.

'You fucking bastard!' he shouted and brutally kicked Baader's body in the ribs.

'It's almost the same as the house servants, Master.' Tom said, squatting down next to the bodies. 'They've been butchered like cattle.'

Thomas gazed at the carnage on the floor in stunned silence. He could recognise Sir Nicholas's mutilated bulk, as it lay spread eagled in the blood. His stomach was a mass of criss cross cuts. Next to him, facing the wall was Cawthorne's body, still dressed in black and seemingly untouched apart from the wide, deep slash across his throat. It was the body of the girl that pained him the most, almost rooting him to the spot.

Tom realised that Thomas was reluctant to move any closer. Without waiting he stood up and stepped over the magistrate's body. The girl lay face down on the blood stained floor, her long, russet hair obscuring her features. By her pale skin and slim nakedness he could see that she had been very young. Slowly he knelt down beside her body. 'It's going to kill the squire, when he finds out what happened to her,' he thought to himself.

He reached out and carefully brushed the matted hair away from her face, readying himself to gaze upon the innocent face of Mary Danvers. When he saw the face he gasped and pulled his hand away.

Thomas saw the reaction and stepped forward.

380.

'What is it? What's wrong?' he asked.

'It's not her, Master.'

Thomas knelt down next to Tom and looked at the dead girl's face, even though he had never seen her.

'Are you sure?' he asked.

'I've seen her many times in the village, Master.' Tom said sounding confident, 'I tell you this isn't her.'

Thomas couldn't tear his eyes away from the dead girl's face.

'Who is she then?' he said quietly, still concerned even though this was not his estranged daughter's body.

'I've no idea. I'm pretty sure that she's not from the village though, I would have seen her.'

'She's still some poor soul's daughter.' the Sergeant muttered from behind them.

Thomas crossed himself.

'You are quite right, Sergeant.'

'So does this mean that the magistrate is not Baphomet?' Tom asked cautiously.

'It would appear not.' Thomas replied.

'So, we still have to find Miss Danvers,' Broadhead said, 'and discover who this Baphomet character really is.'

Thomas stood up, the realisation finally dawning on him about who they were actually

381.

dealing with.

'Tonight, I hope to have the answers to both of those questions, Sergeant,' he said energetically, 'now though we must return to the tavern. We have little time.'

CHAPTER 36.

Mary woke with a start. She still expected to
see her horse, Lancelot, standing in front of her.
But slowly the memory of her dream faded and
she realised that she was still where she had
been for the last few days. Blindfolded, gagged
and trussed up, in total darkness.

She tried to push herself up into a sitting
position, which was made awkward because her
hands were tied tightly in front of her. As soon
as she had sat up she stopped moving and
listened to see if she could hear the noise again.
She wrinkled her nose at the foul smell and the
dampness, from where she had soiled herself
hours before.

The moment of her capture was still imprinted
on her mind. The kidnappers had grabbed her
from behind, whilst she had been in her father's
stables.

She was immediately blindfolded and her
riding clothes were ripped off. Then a foul
smelling, rough linen gown was pulled over
head before her hands were tied.

She didn't remember much of the journey to
her makeshift prison. She was aware, though, of
how bruised she was from being lain across her

kidnapper's saddle. Since she had arrived she had been sitting in the dark, huddled up, freezing from the cold. Her stomach was also cramped from hunger, it had been hours since she had last eaten.

Then she heard the sound again and gasped in surprise. She was now listening more intently, trying to gauge how close the sound had been. She tried to call out, but the gag over her mouth was too tight. There it was again. It sounded like shuffling feet. This time, though, it was much closer.

She tried to turn her head in the direction of the noise, even though the blindfold made it impossible to see, but the sound had stopped. After a few moments of silence she started to cry. The feeling of fear and utter hopelessness became stronger.

There were times, since her capture, when she had woken and would swear that some one had been standing close to her. On one occasion, not long after she was taken, her gag had been removed and she was allowed a few bites from a bitter tasting lump of bread. At other times she had felt a cold, soft hand brush against her cheek. But when she tried to speak to who ever it was, no one would answer. She couldn't decide whether it was a mocking gesture or a sign of sorrow, possibly even regret? She often prayed that someone would save her. She had done a lot of praying since she had been captured.

Suddenly, two hands touched either side of her face and she flinched. Before she could react her gag was pulled away from her mouth. She waited for a lump of bread to be shoved into her mouth, but nothing came.

'Is someone there?' she asked quietly.

'Be quiet.' a voice whispered back.

'Please, let me go?' she begged, feeling relieved and frightened at the same time, after hearing another voice.

'Don't worry, my sweet,' a soft, female voice answered. 'I'm going to get you away from here, but you have to stay quiet.'

Tears started to well up in the corners of her eyes.

'Thank you.' she whimpered. Then she felt her hands being untied.

'Leave your eyes covered, sweetie,' the woman whispered. 'I'll lead you out, don't you fret.'

'Ok.' Mary answered, rubbing her sore wrists.

'Let's get you up then.' The woman said helping her to her feet.

Mary stood up and tried to stretch the cramp from her legs. Her mind was full of questions.

Who was this woman? Why had she been kidnapped? She was about to risk asking where they were, but she felt the woman gently take her hand.

'This way and be quiet,' the woman said softly, before leading her off. 'Keep your head bowed, my sweet.'

Mary stumbled as the ground rose up unexpectedly. Something brushed the top of her head.

'Keep your head down, luvvie, or you'll crown yourself.'

Mary walked the next few paces with her head bowed. Then all of a sudden a cold breeze hit her in the face, chilling her instantly.

'You can stand up now dear, you're outside.'

Whilst they walked, she could hear the wind in the trees. She wrapped her free arm around her waist, in a vain attempt to ward off the cold. After a couple of minutes they stopped. She then felt herself being moved by the shoulders.

'I'll point you in the direction of the path that will lead you to safety,' the woman's voice was now behind her. 'I'm going now, my love. Please wait a few moments before you take off your blindfold and would you also give Master Wayland a message for me?' Mary nodded. 'Tell him he must go to the Rollrights, not the

Knights. He'll know what you mean.'

'I will,' she answered nervously. 'But where will I find him?' she waited but there was no reply. Tentatively she removed the blindfold.

She saw that it was almost dark and that she was alone. In front of her was an overgrown path that led through the trees. She glanced around her one last time before sprinting off along the path.

Titus glared at Thomas from across the table in the taproom. The look of anger and frustration was obvious to all.

'My men and I could end this now!' he cried, 'And where on earth is Mr. Bolton?'

Thomas regarded his friend, as he was tightening the buckles on his breast plate.

'I appreciate the offer Captain, but unfortunately there's no time to get your men into position without them being seem.' He smiled warmly, knowing his friend's blood was still up, after hearing the unexpected revelation from Baader before he died. 'I don't even think Tom Allen could get close enough before they killed her.' He pushed a dagger into the back of his belt. 'As for Samuel, I'm sure he will appear, all in good time.' He pushed his last two knives into place, one in each boot. 'No, it has to be me Titus old friend, unarmed and alone.' Finally, he banged his two ornately carved, Italian wheel lock pistols and his sword down on to the table and winked.

Isaiah was standing on sentry duty, just outside the gates of the stable yard. Daylight had disappeared altogether now, plunging the road and the surrounding woods into almost complete darkness. Moments later Will Spink appeared next to him.

'Well, that's the last torch lit.' he said.

Isaiah looked along the outside of the stable wall. In both directions long lines of pitch soaked torches burned, brightly enough to light to the opposite side of the road.

'My feet are bloody freezing!' he said stamping his heavy boots on the road.

'You really are just a moaning woman, aren't you?' Spink said grinning.

Isaiah looked at his friend blankly.

'Next time we all go training, I'm going to shoot you in the face!' Will laughed at him. 'No, really! The rest of the lads will think it's because I'm clumsy and I'm still learning, but I want you to know that it'll be murder.'

Will's smile suddenly disappeared.

'Quiet, you girl.' he said holding his hand up.

Isaiah realised that his friend wasn't joking.

'What's wrong?' he asked and gripped the hilt of his sword.

'Listen.' Will snapped.

Isaiah took his hat off and opened his mouth. He remembered Tom Allen had told him that it would help you to hear better, especially at night. Sure enough his hearing did seem a lot clearer. At once he realised that Will was right. Someone or something was coming towards them.

'There!' Will said pointing up the road.

Isaiah strained his eyes, but all he could see was blackness. Just then a pale shape appeared, illuminated by the furthest torches. Panic gripped him and he started to draw his sword.

Will reached out and stayed his friend's arm.

'No, it's just a girl and by the look of her, she's in a right state.'

Isaiah breathed out.

'Jesus Christ! I thought it was a phantom or something.'

Will grinned again.

'So what good would you have done with your sword then?'

Isaiah shrugged before looking back at the girl

that was running towards them. He could see now that she was wearing a short, dirty gown and by the streaks on her face she had been crying. When she reached them she headed straight for Isaiah and collapsed into his arms, sobbing and panting uncontrollably. It was then that he realised who she was.

'Bloody hell, Will, that's Mary Danvers.'

'Are you sure?' When he looked at his friend's face he knew that he was. 'Shit! We had better get her inside.'

Without warning another voice boomed out from behind them.

'Spink! Cooper! What's going on?'

Isaiah glanced back over his shoulder to see Titus striding across the stable yard towards them.

'Sir, we've got Miss Danvers.'

'Have you now?' Titus answered, not entirely believing him. Then he reached the gate and saw the girl, 'Bugger me! Is that her?'

'Yes, Sir.' Isaiah answered.

'Right! Cooper, get her inside the tavern. Spink, you stay here.' Titus ordered. Isaiah passed him as he walked the girl towards the back door of the tavern. 'Ha!' he barked, turning back to will, 'It looks like we will be busy tonight after all, eh Spink?'

Moments later Mary was sitting in the taproom next to the fire. One of the men had wrapped a blanket around her narrow shoulders and shoved a mug of warmed ale in her hands. The room was almost empty as a lot the men were in the stable yard, readying their horses.

'I didn't see who it was who took me, Sir.' she said looking up at Titus.

'Hush now lass. It's all over now.' he replied calmly. There were stifled grins and surprised expressions from the few men who were within earshot, most of them had never heard their bombastic commander sound so soothing and gentle.

Mary smiled. She felt more relaxed, and she liked Captain Barnard. But when she looked up and saw the black beard and one staring eye of Master Wayland, she started to feel frightened again.

The first time she had seen him was in the village. He had been with his fierce looking companion, all the village had been afraid of them. The one time she had actually spoken to him, in passing, he had been very pleasant. Now though, his face was a mask of anger, and it terrified her.

'Please Sir, can I go to my father now?' She was surprised when Master Wayland turned away.

Titus laughed nervously as he looked at his friend.

'I've sent one of my men to fetch him, lass. Not to worry.' he said trying to distract her from Thomas's behaviour. 'While we're waiting for him, do you think you could tell me anything more about this woman who freed you?'

'Not really Sir, just that she was very kind. Oh! And she asked if I could give Master Wayland a message.'

Thomas spun round.

'What message?' he asked, more abruptly than he meant to.

Mary flinched at the sudden movement, but she held his gaze.

'She said that you were to go to the Rollrights and not the Knights.'

Thomas lifted his eye patch and rubbed at the empty socket, a habit he usually displayed when he was thinking.

'Was there anything else?' he tried to sound more affable.

'I'm sorry, Sir, that's all she said,' then she paused, looking thoughtful. 'But I do think I have heard her voice before.' At that moment the taverns front door burst open.

Everyone turned to see the squire standing in

the doorway.

'Where's my daughter?' he cried. Then he saw her, as she stood up. 'Mary!'

'Father!' she cried. She pushed her way past Barnard's men and ran into Robert's embrace.

Thomas, reluctantly, walked towards them, trying desperately not to frown at the display of affection. The Squire looked up and saw him coming towards them.

'Thank you, Thomas, for returning her to me,' he said his voice heavy with emotion.

'I just thank the lord that she is safe,' he answered forcing a smile, 'but I would like to ask Mary one more question, if I may?' Danvers looked if he was about to refuse, but Mary was already pulling away from him.

'Of course, Master.' she replied eagerly.

'You said that you recognised the voice of the woman who released you?'

'I did yes.' she answered. 'It was Sarah Hawkins, the landlord's daughter.'

An hour later he was stood in the chill night with one thought on his mind. Baphomet or Simon Hawkins, as he now knew him, will be stopped. Tonight he will die.

CHAPTER 37.

Thomas carefully walked across the narrow footbridge, leaving behind the safety of Barnard's company. He briefly glanced over his shoulder and saw that Titus was still standing in the tree line, watching. He gave his friend a last wave and turned away.

When he reached the other side he stepped off the end of the bridge. The clouds had drifted slightly and the countryside was now bathed in a dull silvery glow. He scanned the trees in front of him for any signs of life.

After a few moments he accepted that he was alone. He would have been happier if Tom Allen were with him, or better still Samuel. Briefly, during the day, he had started to become concerned about his companion's whereabouts. But later he chastised himself for not having the faith to realise that Samuel was capable enough of looking after himself.

He set off towards the woods, happy that he could still feel the reassuring jab in the back, from the dagger that he had hidden in his belt. The knives that he had in his boots he sometimes forgot he had, they were weapons that he had always carried. Titus always mocked his love of knives, saying that they were good for chopping fruit with but nothing else. The truth was that most of the men were in awe of Thomas's skill with knives and he liked to think Titus was too, even though he would never admit it.

As he walked he knew that, in his mind he had already decided on the outcome of tonight's events. He could recall the last conversation he had had before leaving the sanctuary of the woods to cross the footbridge.

'Your men are ready, Titus?'

'Of course!' Barnard answered sounding hurt. 'In fact I'm somewhat offended that you feel the need to ask.'

Thomas smiled.

'Please forgive me, old friend? I meant no offence.'

After a few moments, Titus nodded in acceptance.

'Think on it no further.' he replied with a chuckle. 'Although I had always hoped that you considered the loyalty and courage of the company to be two of the few constants in your life, Master Wayland.'

Sergeant Roach made a subtle interruption by clearing his throat, which stopped Thomas from replying.

'Master, might I ask what will happen to Mr. Hawkins, once he is arrested?'

Thomas's smile then disappeared, to be replaced with a look of cold malice.

'Mr. Hawkins will not be arrested.' he answered bluntly.

'Oh, but…' Bartholomew stopped when he felt someone tap his arm. He looked around and Titus was shaking his head. The realisation of what was going to happen suddenly dawned on him. 'Forgive me, Master.' he replied with his head bowed.

Now, walking through the shadowy woods he remembered Bartholomew's hurt expression. He dismissed the memory and brought his mind back to the task at hand. With grim determination he set off in the direction of the Rollright Stones.

Sarah walked quietly through the trees, making her way towards the old ring of stones. It didn't matter any more, she thought to herself, nothing mattered any more. All she knew now was that she wanted an end to it. The trouble was, that she knew that there would only be one way she could be free. When she was younger it was something she would never have thought about, but now it was the only way.

Up ahead she caught sight of the glow from several fires. She was close. After a few more paces she could start to see the ring of stones, through the trees. All of them silhouetted against the orange glow of the burning torches.

Then she noticed that there were more shapes highlighted by the flames, namely the other twelve members of the coven.

Thomas followed the path through the trees and eventually reached a wide clearing. He silently cursed the overcast sky that had now completely blocked out the moonlight, plunging the woods into almost total darkness. Then he hissed in pain, as his shin glanced off something very hard.

'Damn and blast!' he swore, through gritted teeth. He bent down and attempted to rub the pain away from his bruised bone. Just then there was a break in the cloud and a bright ray of moonlight shone through. He looked up and saw that the bright grey light had illuminated a wide, perfectly round, waist high circle of stones.

No sooner had it appeared, the light vanished and he again stood in darkness. He waited for a while, his feet rooted to the spot. Question after question had started to run through his mind. 'Where are they?' Is this the right place?', 'She said that they would be here!' Then it hit him like a thunderbolt. He knew what Sarah was going to do. 'The stupid girl!' he said and he turned and ran back into the woods.

The twelve members of the coven stood in a circle, just inside the ring of stones. All of them were clothed in their long black robes, with large voluminous hoods pulled over their heads.

Sarah had heard them before she saw them. The low rhythmic chant had resonated through the woods. It didn't matter that their faces were hidden, she knew who they all were. She was one of them, although tonight was different. Tonight she was going to leave the coven.

'Ah! Daughter.' a voice called out.

Sarah glanced around the gathered circle as she stepped into the light. She recognised her father's short, squat silhouette before he pulled his hood back.

'I see you have finally arrived,' he called out. He then looked puzzled, 'Where is the Danvers girl?'

Sarah saw the twisted look on her fathers face. With his feral smile and piercing eyes, she knew he was in the full grip of his demonic alter ego.

'Speak girl, where is the sacrifice?' he snarled. 'The interloper will arrive soon and everything must be set.'

'She has gone, Father.' she answered in a calm voice.

His eyes widened in surprise.

'Gone?'

'Yes, gone. I have released her.' she stepped closer, to where her father was standing. The chanting had stopped. The coven was now watching her, doubt present on some of their faces.

'What do you mean, you have released her?' he shouted as he stormed across the circle towards her.

She readied herself for the inevitable slap across the face, but he stopped a few paces from her. Now that he was closer, she saw that he was seriously out of breath. Spittle bubbled from his mouth as he breathed. She was well aware that it was more from the result of his mania, rather than from the effort of suddenly moving his vast bulk across the circle. In this state, she had seen him murder and mutilate countless young girls and, as on those occasions, she was terrified.

Swallowing her fear, she continued.

'Father this has to stop, tonight! We could go now, before the witch hunters get here. They will now know who you are.' She pleaded with him frantically, but he just stared back her, his eyes cold and impassive. 'Father, please?'

'Your Father is not here Sarah. I am Baphomet, your Lord and Master.' Without a word of warning, he backhanded her across the face. The force of the sudden blow spun her around before sending her sprawling to the ground. 'Seize her!' he ordered. And he turned away.

Sarah massaged her throbbing jaw as she lay crumpled on the ground. Just then two of the coven members lunged forward and grabbed her arms, roughly hauling her to her feet. As usual, when he hit her, tears started to roll down her cheeks. This time they weren't tears of pain, they were tears of hate. Hate for the man that she had been terrified of since she was a little girl. Tonight however was different, tonight she wasn't scared of him any more. After tonight she would be free.

'Why Sarah? Why do you betray the coven?' he had his back to her as he spoke.

'I never wanted to be part of any of this.' she replied, trying to sound as calm as possible.

'But you are part of this, my dear,' he turned

400.

around to face her; 'you have no choice.'

She saw that he was holding the athame, the large black handled knife. 'Is that how it was for Beth? Did she have 'no choice'?'

'Ah! Your curious sister,' he smiled as he fingered the point of the blade. 'Your Father chose her as his first offering to me. And all because she could not leave well alone.'

'She was just a child, Father!' she screamed at him, deliberately ignoring the third person reference he made about himself.

'Yes, tragic really.' He said as he walked to the other side of the altar stone. 'Did you know that you were meant to be the offering? Oh yes. Well, you were his first born.'

Sarah ignored his mocking and carried on.

'Beth was my sister, your daughter and you murdered her. How could you?!'

'I've told you your father is not here any more,' he answered, unaffected by her words, 'We are your family now.' He raised his arms and gestured to the coven members present, 'And I am Baphomet, your Lord.'

One of the coven, closest to Hawkins stepped forward.

'My Lord, now that the Danvers girl has gone, we have no sacrifice?'

'You do have a sacrifice and a willing one at

that.' Sarah interrupted. She stared defiantly at him, expecting a terse remark. But as he looked at her, she didn't see the evil face of Baphomet any more, it was the familiar, lost look, of her father.

'Sarah what are you saying?' he asked timidly.

'I willingly offer myself, in sacrifice, Father.' she replied confidently, deliberately ignoring his change of character.

'No, Sarah. Please don't do this.'

'Why not?' she cried out, struggling against the tight grip of her captors. 'You have taken the children of other men, Baphomet.' she hissed the last word angrily. 'You've even murdered one of your own daughters. Well, I can't watch innocent girls die any longer and if my dying is the only way for me to leave this nightmare, then so be it.'

'I can't kill you Sarah, my love. You're my only daughter.'

'I am your daughter, no longer!' she screamed.

Hawkins reeled as if he had just been struck across the face. In that instant his expression changed from hurt bewilderment to a feral snarl.

'Bring her closer to the altar.' he growled. Sarah's two captors almost lifted her off the ground, as they dragged her to the altar stone.

'Lay her down and hold her still.' he snapped

at them. He then raised the knife to the sky and started to utter a strange incantation. The two men roughly laid her out over the large, ancient stone. One of them held her by the wrists and the other by the ankles.

Hawkins lowered the knife until he held it directly over Sarah's chest.

When she looked up and saw the tip of the blade poised over her heart, panic set in and she started find it difficult to breathe. Please father finish it, please, she thought to herself.

Hawkins closed his eyes.

'Lord! Please accept this, our sacrifice, for….'

'Stop!' a loud voice interrupted from the darkness, outside the ring of stones. Every member of the coven turned in the direction of the voice. 'Put the knife down Hawkins,' Thomas demanded harshly, as he walked into the torchlight. 'Release her, now!'

'Master Wayland! By your unannounced appearance, I assume you have immobilised my watchers?'

Thomas casually walked around the outside of the circle.

'I encountered no… watchers you say?' he chuckled. 'Perhaps they finally realised what a fool you were and simply ran off.' On the far side of the circle, he stopped.

'I am a fair man,' he announced in a loud voice, '…so I give you all this warning. Once I have stepped into the stone circle,' he looked at each face, '…those of you, who still remain, will die!' he paused to let the words sink in. 'Your chance for freedom is now!' Some of the coven members started to look nervously at each other. One of them turned to look at Simon. 'Do not look to your Master for guidance, he is the only one here tonight, that I guarantee will die. He cannot help you now.'

At that point three of them turned and sprinted out of the circle, disappearing off into the trees. Two more slowly backed away, their eyes never leaving Thomas's baleful stare, before they turned and followed their fleeing companions.

'Well, well, Simon. It seems that some of your followers are not so devout.' He saw that Hawkins, who still held the knife above his daughter's bosom, was staring at him with a look of undisguised hate. He then regarded the remaining members of the coven, none of whom looked like they were about to run. Slightly better odds, but he still only had three knives. Too late now, he thought and strode into the circle.

'Kill him!' Hawkins suddenly screamed,

pointing the knife at Thomas.

The two cloaked figures closest ran towards him, but he had already retrieved the knives from his boots. He stepped to one side and let one of the men grab hold of him, which straight away blocked the path of the other attacker. Before the man could react, Thomas had gripped the front of his tunic and driven the knife into his throat. Blood sprayed down the front of the man's robe.

Thomas swung the dying man into the other attacker, knocking him to the ground. He immediately leapt over to the body and kicked the other man savagely in the head, knocking him unconscious.

He quickly turned to face his next opponent. To his surprise he saw that two more robed figures lay on the ground, dead. When he looked closer and noticed short feathered shafts poking out of their chests and he laughed.

The two remaining members of the coven stood, in a state of shock. They had just witnessed four of their members despatched in almost as many seconds.

Thomas looked at them, knowing that the fight had left them and they were of no more immediate concern. Then over their shoulders he saw Hawkins raise the knife to strike.

'Stop him!' he shouted quickly.

Another crossbow bolt immediately buzzed out of the shadows, hitting Hawkins in the wrist. The fat man howled in pain and dropped the knife. He then collapsed to the ground and curled up into a ball.

One of the two coven members, that remained, saw his chance and ran out of the circle. Thomas spotted the movement out of the corner of his eye and snatched the knife from the back of his belt, turned and launched it at the running man. The spinning blade hit him in the small of the back, dropping him on the spot. Thomas looked around for the other man, finding him where he had left him, rooted to the spot with a look of raw terror on his face.

The man dropped to his knees and held his hands out in front of him.

'Please, Master Wayland, mercy!' he pleaded.

Thomas smiled warmly and walked over to him.

'Hush now friend.' he crooned, gently placing a hand on the man's head.

The man seemed to relax slightly, thinking he was going to be granted the mercy he begged for.

Thomas grabbed a handful of the kneeling man's hair and violently yanked his head back.

The man gasped in pain as he felt his hair being ripped out of his head.

'I gave you all the chance for mercy, you murdering scum,' he screamed into the man's face, before drawing a knife across his throat.

The last coven member died with a look of horror on his face. Thomas pushed the body to the ground and stood upright, closing his eyes. He could feel his hands trembling as his anger started to dissipate. It was then that he could hear Hawkins whimpering over by the altar stone. A twig snapped off to his side.

'Good shooting Tom.' he said loudly opening his eyes, 'especially the one in the wrist.'

Tom Allen walked into the circle of stones with a crossbow on his shoulder.

'Thank you, Master, but the last shot wasn't mine.'

'Oh?' Thomas genuinely sounded surprised.

'It was mine.' Isaiah answered, appearing next to Tom, grinning.

'Mr. Cooper, I must congratulate you. That was a remarkable shot.'

Isaiah looked sheepish.

'I was actually aiming for his hand, Master.'

'Well, my thanks to you anyway.' He stepped over a body as he walked towards the pathetic figure of Simon Hawkins. He saw the trembling landlord was still nursing his damaged wrist. Whilst he stood there he considered all the terrible things the man had done and felt nothing but revulsion.

'Samuel,' he called out without looking up.

'Good evening Master,' Samuel answered striding out of the trees, behind the altar.

'When did you get here, old friend?' Thomas asked casually. He was aware that Samuel had been in hiding, as soon as he arrived.

'I've been here all afternoon, Master,' Samuel replied. 'I didn't think you'd heard my signal.'

'I did hear the signal Samuel, yes and if I'm not mistaken I've told you many a time not to use a robin.' Thomas admonished playfully, 'a barn owl would be much more accurate.' His large companion smiled in response.

'We had no idea that you were here, Mr. Bolton?' Isaiah said sounding surprised, 'We even looked around the area when we got here, before we got into position.'

Samuel didn't seem to hear Isaiah whilst he was stood by the large altar stone, looking down at Sarah.

'I'm afraid she's dead, Master.' he said making the sign of the cross over her body.

They all saw that Sarah was still spread eagled across the altar stone. The black, rune marked handle of her father's knife now protruded from her chest.

'Why didn't she try and escape?' Isaiah asked.

'She has escaped, Mr. Cooper.' Thomas answered, 'For years she has lived with the fear and shame of what her sick, depraved father was doing. She meant for herself to die tonight, that's why she sent me to the wrong location first.' Samuel draped one of the coven's robes over her. Just then Hawkins mumbled something inaudible, causing them all to look at him.

'What did you say scum?' Samuel snapped.

'I'm sorry Sarah, my love.' the fat man said through his sobs.

'I think it's a bit late for sorry?' Thomas said angrily as he stepped closer.

Hawkins pushed himself up into a sitting position, wincing as he did. His other hand still nursed his shattered wrist. Surprisingly, once he was up right his face changed into a wide beaming smile.

'Looks like you might have to arrest me then?' he chirped.

The four men stared at him in disbelief, none of them able to accept his sudden change of character. Thomas was the first to regain his wits.

'I'm pleased to say that you will not be

409.

arrested today!' He held his hand up to stay any protests from the others, 'In fact we're going to set you free.'

'Really!' Hawkins answered.

Thomas smiled coldly.

'Of course. Well because of what has occurred tonight, I think arrest is hardly the appropriate course of action.' He knelt down and wiped the blood from his knives on the robes of one of the bodies. Once he had replaced the clean blades into his boots he stood up and clapped his hands enthusiastically, 'Right gentlemen, back to the tavern, I think!' He turned to walk off but stopped and glanced at Isaiah, 'Mr. Cooper would you be so kind as to see Mr. Hawkins on his way. Don't worry about the bodies, I'll have Captain Barnard send some of his men to bury them later.' He looked as if he was going to walk away, but he paused. 'Mr. Hawkins, why don't you tell Isaiah here, how you had his younger brother murdered?' Thomas's cold eyes briefly locked with Isaiah's before he turned away.

Thomas, Samuel and Tom Allen walked back towards the village, in silence. The only sound they could hear were the tortured screams of Simon Hawkins, echoing through the trees.

Tom glanced at the two grim men as they walked along side him. For the first time in his life he was afraid. Then the screaming stopped.

EPILOGUE.

Thomas headed towards the ministers office, looking for a place to sit quietly and reflect on the day's events. The house seemed quiet. He walked into the office and closed the door behind him. He turned around expecting to see that the room was empty.

'Good evening, Your Grace.' he said, seeing the other presence in the room.

'Good evening to you, Master Wayland.' Sir Robert Cecil replied as he stood by the hearth. He continued to prod at the dying embers as he spoke, 'May I congratulate you on bringing His Majesty's matter to a conclusion.'

Thomas seated himself in one of the vacant hearth chairs.

'Can I ask how you are going to explain the events that have occurred at the manor?' he asked wearily.

'I thought a Catholic plot.' Salisbury replied, sounding pleased with himself.

Thomas raised his eyes, 'Ah! The Catholics again.'

The Earl ignored the flippant comment and continued.

'The threat of Catholic vileness is constant,

Master Wayland.' he answered, smiling in triumph when Thomas didn't reply. He sat down in the other hearth chair and sighed.

'You have something else to add, Your Grace?'

'I'm afraid that I do.' he answered. He then cleared his throat, 'His Majesty has another matter, he requests you to attend to.'

'Requests?' Thomas pursued cautiously.

'Of course! The Earl replied, 'His Majesty has also instructed me to inform you that he is keen to continue his patronage of your order, should you resolve this matter successfully.'

Thomas could feel his anger rising at the helplessness of the situation. He glared at the Earl and considered the consequences of opening the man's throat, here and now. After a short while he sat back into the chair, silently admitting defeat.

'Another matter you say?'

Salisbury felt relief wash over him when the grim man, sitting opposite, acquiesced.

'Good. Well, the matter is this. There are problems occurring in His Majesty's provinces in Ulster.'

'Problems?'

'Yes, it seems that some Crown officials and a few of the plantation undertakers have, well… disappeared.'

Thomas rubbed his eyes, 'It sounds to me as if the Irish Earls are starting to organise some form of resistance again.'

'So it would appear, but the last disappearance was, one of the Irish Earls.'

'And what does His Majesty expect me to do about it?'

Salisbury held his hands up in supplication.

'Please be calm, Master Wayland. All His Majesty asks is that you inquire into the disappearances and, if you will, bolster the authority of the Crown officials, whilst they oversee the allocation of tenants.' He tried to smile warmly, but it felt more like an uncomfortable grimace. 'It's unlikely you should encounter any major obstacles, especially with the aid of that lunatic Barnard and his company.'

'And what am I to do if Captain Barnard has business else where?'

'Fear not, Master Wayland, Captain Barnard and the advance parties of his company have already departed for the provinces.' He saw Thomas narrow his eyes, 'It seems he was keen to speak to several members of the provincial court, who are over there. It appears some of them were with him on the Continent, some years back.'

Thomas sprang to his feet.

'You damn fool!' he said vehemently, 'Do you have any idea what you have done?'

THE END?'

AUTHOR'S NOTE.

This is my first novel so I use the title 'Author' in the loosest possible sense of the word.

When I had the idea to write a book I decided to write one that I would want to read. I read a lot of historical fiction (I do often bend a knee at the altar of Cornwell and Iggulden) and reference books, because it interests me. I'm not arrogant enough to call myself an historian; at best I'm an enthusiastic amateur.

My interest in history naturally draws me to the darker side of the past, so the persecution of witches or the witch hunts, that were fuelled by religious zealots and ignorance in general, were right up my street. When I looked deeper into the whole subject I found that it was an incredibly dangerous time in which to live, but it was an ideal time for a sadistic opportunist to thrive. After a while I also realised that if you take a poorly educated populace, who are ill fed and have little income, add a liberal amount of mental illness and top it all off with intolerant religious paranoia and you have a host of victims literally lining up to be persecuted. You could add to all that the recently crowned King of England (James 1st/ 5th of Scotland), who not only wrote his own book on persecuting witches (Demonologie...remember I mentioned mental illness!), but he also commissioned his own version of the Bible in which he personally added the line 'thou shalt not suffer a witch to live' and you have a very difficult situation. Modern day witches and cunning folk call this period 'The Burning Times'.

Now here are a few notes of explanation about some parts of the story. Firstly all locations are real apart from Poden (which is the name of a prehistoric settlement not far from the village of Honeybourne), The Black Dog Tavern, which is the main pub in Honeybourne (but it's actually called The Thatched Tavern and it is from the 13th century). I have also added a little artistic license with Bretforton Manor and some of the distances are approximate (sorry folks...my book, my rules).

Some of the objects, words and descriptions are a bit obscure so I will briefly explain a few of them, so you don't think that I'm a complete lunatic who makes it up as he goes along.

The first object is the Athame. It is a black handled knife, sometimes with runes and/or sigils inscribed on it. But it is used for spells and rituals (like a wand) not for human or animal sacrificial purposes. Authentic witches and pagans don't make human or animal sacrifices and they don't worship Satan (The Devil is a Christian concept).

You might have already worked out that being 'Skyclad' means that you have no clothes on, you are clad by the sky.

The obscene kiss is something that Christian accusers alleged that witches did during their sabbats (periods of worship). I will take this moment to challenge anyone to find a modern day witch who is willing to kiss a goat's backside as part of their worship.

Baphomet is the name of a medieval demon which was first used in the 11th century. It was actually the name of the demon that Phillip II of France accused Knights Templar of secretly worshipping, a heretical act that led to there downfall (I'm sure it couldn't have been anything to do with the fact that they had made themselves incredibly wealthy, after setting up the first international banking system worth millions… could it?).

A few times I have mentioned Treves in Germany (Now modern day Trier) another true event I'm afraid. Towards the end of the 16th century, just outside Treves, 386 people were found guilty of practising witchcraft (Maleficia) and burned at the stake, wiping out two entire villages.

The Pillory, a contraption used for public humiliation (sometimes called the stocks) and The Gibbet, a metal cage, hung from a gallows, where the bodies of executed criminals were hung on display were common in most British villages and towns. Some still have them today.

Strappado was a torture method actually used by the Inquisition and happened exactly as I have described (A papal edict said that no blood was to be spilled in the name of the Church...how thoughtful!)

I would also like to ask anyone who has been, or who is going, to the market square in Evesham to spare a thought for Elizabeth Moreton, who in 1755 was burned at the stake after being found guilty of murdering her husband (I don't question her guilt, I just think it was a terrible way to die).

To finish, all the names that I have used, however bizarre they sound, were in common use in the period and I'm sure that's where they will stay...I mean, who would call their darling child Troilus?

Bye for now.

Thank you Jo, my long suffering Wife, for putting up with me.

WHO IS ANDY O'HALLORAN?

Well, apart from other things he tries to be a devoted Husband, Father, Son, Brother, Uncle, Nephew, Cousin and Friend. He is also a former Grenadier Guardsman, all-round know it all and smart arse. Most of all he is just a thoroughly, bloody nice bloke!

When he dose manage to have a moment to himself you will probably find him listening to rock music, reading or enjoying a pint of cider (probably all three). He is currently employed in the Hardly Mentioned Public Service.

Made in the USA
Charleston, SC
30 September 2011